A Dopeman's Riches

Lock Down Publications and Ca$h
Presents

A Dopeman's Riches

A Novel by *Nicole Goosby*

Lock Down Publications
P.O. Box 1482
Pine Lake, Ga 30072-1482

First Edition November 2017
Printed in the United States of America

Lock Down Publications
Like our page on Facebook: Lock Down Publications @
www.facebook.com/lockdownpublications.ldp
Cover design and layout by: **Dynasty Cover Me**
Book interior design by: **Sunny Giovanni**
Edited by**: Kiera Northington**

Stay Connected with Us!

Text **LOCKDOWN** to 22828 to stay up-to-date with new releases, sneak peaks, contests and more…

Thank you!

Submission Guideline.

Submit the first three chapters of your completed manuscript to ldpsubmissions@gmail.com, subject line: Your book's title. The manuscript must be in a .doc file and sent as an attachment. Document should be in Times New Roman, double spaced and in size 12 font. Also, provide your synopsis and full contact information. If sending multiple submissions, they must each be in a separate email.

Have a story but no way to send it electronically? You can still submit to LDP/Ca$h Presents. Send in the first three chapters, written or typed, of your completed manuscript to:

LDP: Submissions Dept
Po Box 1482
Pine Lake, Ga 30072

DO NOT send original manuscript. Must be a duplicate.

Provide your synopsis and a cover letter containing your full contact information.

Thanks for considering LDP and Ca$h Presents.

Acknowledgments

My purpose in life is to honor my Lord and Savior. It's because of God I have a gift to write. Pepper, you always told me the storm will pass and it did, you always will be my guardian angel. Thanks for the love and support you're always giving me to keep pushing through. Mama, I love you more than life itself. You always told me let the negative be negative, you're right. My sisters, Erica and Lolo, you're the best thing that happened to me. Even though we don't get along at times, I wouldn't have it any other way. I love you dearly, thank you for the support and love. J-boy, keep them CDs coming, love you, bro. My BFF, Demia Brown. You have been my rock, my angel. I can't change it, only words can explain. I love you, girl. Tara Allen, no matter what, when times get hard you're there. You always tell me to reach for the sky, you're such a sweetheart. Katrina, you're a rider. I have so many shout-outs and this list would be longer than a movie. I tried to keep it short and simple, but the way I talk, it just didn't happen. To the love of my life, Nikolvien, you are my world, my everything. Every day, you put a smile on my heart. You are the reason I keep breathing today. Nick, thank you for all you do to give me time to write by keeping our son, and being the best father that you can be. No words can explain. Cory Walker, you're an angel in disguise. Thank you for pushing me to write, and letting me know to never give up and never put the pen down. You always have that place in my heart, stop smiling. Fatima Ransom, you my girl. Keep your head up, stay strong. I did not forget about you this time. Thank you for my fans. My love and support to all the women that are locked up and away from their kids. Know the sun is going to shine, all this should pass. Stay positive always. Fellows on lockdown, you do the same, stay positive.

Angelina Concepcion, I know I work your nerves at times, but I know you have my back. You're in my life for a reason, so just know we have work to do. Thank you, girlfriend, for all that you do. Teri Brown, AKA Ms. T, I thank you for all you do. I

appreciate you. I can't forget about my cousin, Torreon Lewis, Tee, thank you. Cash # LPD and family, thank you for giving me a chance and treating me like family. To my friends that don't know me and will get to know me, thank you for supporting me. The ones that always had something to say, thank you give me the reason to keep pushing this pen!

PROLOGUE

A welcoming smoke hovered broodingly in the room. Thanks to the marijuana, CeCe was smoking alongside her buddies: Byrd, Kay, and Willie. There was no room to swing a cat. The cramped condition of the room made it seem as if the four of them were squatters. The walls were bare, except for a rickety clock. The bare wooden floorboards accommodated a four-seater chair, the only furnishing in the room, in addition to the rough-hewn coffee table. Marijuana burns stood out on the arms of the chair, like varicose veins on the skin of an aged fellow. Above them, the ceiling was cracked. It looked as though it was gonna cave in on top of them. There was a washstand in the corner of the room. The threadbare curtains were open, revealing a broken window.

"I need another hit, Byrd!" CeCe said.

"Come on, Cecelia," said Byrd, his voice and demeanor frantic, "your water already broke. You should go to the hospital."

"I'm good, nigga. Just gimme another fix of pot!" CeCe yelled, despite breathing in spasms.

Kay looked askance at CeCe.

"Why the fuck areyou looking at me like that?" Cecelia said.

"Bitch," said Kay, "you are tripping! A motherfucker can't get high while you over there oozing fluid and whatnot. I must say, you look like you are dying. Stupid bitch!" Kay gathered her things, slipped on her shoes, and looked towards Byrd. "Why you ain't making that bitch take her ass to the hospital, Byrd? You see she is dying."

"Fuck you, Kay," said CeCe. "You must be trying to get me to leave, so you can smoke to high heavens!"

Byrd watched CeCe with both concern and compassion. He was worried about her, though more worried about the weed being all gone by the time he did make it back. Besides, he was on parole. Hence, showing up in hospital with a bleeding woman wasn't on the top of his to-do list. He thought of calling 911 a few times, but that would require him running up the street to the Walmart store.

"You sure you're straight, CeCe?" Byrd mumbled, the weed smoke clouding his senses.

Cecelia screamed. "Ouch! I need another hit!"

"I'm getting out of here," said Kay, "coz this dope fiend bitch gone kill herself."

In spite of the pain CeCe was in, she glowered at Kay. "Why don't you just fuck off and leave me alone!"

As Kay flounced towards the door, CeCe said at the top of her voice, "To hell with you, Kay!"

Just before Kay slammed the door behind her, she cast a backward glance at CeCe, and said, giving CeCe the finger, "Fuck you, cunt."

Byrd could only watch as the pool of blood formed under Cecelia's thighs. He'd just hit the joint and handed it to Cecelia, who was trying hard to hold in the smoke she inhaled.

"Y'all hear that?" Byrd asked, looking towards the door. "They are coming," he whispered.

Willie fell silent, trying to hear what he believed to be on the other side of the door. His eyes widened. "They did something to the dope."

"Ain't nobody did nothing to that dope," Byrd said.

"We gonna die," Willie continued. "They gonna kill us."

Byrd glanced over at Cecelia and then at the marijuana she was pulling on. "Now that's ya last hit, bitch. You got to go to the hospital!"

Cecelia barked. "I'm not going to no damn hospital! They gonna take my baby, Byrd." She pulled at the weed and let out a scream of pain.

Knowing there was no way around Cecelia's protest, Byrd let her have her way. Grabbing what looked to him to be around fifteen grams of weed from the coffee table, Byrd crept to the front door, opened it, and slowly walked out. Once I get to the payphone, I'd call the paramedics and catch up with CeCe and Willie later.

After speaking with the 911 operator, Byrd walked into the Walmart store for a bag of chips plus bottled water. Seeing fresh fruits, he strolled several aisles over, and ate a few strawberries and grapes. He even thought about buying some fruits for Cecelia, but decided against it. I believe the paramedics would have been to take her to hospital already.

Walking toward the counter, he noticed the items displayed: baby diapers, formulas, pacifiers, and all sorts of powders and shampoos. He thought about Cecelia and the child she'd deliver. Her words echoed in his head: "They gonna take my baby, Byrd!"

Leaving the store, he walked down Barry Street- towards the crib.

Two houses from the spot, Byrd looked for telltale signs that the paramedics had come and gone. Seeing no one around, Byrd climbed the steps, pushed the door open, and walked inside. "Willie! Cecelia! Y'all here?" Stepping into the room, Byrd couldn't believe his eyes: Cecelia lay slumped over, half-naked in her own blood. The t-shirt she wore was now soaked. "CeCe, you alright?" he asked the lifeless body. He sensed she was dead, yet hoped she was still alive. What angered Byrd was, the paramedics still hadn't showed. And there was no trace of Willie. He must have left upon noticing Cecelia's condition was becoming critical, thought Byrd.

Byrd knelt down and kissed Cecelia's forehead. It was then he noticed a slight movement close to her chest. He moved her hand. "Oh, shit! He staggered backward. Seeing the baby startled him terribly. "What the fuck, Cecelia!"

Knowing nothing else to do, he hurried to clean the baby under the stale washstand water, and wrapped it in a dirty towel. He and Cecelia had always spoken of getting themselves together and making lots of riches. That was the first name out of his mouth: Riches. It sounded crazy, but that would be the baby's name.

"Jasmine Riches Nichols, welcome to this fucked-up world," he said.

CHAPTER ONE

O'Shay Lewis had been running the east side of Fort Worth with an iron fist. He knew the core principles of getting money, murder. That was how he'd established himself in the game. His ruthlessness was the reason people respected and feared him at once.

"You need to sell some ass or something. I don't give a damn how you get my money, just get it!" O'Shay ended his call and tossed his phone in the passenger seat of his cream-colored Lexus convertible. Today was one of them sunny days and what better way to roll than letting the top fold back into the trunk. When he wasn't in the Lexus convertible, he was in the huge Lincoln MKX or in his recently bought Jaguar. Money was being made and it came with a cost; a cost he was sure to pay at another's expense. His boys on the east side made sure their hustle had the bread rolling in. The fact that neither of them were over the age of fifteen brooked criticism from those that rated his campaign. O'Shay pulled into the tire shop on the corner of Killian and Miller, climbed out, and headed for the door.

"Hey, O'Shay, I need to talk to ya!" yelled a guy on the other end of the shop.

O'Shay threw up his middle finger and smiled, his crowns boasting nearly fifty thousand dollars' worth of diamond-glazed dental work.

"Come on, nigga. You are acting like one of the Riverside hoes now," the guy told him.

O'Shay stopped dead in his tracks, his smile fading. He turned towards the voice and pointed. "Pussy ass nigga, what you call me?"

"Quit tripping, nigga. You take shit personal all the time."

"Personal? Personal?" O'Shay raised his voice. "What the fuck you want anyway, Jay?"

O'Shay had known Jay since middle school. Despite Jay being five years his senior, O'Shay still felt he himself had real seniority. He knew those around him had come to realize that.

"My boy just came down from Kansas and he is looking."

"Looking for who?"

"You, if the price is right."

"What's wrong with your own prices?"

O'Shay knew what Jay was up to. "Well, I believe your boy from Kansas is looking in the right direction. Fine by me." Jacking an out-of-towner and leaving him in some abandoned spot was nothing new to either of them. Plus, if the price was right, it would be done sooner.

"I knew yours were better. Besides, my hands stay clean."

O'Shay smiled again, he knew he would get the lion's share, yet felt he'd better be careful. He knew Jay didn't give a damn and was simply trying to keep his hands clean in the deal, after all. "Come on in here right quick," said O'Shay, his anger abating. "I gotta hear more of what you are talking about."

Byrd was so caught up in thoughts of his own he hadn't realized Riches was no longer in bed, but checking herself out before the mirror. Twenty years had passed since Cecelia's death. Over the years, he had watched over CeCe's daughter like a guardian angel. She was no longer the little girl he'd sheltered and kept away from the world he knew so well. Standing five feet seven and weighing a hundred and fifty-eight pounds, men didn't hesitate when it came to approaching her. Byrd hated hearing them call her brick house. She was light-skinned, wavy-haired, and had brownish grey eyes that radiated warmth.

"Byrd! Byrd! What are you standing there frowning at?" Riches asked with a frown of her own.

"Huh? I was just thinking about something, that's all." He hoped she wouldn't make conversation out of his reply. One thing Byrd Nichols didn't do was lie to Riches. So, he did his best to evade certain topics, especially when it had to do with her mother. But, he was sure the day would come when Riches would start asking questions he hated giving answers to.

"You weren't really listening to me. I called you into my room to tell you something, you know!"

"I'm sorry. My mind was somewhere else. What's up?"

"I'd like to go to Tiffany's this weekend. Her neighborhood is having a block party and everybody's gonna be there."

Byrd sighed. He'd done pretty good keeping her out of the hoods of both the east side and the south side of Fort Worth. But, she was no longer a teenager. She and her friends routinely visited families in the hoods. Thus, sheltering her was getting harder.

"You know I don't want you getting caught up in all that drama shit, Riches. Ain't nothing good happening out there."

Riches plopped down on her queen size bed, grabbed one of the stuffed bears that lined her bed, hugged it. "We not going to be doing nothing but eating, Byrd."

Seeing her pout got to him every time. Each time he remembered how her mother used to control him with the same antics, defeat found him. This was the same pout Riches had gotten used to doing and the very same one he was used to seeing. Her walk-in closet was filled with retro Jordan sneakers, Manolo boots and a collection of designer clothes, because of these one on one sessions and the pouting that followed. In the end, they both knew she'd get her way.

"Who are Tiffany's people?"

"Most of them are Craines and some are Goosbys. They are good people."

Byrd couldn't dispute it. As much as he wanted to have something bad to say about the matter, he couldn't.

"It's alright to go out and have a good time, Riches, but you're going to have to start picking better places to do it. The hoods ain't what they used to be."

"It's not like I want to go live out there or anything. Besides, my friends already know what's up with me."

"What you mean, your friends know what's up with you?" Byrd stood up from the armchair across her bed. He walked towards her dresser, fingered the piece of paper wedged between the mirror on her dresser. He was being nosey, as always.

"They know I don't smoke, drink or hang out with thugs."

He had to smile at the statement she just made. He had taught her well. "I guess that's supposed to make hanging in the hood alright. Because you don't know what they do or talk like they talk, huh?"

"Never know, I might even rub off on some of them. Next thing you know, they'll want to hang out right here."

"Hell naw! Don't bring their ass here!" Byrd laughed, but maintained a serious look. "You know the rules. Don't—"

"Don't be influenced by stupidity, and don't be trying to fit in," she said with closed eyes, completing his words.

"If you get in a jam, you know my number. Don't hesitate either."

"I got this, Byrd. You are tripping."

"And don't be letting them fools drive your car either."

Riches twisted her lips at him. He knew that wasn't likely, because the girl wouldn't even allow him to drive the car he'd bought for her. The Dodge Challenger might have been used, but it was hers. The grades she'd had to make in order to be rewarded in such a fashion taught her sacrifice and that was the very way she looked at it. She worked hard, studied hard and sacrificed way too much, to let someone else to mess things up for her.

As soon as Byrd was out of the room, Riches called her friend, Tiffany. It was a few things they had to get straightened out.

"Tiffany?" Riches spoke into her phone before her friend had time to answer.

"What's up, bitch? You coming or what?"

"Hell, yeah. I had to let Byrd know what was up though. He thinks we're doing the block party thing."

"We are going to do the block party thing."

"That and some, unless ya lame ass can't get out the house for the night."

"Bitch, please, I'm on the up side of the game. You just come on. You are driving, ain't you?"

"Sure."

"You know it's going to be niggas everywhere, balling and waiting to meet some real bitches," Tiffany continued. "Might even get you some dick tonight."

Riches smiled. "Girl, whatever. I don't know why y'all think I'm the virgin of the bunch." She might have talked a good game, but Riches was more virgin than Mary. The only time she'd opened her legs for anybody was for the tailor so he could size her for a custom pair of linen slacks.

"Keep fronting, bitch. A nigga slides a dick across your face and you ain't going to know what to do." Tiffany prided herself on the fact that she could not only take a dick, but she could suck one also. At least, that's what the guys around her way had her thinking.

"Whatever, girl. Y'all just be ready to get it in."

Tonight would be like one of the many nights Riches had lied about, in terms of going to one place but ending up at another. As always, her drinking would be done in moderation and she was only going to smoke weed, provided she was the one to roll it. She wasn't a stranger to things niggas did to get some pussy. Tonight, she was going to do her thing and like always, she'd love it.

CHAPTER TWO

The Stop Six Projects, though a goldmine, was known for the low-income housing and the kinds of people that lived there. Dope fiends, crack heads, casual smokers and heroin addicts busied the sidewalks and parking lots daily. Cops had their eyes on them, but as long as nothing major happened, like a robbery or a white guy getting killed, the police pretty much kept their distance. Finding your vice was as easy as whistling when you were in the projects, because everybody had some sort of product. O'Shay made sure of that. After all, this was one of his spots.

Mike, Pistol, T, Fe and Chubby were the lieutenants of this hood. They made sure the heat stayed to a minimum. T, being the oldest, was responsible for keeping the numbers right and the weight distributed appropriately among the rest of the works. He took his job seriously and at fifteen years of age, he took no shorts and accepted no losses. O'Shay made sure all his guys were straight, as well as their mothers, sisters and brothers.

Without license, insurance or even registration, it was customary to see them in the latest model cars and trucks. The only rule was they had to stay in and around the hood. Catching them outside the hood meant probation. Probation meant you weren't allowed to drive and worst of all, it meant you couldn't make any money for the duration of your probated term.

T was climbing out of the champagne-colored Chevy Sierra when they surrounded him. The guys had been on call because of their next drop, and each of them made sure to be in attendance when it arrived.

"Y'all ready to eat?" he asked them.

With over two hundred and fifty grams of hard butter, five hundred X-pills, several pounds of exotic and rolls of weed, they were ready.

"We gonna shine tonight at the block party!" T told them.

"Hell yeah, hoes gonna be coming from everywhere for the dick tonight," said Chubby.

After everything was distributed among them it was time to get up. By the time Soft Shoulders got to jumping, they'd be damn near out of work and they all knew it.

Cynthia was completing her report and filing documentation of the checks she'd sign for her employees at the end of the day, when her friend, Cherry, walked into her office. It had been a couple of weeks since she'd gotten her package, so she anticipated Cherry's arrival. As their eyes met, they smiled at each other. "You look as if you have some good news," said Cynthia.

"Better than that." Cherry sat in the sofa adjacent her friend and dug around in her purse.

"I got a couple of tickets to the comedy club Saturn You up for something like that or what?" She waved the tickets in front of her friend.

"Who all's going to be there?"

"A bunch of funny motherfuckers." Cherry laughed.

"Let me see what JB got going on. He—''

Cherry cut her friend off. "Fuck JB, Cynthia. You need to cancel his ass anyway." When it was something concerning Cynthia's boyfriend, JB, Cherry didn't care to hear it. His ill-treatment of Cynthia pissed Cherry off.

"Right about now, I wish I was fucking JB," Cynthia continued. Defending both JB and his actions had become habits of hers. Although he often wronged her, she still loved him. She considered his physical abuse minimal, something she had gotten used to.

"If our having a good time depends on what that nigga wants to do, then I'll just find me someone else to go with. A bitch tries to get you away for some fun, the first thing you do is fuck it up talking about his nasty ass." Cherry wasn't a foul-mouthed person, but when it came to taking to and about JB, she didn't mince words. JB was the reason Cynthia started experimenting with cocaine and also the reason she had Cherry sneaking around, meeting with dealers to get it. Cynthia had been the owner of the

Magical Moments Day Care Center for over eighteen years and was a prominent citizen in her community and workplace. Cynthia usually got invitations to events distinguished people attended, and dinners where expensive cuisines were served. People trusted her with their kids, and the chances of any of them finding out she was a user were slim.

"I hope you didn't get that same issue from the last time."

"At a matter of fact, I got another plug and he promised this was a nice drop." Cherry pulled out the envelope that contained one ounce of the powdery substance.

"Girl, don't be pulling that out in here," Cynthia whispered while looking towards her office window.

"Girl, nobody knows what this is. And you're the last person anyone would think got down and dirty like this," Cherry assured her.

"Well. Let's keep it that way, Hell, it's not like I'm a junkie or anything. I only use it to take some of the stress off."

"If you get rid of that no-good ass nigga, you wouldn't have to be stressing in the first place. You are sounding like Byrd when he was doing drugs back in the day."

"I'll never be out there like that," Cynthia said with disgust. Byrd had constantly stolen from the people that loved him, and didn't give a damn about the way they'd felt. Byrd was what Cynthia liked to call a disappointment back then. Regardless of how many times she'd said she'd cut her brother off, she was still his go-to source, asking her for money so he could get high. It wasn't until he showed up on her porch with a baby bundled up in a dirty towel that she told him she was through financing his habits. It was that night she made him promise to do his part in raising that child. That was over nineteen years ago and she was proud of the person her brother had become. Thinking of just that, she told Cherry, "He even managed to surprise me by kicking that habit."

"I wish you could do the same."

"Like I said, I'll never be out there like that." Cynthia closed her file cabinet, gathered her purse and phone, then headed for the door.

Byrd parked his extended cab dodge ram alongside the canopy of his small mechanic shop. He'd been doing car repair all his life, but decided to make something of it when his responsibilities consisted of more than running the streets to get high. After consulting with his sister about a small loan so he could get the spot, she made him promise it wouldn't be for nothing. Knowing how he was and the habits he had, Cynthia made sure he held ownership of the shop. That was nineteen years ago. Today, Byrd was the sole owner of Byrd's Repair Shop and was making a nice living for himself and Riches. His quality of work spread by word of mouth and before he knew it, he was getting so much work he had to hire other mechanics to lighten his load. With four more mechanics and several technicians on his payroll, he was doing well for himself.

Once the stock was checked and several parts were ordered, Byrd kicked his heels up on his desk and leaned back. His mind was on Riches. The girl had grown faster than he'd have liked, and was surrounding herself with the children of people he disapproved of. It wasn't that Byrd couldn't trust Riches. It was because he didn't trust people when Riches was concerned.

"Byrd!"

"Yeah, what's up?" Byrd asked, upon hearing his name being yelled.

"I'm going to need you to give me an advance for next week." Willie had already entered the office and stood by the window facing the lot. He'd been working on and off at the shop for years, but was never called on because he'd disappear for days and weeks at a time. The binges Willie went on usually ended up with Byrd footing the bill for old times' sake. It had taken Byrd much consideration to go on being friends with Willie, since he'd bailed out of helping Cecelia during her labor and childbirth years back while Byrd had been at Walmart. When he'd run into Willie again, a month after Riches was born, Willie had been profuse with apologies and asked for forgiveness. He cited fear and nervousness as the reasons he'd run away during Cecelia's condition at the time.

"I'd like you to drop that transmission on the pick-up around back." Byrd looked up at his friend and continued, "we need to get that one out of here."

Willie began thumbing the magazine on the office desk. "Man, fuck that shit. Ain't nobody tripping over that old ass truck."

"That's beside the point. Business is business, Willie, and we need to keep it straight."

"You gonna give me the money or what? I'm not trying to hear that shit. You know what time it is."

Byrd sighed heavily. Getting his friend out of the funk he knew so well wasn't as easy as it sounded. He'd made sure Willie had a gig where he could make a few dollars, so he wouldn't have to be in the streets doing shit. However, it baffled Byrd that Willie just stayed at the shop doing nothing and expecting something.

"I'll give you a couple of hundred, Willie. But, I need you to—"

"You are letting these motherfuckers get in your head," Willie said, interrupting Byrd while pointing towards the other guys outside. "I don't give a damn about you getting all self-righteous around them but I know who you are, nigga. Once a crackhead, always a crackhead. A leopard doesn't change its goddamn spots!"

"I'm just trying to get you to finish the job you started. Well, they paid you already and you still dragging on their shit. I haven't forgotten where I came from. The only difference is that you still there and I'm not going back!" Byrd was now standing also, his hand around the glass ball he used for a paper weight.

"Come on, Byrd, you know I was just talking. I'm going to finish that job before next week is out."

"That was the same thing you told me last week and the truck is still out back." Byrd counted three hundred dollars and slid the money across his desk. "Don't even worry about it anymore. I'm going to have one of the boys do it."

Willie took the money. "I appreciate it, Byrd. You know how it is, man. I'm trying through. You've got to give me credit for that."

"You really think that, huh?"

Byrd didn't wait for an answer and Willie wasn't waiting around to give one. With three hundred dollars in his pocket, he was ready for the entire weekend. "I'll get back to you later." Willie stopped, faced Byrd and asked, "You sure you don't want to kick it?"

"Get your pipe-sucking ass out of here and don't do nothing stupid either."

Knowing there was going to be more to the story, Byrd closed his eyes and sighed. If no one else understood, Byrd Nichols did. If no one else was grateful for anything, he was grateful for everything.

Willie crossed the shop's lot, climbed into the late-model Malibu Byrd had loaned him, and headed for the east side. Not only did he have a couple hundred dollars to use for front money. He had a plan. If things went accordingly, he'd be set for a while. Feeling the need to wake up, he pulled his glass pipe from over the visors, pushed a nice dub into the Brillo, and set fire to the underside of the stem. "Um," he mumbled, liking the taste of the crack.

CHAPTER THREE

After filling Jay in on the way the deal would go, O'Shay headed to one of his many girlfriends' apartment. His habit of keeping large sums of money and products in the girls' apartments worked for him. As long as he was able to reward most of them with sex and a shopping spree, he'd stayed ahead of the curve.

Shannon, the girl O'Shay was visiting at present, was a nineteen-year-old single mother. She was happy to house whatever O'Shay had for her, especially because of the benefits she got from him, as evidenced by her deluxe wardrobe, amongst other goodies she gained as well. She liked how O'Shay catered to her every want. Besides, she relished the sex he was sure to bring when he did come. That was the reason she answered the door naked.

O'Shay smiled before walking past her. Not only was he used to her brash act, he looked forward to them. "That pussy stay hot, huh?" he said, before kissing her full lips. Shannon's body was what men called magazine material. What enhanced her appearance was her constant visit to beauty parlors, the pedicurist and boutiques.

"And tight," Shannon said. She grabbed his hand and placed it between her legs, eyeing him seductively. Her being clean-shaven was a plus and to O'Shay, she had the prettiest asshole he'd ever seen. Before he could settle into one of the leather seats he'd bought for Shannon, she pushed him backwards and began straddling his face. Before anything else, she'd get hers. And, before all was said and done, he'd be happy as well.

Riches was sitting at the wheel, observing the traffic lights at the intersection of Stolcus and Raney. She was waiting for her cue to go on, when the turquoise Yukon pulled alongside her, its stereo system vibrating her rearview mirror. She'd seen the exact same truck several times and noticed it had different drivers on those different occasions. A couple of years ago, tricked-out cars and trucks did catch her attention. She'd grown to learn that young dope dealers constantly put themselves in the limelight and under the radars of the very people they hid from. Respecting the hustle and the player, she looked over at the driver and threw up the deuces.

Seeing the girl driving the burnt ochre Challenger on the twenty-two inch Lexani spiders, Chubby nudged Mike. "Man, look at this bitch. Ever seen her before?" Mike leaned over Chubby for a better look. He knew her face from somewhere but couldn't quite place her.

"I've seen her somewhere before," said Mike.

Hoping she wouldn't be a threat to their money, Chubby asked, "You think she is moving weight or what?"

Mike shook his head and remembered where he saw the car before. "The south side. Everman," he said, speaking of the high school she'd attended. "Yeah, she one of them southside hoes. Bitch look like she got a little money, the way she is rolling." Mike hit his horn, gaining her attention a second time.

The wave of an arm was the only reason Riches looked over and after seeing the driver signaling for her to pull over, she smiled. Too often, girls would see guys driving nice cars and vie for their attention. Of late, men had been the ones stopping her. Knowing they couldn't have been a day over sixteen and pushing someone else's ride, she lowered her window and asked, "What you want, little boy?"

"Damn, it's like that? I'm just trying to get to know ya pretty ass," Mike grinned, showcasing his diamond grille.

Chubby looked over the Challenger and cut in," You trying to sell that bitch you're riding?" Wanting her to know he was rolling in it, he pulled out a couple of racks of cash. "I'll give you ten grand for it right now."

"My paint cost that much," Riches boasted. Byrd had been able to get the Challenger painted the color she liked, because of the work he'd performed on a couple of a cars belonging to a guy that owned a paint and body shop. In addition, all of her accessories were bought by Byrd, solely because he wanted her to have her own and not be so eager to climb into a guy's car just for the sake of transportation. When the traffic lights changed, Mike said, "What's your name?"

"Riches."

The noise surrounding them hindered Mike's hearing and instead of chasing her, he turned and headed for the cut.

"What she says?" Fe asked Chubby.

"I think she said Rich Bitch or something."

Mike liked what he saw, the car, the girl, her swagger. He'd surely run across her again one day. "I'm going to get at her later."

"Yeah, she was nice," Chubby said.

Cynthia led Cherry to the dining table in the kitchen, reached for the empty tray above the refrigerator and handed it to her. "Put me a little something on there. She'd already called JB a few times and even left messages on his voicemail. He knew the codes at their conversation, so he got back to her at his earliest. Tonight, she planned on scratching the itch she'd been having. Several of her co-workers wanted to get at her on personal levels, but feared losing their employment. Some of the guys that came there to register their kids even tried their luck, but felt intimidated after learning her position and prominence. Bee was the only one that could handle her thirst for the things she liked. With her, the more aggressive the better and that's what Bee brought to the table. That and the watered-down game he was used to.

"I need to hire a maid," Cynthia told herself upon seeing the dust on the tips of her fingers after rubbing the mahogany table, just before she left to change out of her night clothes. Her maintaining the cleanliness of the house was a must because of the company she kept. She paid well over $260,000 for the palatial house in the gated community of Forest Hills. Her neighbors were executives of multi-million dollar companies, owners of social media sites, and realtors. She prided herself on the fact that she was able to move herself out of the suburbs of Fort Worth, into the more prestigious areas. At forty-four years of age, most people considered her successful.

"You need to be paying me for pulling strings to buy this stuff," Cherry said while forming several lines on the tray.

Cynthia rolled a twenty-dollar bill and snorted the entire first line, wiped her nose, looked at a smiling Cherry.

"Good, ain't it?" said Cherry.

Cynthia lowered herself into the high-backed chair and nodded. "Where you get this shit from?"

"Don't start that shit. Get that purse and give me my hundred and fifty dollars." Cherry made sure the party didn't start until she got her service fee.

"I must say, you earned it today." Cynthia pulled two hundred-dollar bills from her purse and handed them to Cherry. One thing Cynthia didn't mind paying for was something she wanted for herself. Her home spoke volumes in that regard.

"I might as well get me a couple more of these. What do you think?"

"You're getting out of control now, Cynthia."

"Girl, please, I rarely do this shit." That statement would have been true had she said it two years ago, but at this moment it was something she was enjoying.

Byrd had an uneasy feeling the moment Willie exited his doors. They'd been a part of each other's lives for years and he knew when something wasn't right with him. Willie was on something untoward and Byrd was sure of it. He had one rule with Willie, no bringing any wacko to his establishment or his home. Not the one to pull a punch when it came to Riches' safety, Byrd let it be known he would trip out when she was concerned.

Shannon's screams and yelps were muffled by the pillows she was biting. Face down and ass up was the way O'Shay liked banging her, because he found her asshole irresistible. After numbing the head of his dick with Baby Orajel, something she made him do when she wanted to be fucked in the position they were in at this moment, he tongued and fingered her, leaving her pussy aroused. O'Shay slapped her ass umpteen times, so much so, it hurt and elicited grunts from her.

"Make that pussy curl, bitch, make it curl," he said in a sing-song tone while thrusting into her with strikes that allowed him to hit the bottom of her vagina. Seeing his cum-streaked dick and hearing her muffled screams, he kept pounding. The more slaps he unleashed on her ass, the harder she bucked like a bronco gone wild. And the sensation emanating from her pussy walls made her vagina greedier for his cock, which didn't relent in its hard, aggressive fucking as though the dick was hell-bent on turning her pussy inside out. Shannon begged for more. "Mmmmmmm! Fuck that puss, nigga. I feel you all the way. Oooooooooooh, fuck me! Fuck me, I can take it! Yessssssssssssss!" Her scream was music in his ears, inflaming his brain. He sucked his middle finger, slid it inside her ass. Shannon let out a long groan, sensing her vaginal muscles and asshole squeeze real hard at the same time. Orgasm gripped her, seizing her nerves as if she were in the throes of electrocution. As her cum burst forth, she gasped, "Get yours, baby, get that nut!" Seconds before he felt his release on the way, he pulled out of her pussy and shoved his ten-inch dick in her asshole. Shannon tried to protest, but her screams only hardened his already throbbing dick more.

"Uhgggg! Nigga, damn, you trying to bust a bitch open." She put a hand back hoping he would slow his stroke, but he only grabbed both of her arms and clamped them behind her, leaving her nothing to defend his assault with. With one hand holding both of her arms and his other gripping the front of her thigh, he pushed deeper.

"Take this dick. Oh, that ass! That ass!" he grunted before coming deep inside of her.

When she collapsed onto the bed, he asked, still thrusting with slower strokes. "You need some money or something?" He sucked softly on her neck and ear while reaching around for a palmful of breast. He fingered her nipples. Feeling his dick throb on and on, he pulled out of her. "Roll over right quick." Loving the way her body glistened with sweat, he parted her legs, licked her inner thighs and covered her clit with his mouth.

"Nigga, you're the devil," she told him before placing her right leg over his shoulder.

CHAPTER FOUR

Willie watched as Mike and Chubby pulled into the projects from across the street. He had scored from them several times. Having spent hundreds of dollars with the young hustlers, he felt they should at least sell him crack on credit sometimes. but that wasn't the way these youngsters treated the game. A couple of weeks ago, that was exactly what had happened. He'd spent well over three hundred dollars and when he came back a couple of days later, in need of a boost but having no money, Mike and Chubby rejected him. Willie had been on these streets before most of them were born, thus he didn't like the lack of respect they showed him. I won't tolerate such disrespect, thought Willie, checking the cylinder of the six-shot .38 he'd brought along. The huge crack rock he loaded on his stem lit up his brain the moment he inhaled the smoke. "This some good ass dope," he told himself before stuffing the pipe over the visor and pushing the gun into his waistband. "Punk motherfuckers ain't got no game for Willie," he said to himself and climbed out.

Mike handed Chubby a bulging Crown Royal bag. "Here, you go ahead. I have something to do right quick." Chubby smirked. He knew what time it was. On the ride there, Mike had been on the phone with one of his chicks. Seeing her watching from the doorway of her mom's apartment really got to Mike. "Do your thang, man. I got this end," Chubby assured him.

"Sure?"

"Yeah, I got it." Chubby nodded at the girl and headed in the other direction. These things were routine for him. Counting money was something he'd been doing for months now.

Chubby had climbed the steps and was fumbling with the keys in his pocket when Willie approached him. He'd seen Willie a couple of times and figured it might be time to bless the junkie, only if he was scoring something and not begging.

"Hey, youngster, what are you are holding?"

Chubby acknowledged Willie with a glance. "What you trying to do?"

"I want the usual," Willie told him, before pulling out the huge wad of cash.

"How much you got there?" Chubby asked, seeing the cash.

"About eleven-hundred. I got another grand in the car, just in case . . ." Willie looked around them to see who else might be watching. Seeing no one, he heaved a sigh of relief.

Liking the possibility of another lick, Chubby nodded. Against his better judgment, he did something his shouldn't he shouldn't have. "Come on in right quick, I got a little something for you."

Once inside the apartment, Willie waited to see if anyone else was there. Hearing no one, he bit his bottom lip. Chubby knew how heads swelled with ego when it comes to the dope and that was the reason he began smiling. The dope he and Mike had was strong and purer than ever. He knew it was only a matter of time before Willie was back scoring more.

"I'll give you two ounces for the eleven hundred." Chubby had led Willie to the kitchen area and pulled the shoe box from over the refrigerator. As soon as he turned to face Willie, he noticed the pistol pointed at him. "Damn!"

"Where the rest of that work at?"

Not believing the position he was in, Chubby placed the shoebox on the counter. "You for real, man?"

"Oh, you one of them punk motherfuckers that need to see some blood, huh?" Willie raised the gun to Chubby's face.

"Hold up, old school. You can have all this shit, man. I'm not tripping." Chubby felt he had to do something there and then, knowing full well Mike wouldn't be returning until later. Having to take a loss like this wouldn't go down very well with O'Shay, thought Chubby.

Willie observed Chubby's body language; he knew the youngster was trying to buy time. "I want everything you got right here and right now!"

"All I got right here is a couple of ounces. I told you I got…"

Chubby swallowed the rest of his words the instant Willie grabbed his neatly trimmed afro and shoved him into the counter top. "I'm not playing with your fat ass!" Willie hit him upside his face with the pistol three times. The hit was so hard Chubby could both feel and see the blood now pouring from the gash by his left ear.

"Alright! Alright! Just don't kill me, man."

Riches parked behind a marble green CTS Cadillac. She was sure this was Tiffany's home, because of the address she'd been given. As this was a first time for Riches, she'd been told her friends would be waiting outside when she arrived. "Where this girl at?" she asked herself before texting Tiffany again. Seconds later, Tiffany emerged from the passenger's side of the CTS, applying a coat of lip gloss.

Tiffany climbed into the Challenger and smiled at her friend. "I didn't think you'd get here that fast."

"Who is that?" Riches asked before the car pulled from the curb.

"Girl, that was Butter. Remember, I was telling you about him."

Riches frowned. "The old guy who's been giving you money?"

"Yeah, he just wanted his dick sucked." Tiffany pulled five hundred dollars from her purse. "Head game vicious, ain't it?"

"Go brush your teeth or something, Tiff! Your mouth reeks of cum. I'm not riding with your breath smelling like that."

Tiffany sighed, "Ughhh, I'll be right back." She alighted from the car and ran into the house.

"Tramp!" Riches murmured under her breath. She knew Tiffany was hood. However, she felt she had to put a boundary on their friendship. Byrd had always told her, If you didn't set any for yourself, no one would.

Tiffany jumped back in the car. "You happy now?" she smiled at her friend, checked herself in the visor's mirror.

"What you did makes no sense, girl. And you did it in front of your home."

"He said he had something else to do. Besides, his wife be texting him every five minutes."

"So, he gave you all that money for some head?"

"I let him fuck me sometimes. This is how I eat, girl. Everybody ain't got it like you. You are rolling a Challenger, you keep money and you got a rich auntie. You got it made, Riches. But, some of us out here got to hustle for daily bread."

"Yeah, well, I still wouldn't be out there like that. I'll just get me a job or something."

"Bitch, who gonna hire us?" Tiffany turned in her seat and faced Riches. "Huh, who gonna hire somebody like us?"

"No offense, Tiff, but if truth be told, it's you who's made yourself unhireable. I, for one, would prefer to keep a job, rather than act like a rolling stone. I have acted as a reference for you in several jobs, yet your habit of using dope during work hours would always get you fired. I do have it better than most of my peers, but that is because both Byrd and my Auntie Cynthia made something of themselves and touched me with the same values."

"No offense taken, Riches. I get your point."

"Good. Anyway, you can come work for Auntie Cynthia. I'm more than sure I can get you a job¬, if you really want one."

"Is she going to pay me five hundred dollars for ten minutes of work?"

"Not sure."

"I don't think she could pay me that. The only way people out here getting that kinda money is by doing what it takes to get it."

"Well, you just keep on wetting a nigga's whistle, if it really pays you."

Cynthia and Cherry were sitting in the pitched den when JB showed his face. When he took off his shades, they could tell from his glossed-over eyes that he was high. Bee, as JB was fondly called, smiled at both of them

"What you both doing?"

Cherry rolled her eyes at him. "It ain't nothing to do with your tired ass."

JB focused on Cynthia. "Hey, baby. About time you showed up. I thought I was going to have to call somebody else that knew how to oil my dick."

Cynthia stood, and JB saw that she only wore a t-shirt.

"Well, I guess that's my cue. I'm going to leave you two freaks alone." Cherry grabbed her keys and headed for the door. "I'll show myself out."

Cynthia pointed to the tray on the endtable. "Get you some of that right quick. I got something for you."

"Where's my juice?"

"In the back of this pussy."

"Mmm, I like the sound of that." Bee snorted two lines, looked up at Cynthia, and snorted half another.

"Take that shit off. You've been begging for an ass whopping all day." He pulled the belt from his pants, rolled it around his hand, walked towards her.

"I'm sorry, daddy." Cynthia smiled, backed away until her back touched the wall. I didn't mean to make you mad, baby."

"Turn that ass around." Bee looked over Cynthia's dark chocolate skin. Her short frame carrying a forty-four-inch ass, she was plump, thick and curvy altogether, but had some of the prettiest feet he'd ever seen.

"I'm going to fuck the shit out of you today." He spanked her ass hard.

Cynthia jumped. "Harder, baby. Spank that ass!"

Bee was spanking a willing Cynthia and getting out of his clothes at the same time. She loved it when he spanked her and right afterwards, massaged her welted flesh. The coke and the excitement, the pain and the pleasure, it all was something Cynthia couldn't get enough of. Once he saw the welts forming on Cynthia's butt cheeks, he pressed his manhood against her. She pushed herself from the wall, knelt down in front of him facing him, then took him into her mouth and moaned, causing him to grab the sides of her head.

"You like that?" she mumbled with a mouthful of dick. The girth of him excited her to no end and being able to deep throat the same dick baffled her.

Bee stood watching the almond-eyed, chocolate woman devour his throbbing dick. Feeling himself swell, he pulled out of her and pushed her on her back. She immediately opened her legs, inviting him to a hairy pussy opened slightly at the entrance. Her clit was bigger than normal and when positioning himself between her, he used his dick to spank it repeatedly.

Using her elbows to prop herself up, Cynthia eyed the dick hungrily. She wanted all of it in her.

"Mmmmmmmmm! That's right!" She squirmed under him. "Yeah, punish that pussy, baby." She reached down, grabbing his shaft and placed it at her opening, the pussy lips embracing the mushroomed head of his dick.

Bee pushed her legs to her chest. He pushed inside of her. His thickness was wont to put her pussy in a helpless state, with the positions she found herself in. His thrust was slow at first, then faster; shorter in the beginning, then deeper. Hearing her moans, he pushed deeper, harder and faster, causing her to moan more and more.

O'Shay was a frequent customer at the Ridgemore Mall. He had a few girlfriends managing a few of the high-end boutiques there, and sending a few grands did both favors and wonders for him and them. Shannon being the juiciest of O'Shay's bootilicious fruits, clothes dealers loved to dress her, make-up artists loved painting her, and niggas dreamed of fucking her.

"What do you think about a couple of pant suits?" she asked O'Shay after gathering her bags from the counter of the Victoria's Secret lingerie booth.

"Whatever you want, get it," said O'Shay. He conducted several calls while following Shannon through the traffic of patrons and employees. This was the getaway he needed from the hood at the moment. The calls he answered were more than favorable, as was the money he was sure to pull in.

"I'm going to make a stop right quick at World Foot Locker, text me in about fifteen minutes." This was the excuse he used to get a closer look at the two girls across the way. He recognized the shorter one, but the mare with her was what caught his attention. Seeing guys walking over to her was the reason he was walking in their direction himself.

Riches had to literally pull Tiffany out of the music store because of the hungry eyes looking in their direction.

"Girl, bring your fast ass on," said Riches.

"If I knew it was going to be like this at the mall, I would have worn something more enticing," said Tiffany.

"Even if you'd worn a choir robe, they still would have been chasing your ass."

"As if you're not getting attention too."

"Yeah, because of you and your freaky ass." Riches laughed.

"See, you've got to be able to sort out the ones that got the money to give and the ones that ain't."

"That's what's wrong with you. Should you end up catching something you can't get rid of, you'll be wishing otherwise."

"But, we both know that day has to come before I quit the game." Tiffany winked at Riches and pulled down the powder pink Air Max from the display shelf.

O'Shay was standing by the counter, talking on his phone when Tiffany and Riches walked up. He nodded at Tiffany and smiled at Riches, making sure he showed her the diamond display in his mouth. Riches smiled back.

"Damn, you're beautiful," O'Shay said to Riches as he held out his hand. "I'm O'Shay."

Sensing the guy was interested in only Riches, Tiffany excused herself.

"Thanks. I'm Riches." Her guess was that the guy must be ten years older than she, and was definitely a thug. His attire, his teeth, his swag, everything told her to walk away. But, he was handsome, clean-cut and smelled good. Riches had to make herself look away from his hazel eyes, which she found captivating. His jet-black waves accentuated his chocolate complexion and he towered over her. Before she could excuse herself and catch up with her friend, he continued.

"Riches, I see a treasure when looking at you. Do you model?" He looked her over. Even in jeans and a Texans jersey, the girl was turning heads. He noticed her slightly-bowed legs, hips and thighs that were shapelier than he thought. This girl is definitely giving Shannon a run for her money.

"No, modeling is not for me, but thanks for the compliment." Riches looked around for Tiffany.

"If you don't mind me asking, how old are you?"

"I'll be twenty-one in a couple of weeks."

"Sounds great!"

"Mm." Riches saw Tiffany return from wherever she'd disappeared. O'Shay was still smiling, staring at Riches as if he'd seen paradise, and his smile wasn't lost on her. "Tell me, how old are you?"

"Twenty-six," said O'Shay.

Tiffany walked up from behind him, placed her items on the counter.

O'Shay couldn't help but look Riches over again. "Babe, you're so fine, I could lick ice cream off your body."

Riches smiled.

"When it comes to ice cream, it had better be vanilla, coz that's her fave," said Tiffany.

"Let me buy this hit for y'all." O'Shay pulled out his wad of cash. This was something that usually sealed the deal.

"I got this," Riches told him and pulled out the Platinum Visa she had.

O'Shay frowned. "What are you doing with the platinum?" Realizing he'd probably put her on blast in front of the clerk, he sat five one-hundred-dollar bills on the counter.

"Oh, she legit," Tiffany chimed in. "Rich people in her family."

Riches charged twenty-two hundred dollars' worth of shoes, socks, jerseys, pullovers and warm-ups, the eight pairs of shoes being the most expensive.

"Can I at least give you my number?" O'Shay asked.

"Why not?" said Tiffany.

"Yeah, sure." Riches rolled her eyes at Tiff. The girl wasn't going to let it rest.

"I'm just going to have to catch up with you later, Riches." O'Shay scribbled down his phone number and pushed it into her hand. "Maybe you'll let me take you shopping or something."

Riches simply smiled.

"Sounds good if you ask me," Tiffany smiled and shook his hand.

O'Shay walked in the direction he'd left Shannon, looked back at the two girls and waved. In his mind, he had to have Riches and if he got it his way, he'd have both of them at the same time.

Willie checked his rearview mirror every few seconds until he made it back to the south side of town. The shoebox did contain two ounces, but the real lick came from the Crown Royal bag Chubby had tried his best to hide. Parked on the side of the automobile shop, Willie counted out nine thousand in cash, his eyes widening with every bill he counted. "Fat motherfucker tried to hold out on Willie," he said aloud. This was his come-up all by himself. Back in the say it would have been him, Byrd, Kay and CeCe, but that was a lifetime ago. The last time he saw Cecilia was the night she died and the last time he saw Kay, she looked as if she was about to. Feeling the win of a lifetime, Willie filled his pipe with huge chunks of the crack he now owned.

He looked around the lot and was satisfied that no one was paying him any attention. This was his moment. Willie laughed. "Ha, you son of a bitch!" Hearing the crack sizzle under the heat of the big lighter, he put the pipe to his mouth and pulled, smacked his lips and pulled again.

Byrd was walking from the garage to the office when he saw the black Malibu pull around the side of the building. Because of the tint, he could see Willie but when he saw the small fire, he knew exactly what his friend was doing. The taste he was once familiar with flooded his head and as bad as he wanted to join Willie, he couldn't. This was a fight he had with himself occasionally. Byrd would have loved to rub a crack pipe between his palms, but he couldn't bring himself to do it.

Byrd stopped at threshold of the number-three stall and watched the Malibu. All he could see was the flickered flame on the driver's side. He swallowed hard, looked towards the service desk and headed in Willie's direction. He could use a good laugh and knowing Willie was most likely over the moon, Byrd smiled mischievously.

Willie was laughing uncontrollably. He felt all his troubles were over, because he knew exactly what to do with the money he'd just acquired. "These haters on my body shake 'em off," he sang along with the radio. He closed his eyes and thought the first thing he had to do was get another ride, just in case someone was able to identify him by the Malibu. Secondly, he'd rent a motel room on Bishop Street and get himself a couple of whores. Willie laughed again. He was on his way, he thought to himself, and it was those thoughts that kept him from seeing his reality and the driver's door being yanked open.

"Get on the goddamn ground, you son of a bitch!"

Willie tried to reach for the .38 he had on his person. Before he could scream for help, the dark figure pressed against him.

"You motherfucker!" was all he could manage, because he knew he was dead.

Byrd was laughing so hard, he lost his footing upon seeing Willie reaching for the only protection he had. Fucking off a good high was something he hadn't done in a while.

"What's yo' scary ass doing in here?" Byrd was still smiling at the terrified look on his friend's face.

"What the fuck wrong with you, nigga! You damn near got smoked, fool." Willie checked for his pipe, making sure it hadn't shattered in the event.

"Yeah, I can tell by the way you were screaming and looking. Ya eyes got so big ya eyebrows disappeared." Byrd couldn't stop laughing. He knew Willie was mad as hell and had more than likely messed up whatever dope he had left.

"Ya black ass play too much!"

Seeing the revolver, Byrd grew serious. "What are you doing with that?" His eyes darted from the gun to the Crown Royal Bag and the money beside it. "What the fuck have you done, man?"

"It wasn't you who did it, so don't worry about it." Willie's tone of voice was defensive, an apparent action Byrd was used to seeing when his friend was hiding something.

'I hope you didn't rob some store, and use this car for a getaway!"

"Ain't nobody rob no damn store." Willie climbed out of the car.

Byrd watched him, looked over his attire then back to the money in the passenger's seat. "Where did the blood come from?"

Willie's eyes followed Byrd's to his right hand. How could he have not known blood was there? Hoping the conversation would end, Willie feigned ignorance. "Probably cut myself fucking with you a moment ago."

CHAPTER FIVE

Mike hit the stairs two at a time. He smiled contentedly. "Damn, that hoe got some good pussy!" he yelled before seeing the partially open door. Concern now replaced his air of confidenc, because Chubby wasn't known for leaving the door carelessly open like that. Mike walked from the living area to the bedroom. "Chubby! Fat ass nigga, where you at?" It wasn't until Mike had walked back to the front of the apartment to the kitchen that he saw his friend lying bloodied on the linoleum floor. "Chubby! Chubby!"

Hearing his name, Chubby groggily came to. He felt his swollen face as he looked Mike over. "Motherfucker got me bad."

"Who?" Mike asked before looking around.

"Fucking crackheads got me."

"Fat bastard, stop lying all the damn time!" Mike checked the stash above the refrigerator, praying it wasn't true.

"They tried to kill me." Chubby sat up, shook his head and grimaced at the pain. "Ran in on me when I was opening the door."

"Damn it, nigga, what they get?" Mike was now hysterical. There was no way this was happening.

Chubby was slowly coming to. He and Mike were boys, but there was no way he was going to take a loss by himself. He still had his personal money, but that didn't have anything to do with the money they lost. "If you would have been with me, them crack head motherfuckers wouldn't have moved on me like that."

"Don't be blaming me, punk-ass nigga! I asked you if you had it and ya fat ass got bossy." Mike ran to the window overlooking the parking lot for either car that belonged to boss "Man, you know this nigga on his way to pick up that bread. Damn!"

"We ain't lose nothing but nine grand," Chubby reasoned.

"You are bumping like you got it or something."

"Man, I told you them niggas got me," Chubby lied. "I got a little something in the back, if they ain't got that too." He headed for the bedroom, looking over his shoulder.

Worried about the outcome of the ordeal, Mike counted out all the money he had on him. He thought of how O'Shay was wont to preach to them about the repercussions of them walking around with shit loads of cash.

Chubby returned with a handful of cash.

"All I have is a little over twothousand," said Mike.

"That's all? Shit! All I got is seventy-five hundred on me."

"Here, give me that." Mike snatched the cash and counted it again, hoping like hell it was more than the said amount. "Your stupid ass need to be trying to find out where them crackheads be at, 'cause I'm gonna kill them hoes!"

Chubby watched his friend punch the wall in anger. All he had to do now was keep to his story about it being more than one person, and once it was out that the reward consisted of some crack, every crackhead in the hood would have a story to tell, which could help in catching the culprit.

"Somebody must have seen something."

With an iced towel over his face, Chubby continued to conjure his plan. He had to smile at a quote he remembered, "Keep ya losses to a minimum."

Having older cousins and sisters who schooled her on the things niggas paid for, Tiffany made herself a competitor in the game. Knowing the reasons niggas came back for more of what she offered, she kept herself ready.

'I'm telling you, girl," Tiffany was saying to Riches, "you've got to keep the pussy tight. Water and a little vinegar do help in that regard. It's old school, but it works."

"The way you got niggas running in and out of your pussy, you gonna be sore." Riches laughed.

"Nah! The pussy snaps back like a rubber glove, and these niggas love some tight pussy. When they think they are killing it, they cry to keep it for themselves. That's why you only fuck niggas that like to spend the money. Niggas who think they're special and know their wives and girlfriends can't find out." Satisfied with her principles and the point she'd made, Tiffany lowered her visor and checked her appearance. Hell, it allowed her to walk around with hundreds and hundreds of dollars. "In a couple of years, I'm going to be like Mona," Tiffany continued, referring to her oldest cousin who'd made it big. "Two cars, a house, clothing store, and only fuck with niggas out of town."

As Riches kept driving, she thought, Tiffany's made a hell of an argument, but I know better. Not only was Byrd enlightening her from a male's perspective, but her Aunt Cynthia continually educated her on things from a more prominent point of view. Seeing her aunt own and manage several properties, host council members, influence mothers both young and old, and maintain a good name while doing it was an inspiration to Riches. "Well, you keep doing what you do 'cause in due course, I'm going to be a college grad. And with my degree, I'll be sitting on somebody's board and running a business or something. Oh yeah, and living drama free."

"Whatever, girl." Tiffany sighed. "Ain't nothing exciting about that. The shit even sounds boring as hell."

"That's what's wrong with your crazy ass now, Tiff. Drama and chaos excite you and you feel you continually need it."

"What I need is a lot of money, a nigga that knows how to suck some pussy, and somebody that's going to spoil my ass."

Cynthia's pussy was throbbing. She was so sensitive she came every ten strokes Bee dealt to her pussy. Besides, the cocaine was so good, she had to have more. The dick was still hard and Bee wasn't stopping. Feeling herself cum for the umpteenth time, she reached around and grabbed Bee's ass. Pulling him deeper, she yelled. "Ugh, ugh, ugh, here it comes again!" With her knees still pressed to her breasts she had to take all of him, his strokes, his grinds, the pressures and the pounding. "Um-hummm, beat this pussy, baby!"

Bee licked the soles of Cynthia's feet, sucked her toes, and made her feel every inch of his manhood. He watched the sweat glistening on her body, making it look as if her chocolate skin was melting under him. He lowered himself and kissed her full lips. His rhythm slowed. Smiling down at her, he asked: "You good?"

"Mmmmmmmm," she could only reply in a moan. There was no more fight in her, no energy left, only spasms strong and deep in her loins. She couldn't stop, couldn't control it. How she loved every minute of it! She wiped the sweat from his brows, then he squeezed her clit. "Oh, shit. You can't keep doing me like this," she said, her voice full of plea. Bee pulled out and squeezed her clit again. She let out a long-muffled cry. "Don't, don't touch it," she begged him.

"Turn over." Seeing her unable to comply, Bee rolled her over, placed a huge throw pillow under her pelvic area, lifted her ass slightly and entered her vagina from the back. "Cynthia, gimme some more money. You know I'm going to pay you back."

"Whatever you want, Bee. Whatever you want."

Byrd followed Willie inside. "I guess that blood on your arm don't have nothing to do with these cars pulling into the shop now, or does it?" Willie kept mute; Byrd sensed a slight uneasiness in him "So, you did rob somebody?"

"Man, stop sweating that shit. Nigga got caught slipping, charged it to the game and moved on. I know I did."

"Oh yeah, charging it to the game ain't never made no blood spill and the way you were peeping out that window,you worried about something." Byrd pointed towards the door and said, "If some niggas come up in here looking for your ass, I'm going to point you out, 'cause I told you not to bring your shit back here.

I don't give a damn what you do out there, but I've got more than me to worry about."

"Nigga, ain't nobody even saw me. I know how to blind a young ass nigga! You act like I just started doing this shit."

"Like I was saying, it isn't just me thinking about me and the next high. I got to think about Riches."

"Yeah, yeah, I know." Thinking of a way to change the conversation, Willie said, "Know she is hanging around on the east side now, don't you?"

"Yeah, I know. I told her she could go out there for the weekend. Where you see her at?"

"I was a couple of cars behind her earlier. She didn't see me though."

"So, you rob some of them east side niggas?"

"There you go with that shit. Don't worry about that, Byrd. Leave it be."

Having heard that line many times before, Byrd threw up his hands in defeat. He'd seen Willie get his ass beat up umpteen times, but still felt he'd give him the benefit of the doubt. Hell, this wasn't the first time and as long as Willie got high, it wouldn't be the last.

O'Shay was finishing a call when he walked through the doors of the apartment and the first thing he noticed was Chubby's face. "What the fuck happened to you?" He looked from him to Mike, who was engrossed in the video game he was playing.

"It wasn't nothing major. I handled it."

"Handled what?" O'Shay headed to the kitchen. Fighting amongst his workers was totally against the code with him, and if there was a problem he should have known about and they didn't report it, there was still a problem.

"Stupid ass nigga damn near fell down all the stairs and bust his face on the railings," Mike said, preventing Chubby from messing everything up

"That bitch was running up and down the stairs and got in the way," Chubby said, trying to hide his nervousness.

O'Shay looked askance at him. "What bitch?"

"Tara," Chubby replied, quickly mentioning the first name that came to his mind.

Knowing full well that the girl Chubby had named was actually a little girl, O'Shay looked at him incredulously. "Tara?"

Mike exhaled and shook his head. "That little motherfucker is always in the way or doing something stupid."

O'Shay walked into the kitchen, opened the refrigerator and grabbed one of the kiwi juices. He knew they were lying to him because he'd just talked to Tara's mother on the way upstairs. And having heard from her mom about the drama she underwent when picking Tara up from her father's house only confirmed it. These boys are up to something and if I'm right, it has something to do with either my product or my money and that is a big problem. "You both ready with that bread or what?"

"Yeah, everything straight on that end," said Mike, handing O'Shay nine thousand dollars in sequenced bills. Not one dollar missing.

"Where's the Crown Royal bag I gave you both?"

Neither of the two responded fast enough, out of fear one would say something different from the other,another mistake on their part.

"You motherfuckers think I'm stupid now! I'll tell you what, give me my keys and get your asses out!"

"Come on, O'Shay, man," Chubby began. The money is—"

"It ain't about no money, nigga!" said O'Shay, cutting Chubby off. "Why the fuck y'all in here trying to play me? Tara ain't even been here and your fat ass ain't fall down no stairs." O'Shay held out his hands, beckoning for his keys. "Gimme my shit."

"You the one be telling us to cover for each other and have each other's back and all that shit. Now you want to trip about the shit you done told us to do?" Mike said.

"Who the fuck you talking to like that?" O'Shay walked towards Mike.

Seeing things escalating, Chubby stood up and got in front of his boss.

"Let him make it, boss. That nigga been tripping all day."

"I said who you talking to like that?" O'Shay pushed Chubby aside, stood inches in front of Mike.

"I'm talking to you. You told me to keep this shit right and..."

Before Mike could finish his statement, O'Shay slapped him hard across the face, silencing him, the slap resounding through the room.

Stunned, Mike held his cheek, his eyes stinging from the slap.

"Don't ever, ever, show me such attitude again, boy," said O'Shay, his nostrils flaring with anger.

Chubby deemed it fit to be silent, fearing he might get a slap or something if he spoke out of turn. O'Shay counted three thousand from the money he'd been given and handed it to Mike. "Pay your works and get some food up in here."

Mike simply nodded.

O'Shay always made sure Mike and T oversaw the operations he kept in the projects, and Chubby and Pistol added a little muscle to the fold. Now, Chubby was fucked up. Moreover, he and Mike weren't saying anything. As far as I am concerned, thought O'Shay, the issue is far from over.

"Get at T and let them know that I'm going to have something coming through and I'm not waiting on nobody." O'Shay turned and headed for the door. "And keep ya mouths shut, we don't need everybody knowing when and what we are moving," he said to Mike and Chubby. After a couple of calls and seeing a few faces, O'Shay was sure that he'd have the details he was looking for. True enough, he told his boys numerous times to take care of their business and look one another, but he still made it his business to say in the loop.

After several visits and hours of conversation, Riches was ready to get something to drink. She and Tiffany had been debating about the game and the things she felt she knew too well. Once she'd met Mona and had the chance to hear it from her end, understanding Tiffany was easier. Mona's history was one of both abuse and drugs at an early age. And having to drop out of school at the age of thirteen to take care of her sisters was something Riches couldn't fathom. Tiffany was emulating Mona's lifestyle and justifying it as a means of living. She wasn't even willing to turn over a new leaf.

"Mona's been through a lot," Riches said, as if speaking to herself.

"Girl, you ain't listening to nothing I said." Tiffany nudged Riches and pointed out the front dash. "Pull up in there, let's get some wine coolers or something."

"Yeah, I could use a wine cooler." Riches pulled into the corner store on Killian and Miller.

"Get some blunts too," Tiffany reminded her.

Riches climbed out, checked herself in the reflection of her driver's side window and entered the building. The smell of toasted bread and seasoned meats wafted to her nostrils. She smiled. Standing before the beverage cooler, she could feel the coolness inside. "Damn, I haven't even opened the door and I'm freezing," she said.

"Excuse me?"

Not realizing anyone was even around her, Riches looked back to see a tall, dark-skinned brother. She frowned. "Oh, I'm sorry. I didn't even know you were there. I was just talking to myself. My bad." Riches turned back to the cooler and continued her selection.

"Is there anything I can help you with while I'm here?" the dude asked her.

"Just looking for something light to drink." Seeing him smile, she smiled. She could feel the obvious question coming.

"Oh, you're trying to get bent, but not drunk."

"Yeah, yeah, you can say that," she said, then laughed.

"Aren't you the one driving that Challenger outside?"

"Yeah."

"Well, if I was you, I'd be trying to get some bottles of Cîroc. That's if you got the money to spend." He pointed to a different section of drinks.

"You work here?" she asked, taking into account the fact that he also wore an apron.

"I own this place. I'm Yousef, and you are?"

Riches looked around them, then back to the guy standing in front of her. He wasn't the best-looking guy, but he was genuine and more of a gentleman than most guys she'd come across on this side of town. His pock-marked face reminded her of the singer, Seal, but this guy was at least six feet three and had an athletic build. His tapered face, soft brown eyes and neatly trimmed facial hair made her reckon he was much older. "My friends call me Riches."

"Riches?"

"Yep, that's what they call me." This was one time Riches wished she'd worn something different, something that accentuated every curve on her body.

"Riches, mmm. Well, it's not like a person can forget that. You're so beautiful."

Riches smiled. "Thanks for the compliment."

"Come on over here and get you a couple bottles of this Cîroc. Women come in here requesting it all the time," he added.

"Have you been working here for a while?"

"Yeah,family-owned biz." Yousef backed away and headed towards the front of the store. "Pick your poison."

With three bottles of Pink Passion, Riches made her way to the counter. "You're the one cooking too?"

"Yeah, sometimes. But Rodney's back there now."

"Those curly fries sure smell good," she said, looking towards the menu over the cigarette selector.

"It'll take about four minutes for them to fry 'cause we drop 'em fresh and serve 'em hot."

"I guess I could have a few minutes." Riches looked out of the window to the parking lot in an attempt to see what Tiffany was doing. From where she stood, she could feel the vibrations her stereo caused and concluded that her friend was probably on her phone or singing along with whatever song she was listening to.

It wasn't everyday Yousef entertained guests in this fashion, but talking to Riches was something he welcomed. He didn't have to follow her around the store to make sure she wasn't shoplifting. So far, she hadn't come to him with any game to get something for free. He was no stranger to being around beautiful women and therefore wasn't intimidated by that. "Are you celebrating something?"

"Yeah, but not until next week."

"Maybe I could send you a Kissogram or disguise myself as one."

Riches laughed aloud, covering her mouth with her right hand, showing off her Draconian manicure and her five-carat bracelet. She took a step back, hoping he'd notice the belly ring dangling below. She'd tied the jersey she was wearing in the back to show off her small waist.

Riches noticed him watching her. Eager to give him a better view, she turned her back to him and began looking towards the door and that's when she saw Tiffany entering.

"Damn, girl, I thought you got lost up in here," Tiffany said.

Riches faced Yousef and rolled her eyes. "I was just about to come out and ask you what type of blunt you wanted."

Tiffany stopped, looked Riches over then to Yousef, who was staring at the both of them. Hoping her friend wasn't caught up in some sort of shit, she felt obliged to come to her rescue. "Um, is there a problem?"

Yousef frowned. "No."

"I'm waiting on my curly fries, thank you," Riches said.

"Oh."

"Yeah," Riches said before giving her friend the side eye. Seeing Rodney walking from the back with her order, she stepped back in front of the register. "They smell good."

"That will be sixty-five sixty," he told her.

"Damn, girl, what a buy!" Tiffany said, looking over the items Riches picked. "Cîroc? Why you get this bitch-ass shit? You could have got some Jack Daniels or something other than that shit."

"We are trying something new tonight, Tiff. Pick the blunts out and let's go." She could tell that ever since Tiffany walked in, Yousef held back the conversation they were having. Riches hoped it wasn't because he couldn't choose between the two of them.

Once they made it back to the car, Tiffany blurted out: "Why you in there smiling at that ugly-ass man?"

"He ain't ugly. He's got some pretty eyes and he's nice as hell."

"Nice as hell and broke as hell too. Nigga working in a store and shit. Hell, naw, bitch. Don't start that shit."

"Shut up, Tiffany. You act like I was sucking his dick or something. We were just making small talk until my fries got ready." Riches handed Tiffany a couple of the curly fries.

"The way he was looking at your ass, he prolly was behind that damn counter getting off." Tiffany pulled a blunt from the box and emptied the leaf. "Where that exotic at?"

Riches was just about to pull into traffic when the champagne-colored Sierra pulled past her, going in the direction she'd just come. Tiffany told her, "The guys in that car are the kind of niggas you should be spending your time with. Not some broke-ass nigga working in a damn corner store."

"What if he owned the store? He—"

"Owned it? Girl, please. Niggas say such things to get some pussy and if I hadn't come in there, ya ass might have gotten drugged and fucked for free or something."

Riches couldn't help but laugh. The girl might be talking shit, yet Riches knew there was some truth in what Tiffany was saying. After all, she was already going out of her way to attract him. She wondered what might have happened if Tiffany hadn't walked in. "Said his name was Yousef. You ever heard about him?"

"The nigga drives that old-ass Maxima parked in front." Tiff filled her mouth with another handful of fries before continuing, "I think I heard something about him having a kid, and his baby momma fucked over him or something."

"Fucked over him how?

"The hell if I know." Tiffany shrugged. "Probably fucked one of his friends or got caught cheating. Fuck 'em."

"Well, at least you ain't heard nothing about him being a thug and beating up girls, "Riches said in Yousef's defense.

"Ugly-ass nigga ought to be glad a bitch cheated on his ass. Ain't no real bitch being faithful for nothing."

"You never know, he might be a fool with it," Riches said.

"Yeah, right. Ain't no bitches breaking their necks to keep that kinda nigga to themselves." Tiffany pulled the vibrating Samsung from its Gucci case and looked at the caller's picture. "Be quiet right quick, let me see what this nigga trying to spend." Tiffany winked before taking the call.

Riches thought about the guy she'd just met. There was something she liked about him. It wasn't always about the looks to her. Remembering some of the things her aunt Cynthia told her, it was more important to have a man treat you right, than one fucking over you every time. She'd also told her to be careful because there were guys that seemed nice and good, but ended up being abusive and pieces of shit once they got what they wanted. "Don't let yourself get trapped, Riches. It's heaven to fall in and hell to get out of." Those were the words her aunt used to sum it up. Either way, I'm going to see what Yousef is about.

Mike waited until O'Shay had walked downstairs before speaking. Since he still had the keys to both the apartment and the Yukon, he believed he held position in the crew and a shot was about to be called. "I can't wait 'til I get my own shit and make my own money. I'm tired of going through this shit and being kicked to the curb. Imagine all the money we make for this nigga and we still ain't got our own shit." Mike threw the money he was given on the table and flopped down beside Chubby on the couch.

Chubby closed his eyes beneath the towel he had over his face. He'd heard Mike rant hundreds of times and knew his friend was just talking. Money was continually coming along with girls here and there. Chubby wasn't going anywhere and neither was Mike.

"I feel ya. We get that nigga out of the way, then we'll be rich." Chubby watched Mike from under the towel, saw his mind spinning, He knew what was coming next.

"I'm not tripping like that, I'm just saying."

"Yeah, tell me about it. Besides, you'll have to kill T, Pistol and a whole bunch of niggas and hoes he be looking out for."

"Anyways, we drive his cars and trucks, so we can move his dope and collect his money. We live in his apartment, so we'll have a place to stash his shit."

Mike and Chubby were laughing so hard they didn't even hear the front door being opened, let alone the two figures that walked up behind them.

"Break yourselves, bitches."One of them grabbed a handful of Chubby's hair.

"Where is it at, Jelly Belly?"

Hearing the familiar voice, Chubby yanked himself free. "Stop fucking with my hair, you cabbage-smelling ass!" Chubby faced Pistol, who was smiling.

"Nigga already been having a fucked-up day, T," Mike said to the second lad who had accompanied Pistol.

"Damn, nigga, what happened to you?" Pistol asked after seeing his face.

Mike laughed. “Some crackheads got at him earlier.”

“Crackheads?” they asked in unison.

“What they get you for?” T asked Chubby

“They ain’t get me for shit, nigga.”

“Nigga, please. Some crackheads jump you to get something. Niggas ain’t just flexing on you for nothing.”

Mike pointed towards the wad of cash on the table. “Take that and pay the workers. Get one of them hoes to go grocery shopping.”

T looked from Chubby to Mike. He and Pistol exchanged a glance. They sensed there was something Chubby and Mike weren’t saying.

“Yeah, right. I might just do that myself,” said Pistol.

Knowing there was more to what wasn’t being said, T sat down, grabbed a controller and restarted the video game. “Start over, bitch.”

CHAPTER SIX

O'Shay pulled into the Great Western Motel off 820 and parked towards the back. He and Jay had done business here a couple of times in the past, but still he felt it was in his best interest to take precautions just in case and that was the reason he was early.

"Don't worry about all that shit," O'Shay was saying over the phone. "Just do what the fuck I say and get here. As soon as you see me walk out of the room, you and the boys go to work. And don't fuck up. Should one of your niggas get dropped, I'm not waiting. We about to get this money and if y'all come bull-shitting, you are getting shitted on." O'Shay ended this call, thumbed the remote on his Kenwood. The tunes of Young Jeezy's "It's All There" came booming through. He snorted a line of powder and waited. The thought of winning the two hundred and ten thousand dollars from the crack deal made him nod harder to the beat he was feeling. He was glad Shannon was also on her way to provide support.

Seeing the expression on T's face, Mike stood up. He knew he'd just ended a call with O'Shay and was hoping things were still on.

"What did he say, nigga? You are standing there looking like ya dick shrinking or something."

"What that nigga talking about, T?" Pistol asked, noting the concern on his friend's face.

"The nigga said suit up. We got to meet him at the Great Western off 820." T crossed the room, lifted the pillows to the leather sectional and grabbed two of the MAK-90s they stashed there. Seeing his action, Pistol and Chubby reached under the couch to retrieve the AR-15 and the street sweeper they hid there. No words were exchanged until the magazines were checked and fully loaded.

"Somebody get them masks from the bedroom drawer," T told them.

Chubby loaded the guns. The last time they went through these measures, it was only to back a play O'Shay called and he was sure that was the case now.

"We ain't even going to need all this shit. He probably just wants us to pull out on a nigga or something," T said, shaking his head

"What you mean by that?" Pistol asked him.

"The nigga said we got to go to work and that if one of us gets dropped, nobody else is waiting. This shit getting real."

"It sure is," Pistol said.

Mike looked at Chubby's worried face. Neither of them had been given such assignments before and only heard of the times when things got out of hand when O'Shay did call such plays. These were the same plays that got three of their friends killed a couple of years ago.

"You sure he said for all of us to come?" Chubby asked.

"Fat-ass nigga, don't get scared now," said Pistol, in a bid to allay Chubby's fear. "You blast first and live later. Remember that shit.

"Ain't nobody scared," said Chubby. "I'm just saying, 'cause you know how that nigga is."

T faced his three friends. "Yeah, that's the thing, we knew how this nigga is and we know what we gotta do."

Once everything was loaded into the gray caravan and the spot was locked up, they climbed in and waited until the time came. Seeing Chubby stalling, Pistol yelled, "Get your fat ass in the van, nigga. If you that scared, get in the back and lay down." Hearing Mike and T laugh, Chubby climbed in and closed the door. "I got a body under me already. You trying to catch up."

Byrd pulled a couple of files from the repair folder and handed them to Willie.

"What the hell I'mma do with these?" Willie asked.

"Just some parts we need to order. Can you handle that?"

Willie frowned and began reading the files. He knew what he was looking at, but still chose to play the part. "What am I looking for?" he asked.

"Motherfucker, you know what the hell it is. The cost for the parts, nigga!" Byrd shoved more files in front of Willie. "With all that money I saw, you ought to be trying to pay for something around here. At least pay up the money you borrowed from me."

"Man, I got shit to do with my money, nigga."

Willie stood, ready to leave. Byrd stood also. "Nigga, you walk out that door without giving me some of my money back, don't even worry about coming back. You take that shit and tear your ass."

Willie looked at his friend. Every word he spoke cut him like a double-edged sword, but in this game, swords didn't do shit for a nigga. "Well, I guess I ain't coming back then, 'cause I'm about to flip this shit, Byrd and if you can't wait until then, I'm sorry, man."

Byrd couldn't help but to think back to the days he told Cynthia damn near the same things. He sighed, because he knew it all too well. "You might as well find Kay and put her on."

"Fuck that crackhead ass bitch! That hoe already owes me!" Willie said.

Byrd just eyed his friend. "I don't give a damn about all that. We still family and if I remember correctly, you were the one that got her strung out on that shit in the first place."

"Same as you got Cecilia's bitch ass strung out on…"

Before Byrd knew it, he'd rushed Willie, grabbed him by his throat and pinned him against the wall. He didn't mind anyone talking about him to his face in such a way, but couldn't stand anyone speaking ill of Cecilia. "Don't ever let me hear you call her some shit like that again, nigga!"

Willie wrestled Byrd's fingers from around his neck and gasped. There were no words to say and nothing else to understand. The line had been drawn and the boundaries had been crossed. "You shouldn't have done no shit like that, man."

"You heard what the fuck I said, nigga." Byrd walked towards Willie again.

"Watch yourself, Byrd. This ain't for us, man."

Byrd stopped himself. Willie knew how he felt about Cecelia then and now. "Get your punk ass out of here, Willie, before I lose my temper again."

Willie walked out without looking back.

As soon as O'Shay spotted Jay's Corvette, he smiled. It couldn't get any sweeter than this. Before the sports car came to a stop, O'Shay was already standing in the middle of the parking lot. "What took y'all so long?"

"Aw, man. We had to make a stop," said Jay, climbing out of the Corvette at the same time with the dude he'd brought along. "This is my boy, Big Ced. Nigga, this is O'Shay."

After Jay had introduced Big Ced and O'Shay to each other, Big Ced shook hands with O'Shay and spoke to him for the first time. "How's it going, homie? You ready to make some money?"

O'Shay watched Big Ced as they shook hands. He had to have weighed three hundred pounds or a little more and looked as if he'd been through hell himself. The long scar from his left ear to his throat was enough evidence to conclude that the man was the proverbial cat with nine lives, and was probably on his second life at the moment. The thick bracelet and the huge link necklace, along with the canary yellow diamond brace in his mouth, made O'Shay realize the guy was a spender and he liked that. "You damn right," O'Shay said to Big Ced. "I wanna make some money."

"I was telling Big Ced that you had some of the best work around here and that the prices got cheaper every time." Jay looked around them, as did Big Ced.

"I got whatever you need, homie. I am the plug. Where the money?" O'Shay asked, now that formalities were done.

"It ought to be pulling up right about now." Big Ced looked at the top of the entrance of the motel and smiled when seeing the black Denali and the blue Acadia pull in.

O'Shay looked at Jay, who was now looking as if he hadn't seen the move coming. Hate filled his vision because he hated being blindsided and crossed.

"Where the work at?" Ced asked him in return.

Before O'Shay could respond, a ghost white Lincoln MKZ entered the lot seconds behind the Acadia. Shannon pulled alongside the bunch and popped the trunk. She'd done this a couple of times now and knew the part she played. Once the duffle bag was removed, she pressed a button on her steering wheel, closing the trunk without exiting, and pulled off. O'Shay swallowed hard and headed for the room. The last thing he needed was for either Jay or Big Ced to check the contents of the duffle he was carrying, because of the dummies it contained and the twenty-one-shot Glock he stashed there. It was now he prayed his team would not only come, but do what needed to be done. There was no explaining his actions and he also knew they weren't about to accept any.

T watched Chubby and Pistol from his rearview mirror. Pistol was continually reloading one of the MAK-90's and Chubby was just holding his. He looked over at Mike and asked, "You ready, nigga?"

"As ready as I'll ever be." Mike climbed into the back and told them," Let's lay down in the back and after T pull around and see where everything at, we jump out the back door and do what we got to do."

"What if it's bunch of niggas everywhere?" Chubby asked him.

"O'Shay said it wasn't going to be nobody but him, some nigga, and Jay's punk ass," T said.

"A nigga scoring by himself?" said Mike. "That's stupid." He grabbed his ski mask. "I wouldn't give a damn if it was twenty niggas. They game just like we game."

T thought about O'Shay's exact words and reminded them of the words, "You get dropped, you'd better crawl your ass back to the van, 'cause we gonna be on fire if this shit go wrong."

Pistol fixed the eyes of his mask, cocked his MAK and lay back with his feet planted solidly on the rear hatch of the Caravan. "Flame on them!"

CHAPTER SEVEN

Hearing Alina Baraz and Khalid's song, 'Electric', Riches hit a toggle switch on her dashboard, activating the two fifteen-inch subwoofers enclosed in her trunk, and turned up the volume. She and Tiffany were on their third blunt and the second bottle of Cîroc. They sang in unison. Both girls were feeling a bit tipsy and it was showing.

"Bitch, you just ran that light," Tiffany eyes widened.

"Did I?" Riches laughed at her friend's expression. This wasn't the first time she'd run a light and as a matter of fact, Tiffany was the one urging her to so she could catch up with a guy driving a convertible Benz. "Girl, ain't nobody pays me no attention. Hell, the light had just changed."

"Well, let's bend a few more corners, then go to the house so we can change." Tiffany had been talking about the block party and the events surrounding it all day and now that the time was drawing near, she wanted to be ready. And they knew exactly how they were going to make their presence known.

"Yeah, let me stop by Yousef's store and get us some more of this Cîroc." Riches held up the nearly empty bottle.

"That shit got me feeling reeeeeeal good, girl. If we keep drinking that shit, a few niggas might get lucky tonight," Tiffany laughed.

"Tiffany, a nigga smiles at you and get lucky. It ain't got nothing to do with what you are drinking. Your ass just stay horny."

"Paid. Not horny. Paid. There is a difference." Tiffany high-fived her friend and continued singing with the radio.

Seeing the Maxima parked in the same spot as before, Riches smiled to herself. She hoped he'd still be there by the time she'd changed and came back. If Yousef had any doubt in his mind earlier, she was sure he'd replace it with certainty this time. Tonight, she was going to show him something she hadn't before.

Cynthia rolled over and reached for Bee. She faced him. "You okay?" she asked him before rubbing his shoulder, chest and making an imaginary line down his abdomen. She traced his sculpted abs.

Bee rolled onto this back and intertwined his fingers behind his head. There were a few things he had in mind to discuss with her. "I might need you to help me get that janitorial contract with the school district. Don't they bid on that this month?"

She leaned up and kissed his lips. "How am I supposed to do that?" Bee was known to ask her for certain things, but not something like this.

"You know damn near everybody connected with the school district. So, I know you can make a few calls and get my name in the box." Bee squeezed her breasts, fingered her nipples and looked deep into her eyes.

"That's not really a field I deal with. I don't even know anyone who does, but I'll see what I can do. Not making any promises though."

"Ask Cherry. Isn't she still tied in with the registrations office or something?"

"Boy, that girl don't have anything to do with stuff like that. She works in the registrations office at the high school. That's it." Cynthia rested her leg against his middle, placing her thigh over his dick, stirring him. "Besides, if that girl knew it was for you, she sure wouldn't do it."

Bee rubbed her thick thigh, warming it with his palm. "You can be pretty convincing when you want to," he said to her before clasping her buttocks as if they were delicate balloons.

"I might need a reason to be convincing." Feeling his dick rising, Cynthia straddled him. "You think you can do something I would like?" She nibbled his neck.

"I might know a little bit about it." Bee grabbed her by the waist in an attempt to position himself better. She moved when he moved, raised herself and reached between his thighs for that thickness she loved. After placing him at the cleft of her pussy, she lowered herself slowly, placed both hands of his chest and gyrated her hips slowly but surely, warming to the friction of their conjoined organs.

"Fuck me like a whore."

Bee reached for one of the throw pillows they were laying on and placed it under the small of his back, creating a better platform for her and allowing himself to go deeper while guiding her. Hearing her moan, Bee grabbed her ass cheeks and began grinding also. This would definitely be the convincing she needed. "Ride it, baby. Ride it. Ride daddy's dick all the way."

"The money all there, homie. You don't have to worry about shit on my end." Big Ced showed O'Shay the duffle full of cash as an assurance he really meant business.

O'Shay looked over the bills in an attempt to stall either of them from checking the items of the bag he had himself. He'd already noted Big Ced had his guys strategically placed in and outside of the room, or even too close for comfort. It was shortly after the second guy entered the room that O'Shay remembered where he'd met Big Ced before. He was the same guy that tried to step on the toes of another street player named Perch, who'd ruled the south side back in the day. He didn't know Perch personally, but heard plenty of tales about the way Perch handed out hits and contract jobs like free lunches.

To confirm his suspicions, O'Shay asked, "Didn't you used to deal with that nigga named Perch?"

"Who?" Big Ced asked.

"Perch. The old nigga used to make some noise back in the day. O'Shay was still looking over the bills, but also managed to catch the shift in Big Ced's stance at the mention of Perch.

"As a matter of fact, I did. I was a young nigga back then. Why?"

"I just remember hearing something about that a while back. You straight though. Your business is your business," O'Shay smiled and chuckled.

"Yeah, that was the nigga that made me beef up my team." Big Ced put his hand in his pocket, pulled out a small knife and unfolded it. "Might've even killed me if I was alone, like you are at this moment. Now, let me take a look at that work in your bag."

Knowing all eyes were on him, O'Shay placed the small duffle on the bed and unzipped it. This was the moment he'd been waiting for and was hoping like hell his boys were also. He pulled out a brick at a time, placing them neatly before them. Just as he was about to pull out the forth, the door swung open, and one of Ced's thugs raced in.

"We got some company, Ced."

"What they look like?" Ced asked, keeping his eyes on O'Shay.

"Just some youngster acting like he lost or something. He pulled to the end of the parking lot, turned around and parked."

"You expecting anybody?" Big Ced asked.

O'Shay nodded. Everybody knew that O'Shay was known for having youngsters work for him and he was notorious for using their lives to protect his own.

In a flash, O'Shay pulled the Glock, aimed it at the guy closest to the door and fired two shots, hitting him in the upper torso and neck. Almost immediately, he trained the gun on Big Ced, who at three hundred-plus pounds was already scurrying out of the room. O'Shay fired three shots at him and only narrowly missed.

"Dammit!"

Outside the hotel, T heard the volley of shots, but didn't know what to do. His instructions were to wait until their boss walked out of the room before moving.

"What was that? What the fuck they are doing, T?" Mike yelled from the back of the van.

"We on, nigga!" T yelled back before pressing the pedal as hard as he could. Hoping that things were unfolding in their favor, he pulled past the Denali and screamed, "Go! Go! Go!"

Pistol bolted out of the van and was firing at everything moving. Chubby was in tow, opening fire on the driver and passenger of the Denali, spraying multiple rounds into the front and side of the truck. He was so caught up in wasting those guys, he didn't even see the four figures who spilled out of the Acadia to return fire. A cacophony of gunfire rent the air. Before Mike could redirect his aim, slugs ripped through Chubby's forearm and wrist. His body jerked violently, he staggered and dropped to the ground, losing control of his gun.

"Come on, fat-ass nigga!" T yelled, pulling Chubby by the arm.

T returned fire without looking, a mistake that cost him dearly and cost Pistol his life. Six shots from the rifle he was firing tore through Pistol's back and head, sending the lad's skull and brain matter flying.

"Oh shit! Oh, shit!" T screamed. He pushed Chubby into the back of the van, climbed in over him. For a brief moment, he'd locked eyes with O'Shay, who was also firing and running across the parking lot, with a huge duffle over his shoulder.

T felt bound to do something fast. "I have to get us outta here!" he muttered under his breath. With trembling hands, T put the van in gear and sped off, leaving two bodies and his best friend lying on the pavement. It wasn't until after he'd hit the service road that he felt someone pushing his shoulder and screaming in his ear.

"We gotta go back, nigga!" came Mike's hysterical voice. "They got Pistol, man. They shot our homies. Turn around, please!"

T knew there was no turning back. There was nothing to return to. "He dead, bro. Pistol is gone!" He yanked off his mask and looked back at Chubby, who was both crying and bleeding everywhere, "We got to get this nigga to a hospital." T dissolved into sobs. Everything had gone wrong from the beginning; he was sure of that. "Shit!"

"That son of a bitch didn't help us!" Mike went on. "The asshole ran straight to his car and left us!" Both of them had seen

O'Shay make his escape, without making sure they were alive or dead.

"I can't believe we left Pistol laying there. We fucked up, man."

T wiped his eyes to clear his vision. Seeing the Wilbager exit, he swung the van in that direction. The scene of him shooting Pistol replayed itself over and over, continually reminding him of a mistake he made, continually reminding him of the secret he'd either keep or tell. His best friend was gone and it was his fault. If I hadn't tried helping Chubby, Pistol would still be alive. T eyed Chubby menacingly. "You fat motherfucker!"

O'Shay backed his Lexus alongside his ghost white Lincoln under the canopy and parked. He subtly scanned the parking lot. Seeing no danger, he pulled the duffle bag from the floorboard and smiled. I got the money, motherfuckers.

His adrenaline was still pumping and the thrill of the victory surge through him. He knew he'd jumped the gun, but he had to. Leaving his fate in the hands of anyone other than him was something he wasn't about to do. He opened the bag and laughed. The duffle containing the fake drugs had disappeared somehow, but all that mattered to him was the one with all the cash, and that was sitting in his lap. He thumbed through stacks of bills. He smelled the currency. After placing five thousand dollars in his pocket, he counted the rest.

Shannon answered the door in her usual attire, nothing. She kissed him. For the job she'd done in the deal, she knew she'd be in someone's mall and parlor by the end of the next week and for what she was about to do to him now, she'd be in his pocket tonight. She reached for his belt. "Did everything go right?"

"Perfect." O'Shay stepped out of his jeans, unbuttoned his Polo shirt and followed her.

"Damn, nigga. Ya dick already hard," she told him before pushing him onto the leather sectional. "You know what time it is."

Instead of allowing her to straddle him, O'Shay pulled her to the floor, spread her legs and licked her hard, sucking and nibbling her clit at the same time. He rubbed her inner thighs, squeezed her groin and continued his tongue lashing. Before Shannon could respond to his aggression, he pushed both her legs upward and stuck his tongue inside her ass.

"Ooh, nigga. Damn!" was all she could say before grabbing her own calves and holding them for him.

CHAPTER EIGHT

Riches tended to criticize everything Tiffany wore, but when she herself stepped out of the bathroom door in a slinky Balenciaga dress that was slit at both sides, Tiffany's mouth fell open. "Oooooooh, bitch, you are making me wet with that shit you got on. Where the hell did you get it?"

"Marissa Collections."

"Damn! I swear, it must have cost a bomb!"

"Money is no object."

Tiffany walked around her friend in admiration. "Take them big-ass panties off though."

"What?"

"You don't wear panties with something like that. You in violation, bitch." Tiffany tugged at the skintight material. "Niggas want to see that ass and that camel toe."

"I think I'm showing too much as it is. If a nigga can't imagine the rest, then that's on him." Riches stepped into her two-inch Fendi boots.

"I really need you to take them big-ass drawers off. That panty line fucking up the whole piece. A nigga gone be like, 'Bitch can't even dress.' And you won't get looked at with approval and lust. You would get looked at with sympathy."

Riches paused, stepped out of her boots and as she walked back into the bathroom, she said, "You might be right, Tiff. If I'm going to wear it, I might as well wear it well."

Wanting to at least get some attention alongside Riches, Tiffany pulled out the Diaboli mini that came above mid-thigh, a pair of Dolce and Gabbana heels, and pulled off her panties also.

"If a nigga dick doesn't get hard tonight, he gay!" Tiffany yelled to her friend.

Willie pulled into the South Side Motel on the corner of Riverside and Berry, hoping to see Kay. One thing he thought of and felt he could use in his favor was that Kay knew how to bring customers and that's exactly what he needed, clientele. Willie parked, walked to the reception desk and booked two rooms for the night. "Matter of fact, I need the rooms for the rest of the week," he told the clerk. Seeing the short, thick chick standing by the payphones, he called her over. "Where Kay at?"

"What you need Kay for? I'm right here," she said in what she felt was a seductive tone.

"You bring me Kay and I'll give you three grands."

"Three grands? Well, the shit better be real, Willie."

"Bitch, have I ever played you?"

The chick looked at Willie, shifted her stance and placed her hand on her hip. "Are you serious, Willie?"

Willie smiled, reached into his pocket and pulled out a fifty-dollar bill. "Here, bitch. I'll give you another one when you bring Kay."

"So, you're the one she is hiding from?"

"Just go get her for me! I ain't got time to be wrestling with yo ass." Willie turned and started walking to one of the rooms he'd paid for.

"You want me to tell her somebody else want her or what?"

"Just do it! Matter of fact, bring some hoes that want to make some money. We got work to do."

The first thing Willie did when entering the room was check the window to see what vantage point he held over the lot, making sure he could see what was going in and out. Secondly, he began breaking down one of the ounces he'd won for earlier this morning. Setting fire to the blade, he was using he sliced right through the hard rocks of crack. After separating seventy pieces of dope, he hid seven thousand dollars and sixty-five dimes in the vent above the bathroom door. Willie loaded his stem with a nice twenty-piece and fell back on the bed. "Get ready for Willie, bitches! Get ready," he yelled, before inhaling the thick cloud of smoke.

Just as T pulled into the John Peter Smith Hospital's parking lot, the van went kaput. It had been smoking under the hood ever since they left the motel, but they couldn't stop. Half the windows were shattered and the right back tire had been flattened during their narrow escape. Stopping for assistance wasn't an option for the trio.

"This shit can't be happening, man!" Mike screamed upon seeing T wrestle with the steering wheel.

"Motherfucker won't even turn now!" T said.

"Fuck that steering wheel, nigga! I'm dying back here!" Chubby cried. He'd been crying the entire ride and T was growing tired of it.

"Shut the fuck up, nigga! If you were dying you would have been dead, fat-ass nigga."

"What the fuck we gonna do now?" Mike said.

"Get me in the fucking hospital, that's what!" Chubby leaned towards the door.

"Man, ain't no way we can walk in there talking about he got shot. Police gone be everywhere," T said.

"I'm going in with him," said Mike. "Fuck them hoes!" He helped Chubby up the ramp and into the emergency entrance, only to see the place was packed and no one even noticed them because of their own problems. His friend needed help now.

"Help! Help! He's dying over here!" Mike screamed. Once the EMT's came and rushed Chubby through the double doors, Mike quickly slid out of the sliding door at the entrance. The last thing he was going to do was wait around for the cops to show.

T had filled the duffle with both guns and masks and was waiting at the corner of the building when Mike came out. He'd called O'Shay several times already, but got no answer. The thought of him getting caught up crossed his mind and he was now hoping he was all right. "O'Shay ain't answering either of his phones, Mike. You think them niggas got him?"

"Man, we got to get away from here. We'll worry about that shit later." Mike sprinted across the lot with T in tow. All that was on his mind how was getting back to the projects. They'd gain both safety and transportation once they made it back there.

"Excuse me, sir. Would you happen to have the time?" Mike asked the guy in the purple scrubs, who looked as if he had just finished his shift.

Seeing the youngsters walking his way, the guy's gut told him to run, but before he could do so, a huge rifle was aimed at his chest.

"Where the keys at, nigga?" Mike kicked the guy in this groin as hard as he could."

"Ugh!" The guy doubled over with pain.

T grabbed a small clutch purse from the dude's hand and ripped it open, spilling the contents inside, eyeliner, compact and contact lens case. T struck him in the head with the butt of the rifle. "Punk ass!" The guy released the car keys. T snatched up the keys and jumped into the Accord. "Let's go, buddy," he said to Mike.

"What the fuck are you crying for?" Mike said to the guy. "You ain't got no balls no way." The ride back to the east side was mostly done in silence because of the thoughts that captured each of them. Mike watched T wipe a few tears and was certain it was because of what happened to his best friend. He knew T and Pistol were like brothers and having known each other for over eight years, Pistol's death was a blow too heavy for T to bear. Not only was Pistol like a brother to T, but he was Mike's cousin. Both cousins took to the streets and gained employment with O'Shay, because of the neglect from both of their parents. Mike and Pistol were from single-parent homes and with their mothers being sisters, their teaming up to make money was automatic. The two of them had been taking care of their households for damn near a year and as long as Mike was still breathing, he'd keep the promise and the pact they made to each other. "I swear, when I find them hoes that killed my cousin, I'm going to…"

"I feel you, Mike," said T.

Riches pulled into the corner store's lot and parked alongside the Maxima and climbed out. "What all am I supposed to be getting?" she asked a phone-wielding Tiffany.

"Get me a couple of them Berry Punch Jack Daniels and some gum," Tiffany said, before returning to her call.

Riches hoped to catch Yousef behind the register, but he was nowhere in sight when she strolled in. She looked around, spotted him restocking a shelf of canned goods, and headed that way.

"I thought you'd be gone by now," she said, standing behind him.

Yousef turned, gazed at a smiling Riches and dropped the can he was holding. Admiration lined his features. "What the hell you got on, Riches?" He stepped back to examine her further. "Damn, girl."

"Just something I threw on to wear to the block party." She spun around for him. "You like?"

Yousef looked her in the eye and swallowed. He could see her pussy print as clear as day, but forced himself to maintain eye contact. Two years ago, he would have been trying to fuck her right then, right there, but his views on women had changed. Hell, his views of life had changed. For the past couple of years, Islam had been his way of life.

"You are a very attractive woman, Riches, but you don't have to dress like that. Who are you dressing up for anyway?"

Riches looked down shamefully. She wasn't expecting that, but knew it to be true. She'd heard the same exact things from both Byrd and Cynthia many times. Never the one to bite her tongue, she looked up at him and said, "I wore it because I thought you like it. I thought you'd like me."

"I, um, I do like you, Riches. You're a likeable person but you don't even know me, yet you go through these measures to please me. What if I was one those guys out here that wasn't trying to hear no after seeing you like this?" He grabbed Riches' hands and held them waist level. "You are beautiful and queenly and you need to be the one who realizes it. You're to be the keeper of yourself until you find someone worthy of your companionship, then you give yourself fully to that person. Don't be like these other girls that be selling themselves short for nothing. Whoever named you Riches named you that, because that's what you are."

Riches felt as if she was melting on the inside. The truth he spoke and the passion he used to convey his point made her liking for him wax stronger. "Yeah, I hear what your mouth is saying and I'm also seeing you eyeing my pussy."

"I didn't say anything about me being less than a man, are you crazy? Hell, yeah, I was trying to see all of you and if I saw you as being some hoe running around, I wouldn't have looked twice. Truth be told, you are so tempting." He walked towards the front of the store.

Riches smiled and followed him. "Tempting you to do what?" She reached for his shirt to stop him. He faced her and swallowed hard, lust forming in his throat.

"Keep on messing with me and you'll find out," he told her before stepping behind the register. Seeing her laugh, he laughed. "You're going to have me doing all kinds of Duas."

"Duas? What's that?" Riches stopped in front of the counter and placed her hands on the glass tops. She was enjoying his discomfort.

"Those are prayers made when we trip out. That's what they are."

"Oh, you plan on tripping out or something?"

"I thought you had a party to go to," he told her with a smile.

"I might be trying to stay here and see you trip out." Riches laughed at her words.

"See, now you're playing with me. I—"

She cut him off. "I haven't even started playing with you yet. I get real physical when I do that. Might even hurt you or make you hurt me." If there was one thing she learned from Tiffany, it was that guys loved the chase of pussy willing to be caught. They'd also spend generously to do so. After purchasing her drinks, Riches smiled and strutted out of the store. "I'm going to come get my change later, Yousef."

CHAPTER NINE

O'Shay was up at the crack of dawn. As far as he was concerned, the deal with Big Ced the previous day had gone well. O'Shay had thrown the windows open when he got out of bed, leaving Shannon's recumbent form on the king-size bed. He was standing by the window overlooking the courtyard when Shannon woke. He checked his phone, it showed six missed calls. He slid it back into his pocket. Feeling her watching him, he pointed towards the duffle bag. "Put that up for me."

"When did you bring that in?" she asked, not realizing that he'd left her bed.

"Didn't want to wake you."

O'Shay relayed every scene from the day before over in his mind continually. The faces of the guys that worked for Big Ced wouldn't register and therefore, he didn't know who to look for. Then, there was the possibility that Jay was out to play him. He thought, however, if Jay was trying to undermine the lick, then he would have been the one now in possession of over two hundred grand. One thing O'Shay knew was that he had to get at Ced before the dude came to him, and the only person he knew had that contact information was Jay. "Where your phone at?"

Shannon pointed to her dresser, rolled over on her stomach and closed her eyes. "I need to go grocery shopping, O'Shay." She faced him. And I need to get those Louis Vuitton bags I showed you."

He reached down into the duffle and pulled out twenty thousand dollars and threw it beside her on the bed. "That should be enough for you to get what you want. Here, pick the call and ask for Jay." He threw her the phone once he heard it ring. "Put the phone on speaker."

"Hello, Jay."

"Hello."

Hearing his voice through the speaker, O'Shay grabbed the phone. "You got me fucked up, nigga," he told him in a calm but menacing tone.

"Naw, nigga. I saw you take off with the money and I want my shit."

"That's the thing, the money wasn't all there. I counted that shit three times and it's forty short."

"Forty short?"

"Yep."

"Anyways, just give me what we agreed on. I did my part."

O'Shay listened to the calm in Jay's voice. Hearing no stress there, he said, "Meet me at the shop in one hour." Having said that, he laid Shannon's phone down and walked to the door. If Jay was trying to play a trick, there was only one way to find out. "Where your keys at?"

Cynthia peeked at the blaring alarm clock on her bedside nightstand. "Ten forty-eight, shit!" She couldn't believe she'd slept that late. She noticed Bee wasn't with her in bed. She looked towards her dresser for the tray of cocaine she and Bee had been enjoying the night before. The meeting she was to attend was less than three hours away and she still had to shower, eat and call Cherry to let her know she was down for the comedy club thing. Cynthia swung her legs over the end of the bed and grimaced at how sore she was. Everything on her was either swollen or still aching because of her fetish. She looked at herself in the huge mirror alongside her bed and immediately noticed the marks on her neck and breasts.If she didn't know any better, she would have sworn someone assaulted her in her sleep. The welts on her ass and thighs were further evidence that her being abused was obvious. She rubbed her ass and thighs. Cynthia smiled, slipped on her robe and walked inside her spacious bathroom. Bee had taken the rest of the powder she had on the tray, but the stash she had saved for herself was still in the cabinet under the bath towels. After filling her tub with steaming water, she slowly lowered herself into the scented watery beads, speed-dialed Cherry's number and lay back. She knew Cherry was about to go off on her for not returning her calls last night and the sooner she got it over the better.

"I see you still alive." Cherry answered her phone with her normal attitude.

"Girl, please. Why wouldn't I be?" Cynthia asked with a smile of her own.

"You must be alone because if Bee's black ass was there, we wouldn't be having this conversation."

"Anyway, what's up? We still doing the comedy club tonight or what?" Cynthia closed her eyes, shifted position and moaned.

"I hope you ain't over there doing what I think you doing."

"What? Hell naw. I'm just sitting in this hot ass water soaking." Cynthia laughed. Cherry really did think she was some out-of-control freak.

"You over there moaning and all that shit. Knowing you, I wouldn't put it past ya freaky ass."

"I wish, but unfortunately, I'm not. I've got business to attend to today." Cynthia shifted yet again, causing waters to pour over the edges onto the floor.

"Yeah. I'll be over there later tonight and don't tell me shit about Bee coming. I do not feel like dealing with that dopehead-ass nigga today, any day for that matter."

"Well, let me hurry up and get out of this tub so I can get ready. I'll call you later." Before ending her call, she added, "oh yeah, get ahold of your friend and tell him you need another ounce of that same stuff."

"Another one? Bee fucked that shit off already?"

"Yeah, he asked me if I could get another, just in case there was a limited supply or whatever."

"That nigga need some rehab."

"Well, just get it. I've got to go." Cynthia ended her call so she could finish her bath, and the few grams she put up for herself was calling her in the worst way. With the aches and bruises she'd gotten from last night's romp, a couple of lines would definitely do her some good.

Riches awoke to the sight of Tiffany sitting on the edge of the bed. Riches wondered how in the hell she didn't have the same headache from hell. They'd both eaten some of the same things at the block party the previous night, drank some of the same liquor. So, Riches thought Tiff would still be asleep. Not only was Tiffany awake and looking energetic, she was also fully dressed in a burgundy and gray bandage sheath dress, and a pair of front-laced Ferragamo, three-inch-heeled boots.

"One would almost think you didn't catch a wink last night."

"Early bitch gets rich, Riches."

"What time is it, girl?" Riches asked the exuberant Tiffany.

"It's damn near eleven a.m. I thought you ass was dead until you started snoring."

"Snoring? Whatever," Riches told her, knowing very well she didn't snore.

"Ya mouth was opened so wide, I thought I was going to fall inside your throat."

Riches laughed. "Shut up, Tiffany. You're only exaggerating."

"I'm not. You lucky a bunch of niggas ain't in here. Ya ass would've had a couple of dicks in there, as wide as even your pussy was open." Tiffany walked towards her dresser.

"Damn. Bitch, you're making this no-panty thing a habit, ain't you?"

"You don't wear panties with everything and especially no shit like this. You wear thongs and T-backs or nothing and in my case, nothing. Once niggas think you naked, then they dick get hard. The dicks get hard, then the pockets get loose and when the pockets get loose, I get paid. That's the order the shit plays out in." Tiffany fixed the loose strands of hair above her forehead and faced Riches. "You hungry?"

"What you going to cook?"

"Cook? Girl, please. Let's eat out. Denny's and Clair's Kitchen right around the corner after all."

"Well, let me get out of this bed so I can get ready."

"I know just the outfit I want you to wear today. Niggas are gonna be fucked up when they see you today," Tiffany assured her.

"No, they're not. I'm not dressing like that ever again."

"Why not? The way them niggas were throwing money at you last night, we got—"

"What you mean, throwing money at me?" Riches asked, her face looking serious. She might have had a killer hangover, but she was sure remembered last night.

"Girl, you were poppin that ass and twerking."

"Shut up, Tiffany. I was not—"

"The hell you weren't. I knew you were going to say that shit, that's why I recorded it on my phone. Hell, a bunch of them niggas enjoyed the show you put up. That's your money on the dresser." Tiffany pointed.

Riches jumped up and grabbed Tiffany's phone, scrolled over a couple of apps and found what she was looking for. "Oh, shit!" She covered her mouth while watching the two-minute recording. The chants and the music in the background, the faces of all the guys and some girls standing and watching, and the money they showered on her. Riches closed her eyes, hoping it was all a dream, praying that she'd open her eyes and see Tiffany sleeping. When Riches did open her eyes, Tiffany was still standing there. Only difference was, now she was handing her the wad of money that was on the dresser. "Here, bitch. That's your cut."

"Oh, my God! Tiffany. Why you didn't stop me?"

"Stop you? Hell. I had to get in where I fit in, what with all that money them niggas were showering a bitch with. Once them hoes saw us getting money, they jumped in the street and started doing all kinds of shit."

Riches shook her head. Upon hearing Tiffany had to drive them to her house, she fell back on the bed. She couldn't even remember half the things she was seeing on Tiffany's phone. Only God knows who else recorded the same video. "I can't believe this shit. Tiffany! What if Byrd sees this video or even my aunt Cynthia?"

Tiffany sat beside her friend, wrapped an arm around her and held up the huge wad of cash. "This is four hundred dollars. You going to put this shit in your purse, hold your head up and keep stepping. You didn't fuck for it, you didn't suck no dick for it and you didn't get naked for it. You had fun. You made four hundred dollars having fun, Riches. Ain't nothing wrong with that."

Riches knew Tiffany was being as sincere as she could be and that was the reason she burst out laughing. "You crazy, Tiffany, you really are."

"I guess."

Riches grabbed the wad of bills from Tiffany, thinking, I'm not going to drink again. Ever. But, then again, that's what I said last time.

The women had been strutting their stuff for Willie all night and he was rewarding them at every turn. The short, thick chick who' said her name was Momma, proved to be his best strutter because she was bringing the big spenders. Once Kay did show and they got to talking, Willie didn't want her to leave. It was like old times. Seeing Kay enjoying herself made him feel good. The guys she owed were even compensated for the small loss she caused them. They'd entrusted her with a five-hundred-dollar-pack worth of fifties and once they returned to pick up their money, she was three hundred dollars short. The fact that she'd made them well over seventeen hundred that week alone wasn't enough for them to forgive her debt. "Them hoes were trying to fuck over me, Willie, so I just took what they owed me," were the words she told Willie and that was enough for him. The five hundred dollars he gave them was not only to clear her debt, but was enough for Willie to set up shop on their turf. The spot had been a beehive throughout the night and was still rolling. Kay was standing outside of the door, relaying every sale to Willie. Since she was the only one that came in this room with the money, she was the only one that knew about the stash above the bathroom door.

"We need to shut it down for a minute and do a count, Willie," Kay said while walking in. She was closing the door behind her when Willie walked out of the bathroom. It was evident he'd been smoking because his eyes were glossy and he was continually biting at the chapped skin on his bottom lip.

"We good, Kay, don't worry that shit. I know where we at," Willie lied. His desire to be looked at as being on top of his game was a must. But Kay knew Willie better than most and knew the role she was about to play in their come-up. He'd already told her this was their time and if they didn't make something happen with the lick they had, then they'd never do it. Willie was sincere and truthful at first, but telling Kay he had robbed some east side niggas to get the work was something he didn't do.

"Well, give me ten dimes," she said, having kept count in her head. If I'm right, thought Kay, we'd still have something left.

Willie fumbled with his pockets for about twenty seconds, another sign he was high as hell. "Where I put that shit at?" he asked himself before turning on her. "What you do with it?"

"Don't start that shit, nigga. You've been in this room blowing your brains out while I've been out there working." Kay had been going back and forth from both rooms bringing money and taking work, so she knew the numbers and this was something he apparently forgot. "Where my shit at, nigga?"

"Girl, you know I'm going to take care of your ass." He pulled two hundred dollars from his pocket and handed it to her. He walked to the window and peeped outside. "You hear that?"

"Yeah, I hear a whole bunch of shit." Kay walked over to the bathroom door and began removing the vent. The money was good, but what she needed now was some of that same crack she'd been selling and which he'd been smoking all night.

Willie was so caught up in peeping at the people walking around outside, he never once noticed the stash of cash Kay counted and replaced. There was just too much going on out there for him to focus on anything else.

Kay had been running the streets on the south side of town for years and knew damn near everything that had to do with anything. Having heard rumor of some niggas getting hit on the east side, it began coming together. She and Willie had been doing the game favors, as they called it, together for years. Stealing from Willie would have been the easiest thing to do, had she been anyone else, but that was something she just didn't do. Once everything was back in place, she walked up behind Willie. "You should have been a damn cop or something. You—"

"Shhhh! Shut the hell up before a motherfucker hear you," he whispered.

"We need some more of that shit you are smoking. If everybody had some of that, niggas would be quiet as hell."

Willie handed her his stem. "Here, push this." He'd been standing there watching Momma run cars and was realizing how thick she was. The jeans she was wearing hugged her curves and the tight DKNY T-shirt made it look as if her breasts were shapely. He'd seen Momma naked plenty of times, but the sight of her now made him grab his crotch. "The fuck that bitch doing?" he asked Kay, looking towards Momma.

Kay didn't give a damn about what was on the other side of the window, because she was holding in the smoke she'd just inhaled. Willie had packed so much crack in his stem, even after firing it up, you could still see the residue and thick streaks of crack left behind. She smacked her lips.

"This shit gonna get a motherfucker rich," said Kay. She sat back in the chair and closed her eyes before letting out another cloud of the crack smoke.

"Don't smoke all my shit, Kay. You've got one helluva big ass lungs." Willie grabbed his stem from the table and looked at it. "It's coated with your lip gloss, yuck!"

"If I was kissing you, you wouldn't say yuck."

"There is no harm in trying . . ."

Hearing the knock on the room door, Willie looked at Kay, whose eyes were still closed. "Get the door, bitch, get the door!"

Kay got up and looked through the peep hole and ducked down. "It's the cops, nigga!"

In panic, Willie began pulling crack out of his socks.

Kay shook her head. "I knew your lying ass had some more. Scary ass. I was only pulling your leg.

"Bitch! Don't ever fuck with me like that again."

Kay laughed, grabbed some pieces of the crack and walked out.

"Tell Momma to come here right quick!" he yelled after her. Some head would do him some good right about now and for the third time, Willie was about to pull Momma's jeans off.

A moment later, Momma peeked inside the room. "What's up, Willie? Kay said you wanted me?"

"Yeah." He pulled her into the room and closed the door. "That stank ass pussy of yours must be good and sweaty right about now." He'd already given her a hundred dollars and that alone was the only thing prompting Momma to step out of her pants again.

The Crowley Area was a suburb of Fort Worth's south-west side and was also where Jay lived. This morning's weather turned out to be finer and cooler than O'Shay had dared hope. After completing his call earlier and telling Jay to meet him at the shop in an hour, it gave him time to drive out and see for himself if Big Ced was still in play. He'd almost reached the rendezvous when he saw a huge Chevy 3500 pull up in front of Jay's home. O'Shay saw this as his chance to get the drop on both of them and was about to make his move, but had second thoughts when he saw a second and third vehicle arriving seconds later. "This nigga doesn't do shit by himself."

After the little incident the day before, Jay's hand was forced. It was his every intention to let O'Shay split the money and give him his own cut. But now, things didn't seem to be going as planned. Big Ced knew where he and his family lived. He hoped O'Shay would help him straighten things out. Jay answered the door with an agitated expression on his face. "Come on in, Ced." With six of his guys posted outside, Ced closed the door and followed Jay into the living area of his bi-level home. "He called earlier. I already know he was trying to read me."

"What you tell him?"

"I didn't have to tell him shit. He knows he fucked up. The nigga played the shit out on me, homie. I trusted this nigga!" He'd got in touch with Big Ced right after the previous day's shooting, which he'd witnessed from a hiding place in order to avoid being shot.

"He's on borrowed time, nigga. I'll fix him." Big Ced sat down in the heavy armchair, pulled out his phone and pressed a button. "Be ready in three hours," he said before ending the call.

"Man, I had my money tied up with that shit. That nigga fucked me up." It was now that Jay was glad he'd given Ced twenty-five thousand for the purchase, an act which didn't make Big Ced suspect him of being a double dealer The game Jay was in meant playing both offense and defense. "We gotta hit that nigga where it hurt, Ced."

"You sure he doesn't keep the money at that shop?" Ced asked.

"Hell naw, the laws done run up in there two times already. That's the last place he gonna put it."

"What about that little apartment he got on the eastside, where his young ass niggas hang out?"

Jay found that feasible. Although O'Shay never really stayed there, that would have been a perfect place to leave the cash, because no one would think he was stupid enough to leave hundreds of dollars in the care of some youngsters in the projects. "It wouldn't hurt to find out," he told Ced.

"We just need to make sure we bleed his ass for everything."

"Well, let me go set some shit up. I'll get at you later." Jay followed Ced to the door. "Just disappear for a minute." The first thing Jay noticed when Ced and his crew left was that neither of their cars had Kansas plates. "Texas, hmm," he said to himself before closing the door.

When the last car pulled away from Jay's home, O'Shay turned and headed in the opposite direction. He'd seen more than enough and spotting the Texas plates on all three cars made him realize they lived closer to home than either of them had claimed.

"Punk ass Jay," O'Shay smiled. "You want to dance with the devil, huh?" He'd been in the game long enough to know that when they did come, it would be to hit him where it hurt, his pockets. With the knowledge he now had, he was determined to put this advantage to good use.

CHAPTER TEN

Mike was standing at the bottom of the stairs, talking among some guys about Pistol's fate, when the ghost white Lincoln pulled into the complex. They'd been calling O'Shay ever since last night and here he was now showing up. He walked back inside seconds before O'Shay to find T sitting at the kitchen table with tears in his eyes and a revolver in his hand. Mike had seen him crying all night and knew not to crowd his space. O'Shay, on the other hand, saw him and blurted out, "What the fuck you in here bitching for, soft-ass nigga? And what the fuck you gonna do with that?" He asked upon seeing the huge gun in T's hand. "You did what you had to do, nigga! We in this shit for real. We live, we die. All that crying and shit don't heal no wounds and it damn sure don't raise no dead."

"Where the fuck been all night? I've been calling you—"

"I been where the fuck I want to be. No need for you to question my whereabouts."

Mike watched his boss drill T. This was what he wished he could do with the rest of the team, lead like a captain on a ship. Needing to hear more from the boss, Mike sat on the corner of the sectional and listened.

"We just left him there, man," T sobbed.

"Yeah, you did. Would you rather have been laying beside him instead?" O'Shay walked to the window and looked out before continuing, "the shit don't always turn out the way we want it and sometimes, you got to be ready to roll over some motherfuckers so you won't get rolled on. That nigga gave them niggas some licking too and that's what mattered. He wasn't cowering behind shit. He was front line, motherfuckers. That nigga always been front line! That's what I expect out of y'all." O'Shay reached into his pocket and pulled out a stack of bills. "Now we have to patch up and make sure he gets buried right. We're all in this shit together. We gotta stand firm as one family."

"What we going to do about Chubby?" Mike asked him.

"That nigga going to be in there for a couple of weeks at least. Just hope the cops don't start fucking with him."

Mike stood. "That nigga ain't talking to no cops. We already told the people in the ER that he got shot when some gangbangers robbed him at the store, so we good on that end."

"Good, 'cause we got to clean this shit up for a while. Them niggas still out there, so we got work to do."

Those words were music to Mike's ears, 'cause he'd been thinking about the night before.

"Take what we got over to Shannon's. T, you go with Mike. Drop her car off and get my Lexus, then come up to the shop." After exchanging his keys, O'Shay climbed into his Sierra and headed for the shop. Jay should be there and it was definitely time to open the ballroom.

Not only was their boss allowing them to drive Shannon's car, but they were allowed to drive outside of the hood. Climbing behind the wheel of the Lincoln, Mike fastened his seat belt and sat closer to the steering wheel. The last thing they needed was for the cops to pull them over the contraband they now had. Drugs, guns and money had become a part of their lives, but getting jammed up with all they had would definitely change that.

"You remember where she lives, don't you?" T asked, seeing Mike turn onto the on ramp.

"Yeah, the nigga didn't give a new address, so that's got to mean the bitch still stay out there in Woodhaven, Copper Creek or something like that. We'll find it."

T's thoughts were taking him further than the distance they were traveling. How will Mike understand that I, not those guys, killed his cousin? He did want to tell Mike about the accident, but decided against it.

Mike drove, focused on the task at hand. He was hoping like hell Chubby would be all right. Visions of Chubby rolling around in the wake of those gunshots filled his thoughts.

"That fat-ass nigga couldn't even get up," Mike laughed heartily.

"That nigga heavy, man. I was trying to help that nigga up when I lost my balance, and that's the moment I turned around and accidentally . . ."T's voice trailed off as the memory silenced him.

"Fat-ass nigga gonna be back on the cut in no time," Mike told him, never really paying attention to T in the first place.

Realizing his slip-up and the fact that Mike was talking and not listening, T lowered his head and sighed. He soon raised his head. That was when he realized they were getting close to the Copper Creek.

T pointed at the entrance of the Copper Creek Apartments. They drove around back until they saw Shannon, who was standing and waiting. She greeted them with a smile.

"What y'all doing way out here?"

Mike climbed out of the Lincoln and licked his lips. He always did like Shannon,despite her being only four years older than he was. Nonetheless, he still saw her as O'Shay's girl. "Just trying to catch up with your fine ass."

"Boy, gimme my keys. You wouldn't know what to do if a bitch sat on your face."

"I would know what to do if a bitch sat on my face," T interjected, refusing to be left out. They always talked about fucking Shannon. She'd grown to become a fantasy for them.

"O'Shay would kill y'all if I gave y'all some pussy."

T walked around the back of the Lincoln to get the bags out of the trunk. She wasn't lying and if she was, he wouldn't even be tripping. "How he gonna find out?" He looked at Mike.

"What the fuck are you looking at me for? We need to be worrying about your ass." Mike grabbed the keys to O'Shay's Lexus and walked towards the car.

"This pussy so pretty, you gonna end up telling somebody," Shannon said, rubbing her crotch slowly and seductively, like a preliminary to a strip tease.

Mike shook his head when he looked at T and saw his dick already bulging.

"Get in the damn car, nigga," said Mike.

With Shannon still standing there looking at both of them like a fruit platter, it was hard to leave. Watching her walk off in the silky boy shorts and sports bra, made their leaving even harder.

"That nigga got a bad ass hoe for real!" T yelled out the top of the convertible.

"If she would have seen ya lil ole' dick sticking out, you would have scored, nigga." Mike laughed.

"That's what them hoes got asses for." T laughed also.

For the moment all was cool, but moments like these didn't last long in the game they were in. It was moments like these that either knitted the friendships you had or tore that very fabric beyond repair.

"We got to get our money up to fuck that hoe."

"You can say that again," said T.

Since the parking lot at Denny's was damn near empty, Riches pulled up and parked.

"Girl, I'm starving," Riches said to Tiffany before walking into the eatery.

Tiffany reached for her vibrating phone, looked at its screen and smiled at Riches.

"What now, Tiffany?"

"Nigga we met last night."

"We?"

"Oh, yeah, I forgot," Tiffany laughed, referring to Riches' memory loss.

Riches and Tiffany were just about to seat themselves when the familiar face greeted them.

"Hey, Riches." Yousef smiled at Riches and acknowledged Tiffany with a nod. He looked over Riches' attire. "You looking nice today."

Riches smiled. She knew he was talking about her not being provocatively dressed, as she was the night before. "Yeah, I bet

I do. What are you doing here?" She looked around the restaurant for a possible breakfast date of his.

"I eat breakfast too." He continued standing while they sat themselves down. "I just wanted to grab something fast before I opened up the store."

Seeing Tiffany smile and laugh at whatever the caller was talking about, Riches knew there would most likely be something popping off later, and with nothing to do for the minute, she slid over, inviting Yousef. "Here, sit down for a minute."

"You sure?"

"Nigga, sit down, unless you're scared ya girl gonna see you with another chick."

"We already talked about that, remember? You're the one that needs to worry about things of that nature."

"So, where's my change?"

"At the store. You spoke of coming back to get it."

"And I will. But, you know you owe me now, right?'

"Owe you for what, Riches?" He smiled.

"I told you I wanted to drink and not get drunk and that stuff you sold me fucked my whole night up." Seeing Yousef laugh, she couldn't help but do the same. "I'm serious."

He threw his hands up. "Wait, wait, wait. I suggested the Cîroc at first, but you decided to come back and get that other poison." He continued laughing. "You did that."

"Well, you should have warned me." Riches took a sip of her orange juice and said, "You still owe me though."

"Oh, I guess it's my job to keep you from doing things you shouldn't, huh?"

"Isn't that what friends are for?" Riches couldn't help but look at her friend, Tiffany, who was still concentrated on her call.

"Oh, we friends now?"

Riches looked deep into his eyes. "Gotta crawl before you walk, right?"

"If you keep looking at me like that, I'm going to be doing more than crawling."

"Oh really? Riches leaned away from him, getting a better look at his disposition. "You keep on talking like that and I'm going to have to see what you are talking about."

"I'm going to let you two enjoy your breakfast 'cause you tripping, Riches. You're tripping for real." He stood but stayed.

"You the one talking about doing more than crawling, hey, you said that."

"Now you're using my words against me? Nice. Riches, real nice."

"Well, when you ready to stop running from me, then get at me." Riches looked him over seductively, making him frown. Seeing him shaking his head, she continued. "Tempting, huh?"

Yousef pulled fifty dollars from his pocket and placed it on the table. Before walking away, he told her,"That should cover you both for breakfast, Riches. I'll just have to get at youlater."

"I'll be waiting," she yelled after him.

Once Yousef exited the building, Tiffany spoke. "Bitch, that lame-ass game worked. The nigga think you cutting for him for real."

"I do like him, he's sweet, Tiffany."

"Sweet and broke. I bet the nigga does get some pretty ass though."

"I thought you were on the phone talking to somebody?"

"I was, until started you both started flirting and shit. That nigga thinks he gone fuck something, Riches. I'm telling you, girl. I was looking at the way he was watching you and that nigga ready to spend something. "You play his ass right, we gonna be drinking free every weekend."

"Oh, no. No more drinking for me."

"Bitch, please, you told me that several times before."

"Yeah, but I wasn't out of control like I was last night."

"You just can't fuck with that drink that made you run mad, so to speak. You need to stick with that Cîroc shit."

"Hell, you probably slipped something in my drink. I wouldn't put it past you to do that."

"For what? I wouldn't do that."

"Well, I don't know about the not drinking anymore, I just—"

Tiffany cut her off. "What we gonna do for your birthday next weekend?" She watched Riches while digging into her omelet.

"I was just gonna to chill. Why, what's up?"

"Nigga that called was talking about a house party and wanted us to come. He was out there when you started doing your thang at the party last night, and yes, the nigga got money."

"Hell, naw. The nigga ain't fixing to have me on some viral site. You probably got him thinking we strippers or something."

"If the nigga pays right, I'll be a stripper."

CHAPTER ELEVEN

The morphine the doctors had been giving Chubby was beginning to wear off. Both pain and reality started setting in. His arm was in a brace and the screws they used to reconstruct his wrist and forearm were killing him. He tried flexing his hand, to no avail. The two cops that walked into his room caused him to lower his hand and watch them. He and Mike had already rehearsed the lines he was to use, so he was ready for this visit. They'd ask a couple of questions, get the answers he gave and they'd be gone.

"How are you feeling, today?" the black cop asked, before walking around the bed in an attempt to see his wounds better.

"I'm feeling a little bit better." Chubby sat up slightly. "My hand hurts like hell though."

"You already know it's routine for us to at least ask what happened, don't you?" said the older cop, a white guy that looked to be in his fifties.

"Yeah, I already told the nurses and doctors what happened last night." Chubby watched as the cop pulled out a small note pad.

"If you don't mind, could you tell us a little about what happened?" the white guy asked.

"Um, I was standing at the bus stop and some gang members pulled up and started talking all kinds of noise and stuff."

"And?"

"I knew they were high on something and I didn't want any trouble, but they were taking everybody's money." Chubby used his boyish features to assist his spiel.

"Did they have any guns out or anything?"

"Um, yeah. One guy had a gun."

"Could you tell if it was an automatic or a revolver?"

"I think it was an automatic, like a Glock or something like that."

"Hmm." The cop continued writing." You were the only one got shot?"

"I think so, I'm not really sure through."

"How many more people were at the bus stop with you?"

"Ummmm, about four." Chubby looked from one cop to the next.

"So, how did you get here?"

"How did I get here?" Chubby asked.

"Yeah, you were shot on the other side of town, so it says here in this report. I was just wondering how you got here." The white guy eyed Chubby.

"Umm, a couple of people saw me get shot and they came to help me."

The black cop stepped closer to Chubby, adjusted his glasses and smiled.

"You were shot, right?"

Chubby held up his arm, grimaced with the effort and said, "Twice."

"But, they didn't take anything from you. In the report, you never said they took anything, right?"

"Yeah, I mean, no, they took off running."

The black cop leaned forward, getting inches from Chubby's face. "You a stupid, fat motherfucker, you know that?"

Chubby looked towards the white cop and swallowed. This wasn't a part of the rehearsed plan. "What you mean by that, sir?"

"Sir, my ass. Did you think for one second that cameras are all over this place, including the parking lots? Did you forget the fact that you and your two friends were stupid enough to drive a van that had been shot to hell, into a hospital parking lot? That's been the talk of the morning around here. That and the fact that along with you, four other guys were brought in an hour after you in body bags. We looked at the surveillance of last night to see who drove the van here and guess what we found, fat ass? Yeah, you were being carried in here with the help of one of the guys that climbed out of it along with you. Shit creek ain't even the beginning of the shit you're about to swim through."

Chubby's heart fell when hearing the detailed account of the things the cops knew. Hearing them talk about an earlier shootout at the Great Western Motel and the ongoing investigation of that, Chubby knew the cop was right. The cops couldn't place him at that crime scene personally, but witnesses were quick to remember seeing a fat guy getting shot. On top of that, Chubby had no idea that his friends robbed a male nurse in the parking lot at gunpoint, just outside of the emergency department doors. The picture they painted him was as clear as his memory of the things that took place. The handcuffs they used to restrain him to the side of the hospital bed confirmed just how vivid that picture was to them also.

"But, I didn't do nothing!"

"That's yet to be established, son, but one thing we do know is that you know who did."

Chubby knew he was in trouble. The money he made was usually used to purchase solutions to problems, but he was now more than sure money wasn't going to free him of this burden. He needed to make a few calls and most importantly get a few calls made.

Jay parked on the far end of the lot, climbed out and scanned the area. The 9mm Ruger sat loosely beside the driver's door, just in case things went south again. He followed O'Shay through the lobby area to the back, the sounds of high pressure air wrenches causing him to look into several stalls. He'd had customizations added to a couple of his cars, and this was one of the places most people frequented when they wanted luxury added to their cars and trucks. This was also the reason O'Shay was able to roll the way he did.

"I might have to bring my wife's Audi up here so they can tint it and upgrade her stereo," Jay said, making small talk.

"You heard anything from that nigga, or what?" O'Shay asked, seeing where the question led.

"The nigga came to my house this morning. My wife and my kids were there."

O'Shay turned to face him, saw the seriousness in his eyes and told him."If I didn't know any better, I would have thought you were trying to cross ya boy."

"Yeah. I can see why. You put me in a fucked-up position, O'Shay. What if that nigga would have just had some niggas to fuck with my family?"

"That happens when you out here fucking with niggas' money, Jay. You know that the game doesn't give a damn who play or get played."

"Where my shit at, nigga, so I can go."

O'Shay walked him into his office and pulled out a small backpack, sat it on his desk and said, "This is fifty. I've got to make a move and I'll have the rest in a week or so."

Jay closed his eyes, regretting leaving his gun in the car. "Nigga, give me my shit now! You just won for two hundred plus. We agreed on seventy-five for me. Now give me what you owe me, O'Shay."

"That was before I lost one of my workers. We went over that shit over and over and I had to end up taking a loss."

"So, I got to pay for your losses?" Jay asked with raised brows. "I'm putting money in your pocket and you pulling out of mines because your workers can't stay alive?"

"Just need to cover a few expenses. I know you can understand that, can't you?"

Seeing this conversation not ending right, Jay inhaled deeply and let out a long exasperated sigh. "Yeah, whatever. Come on with it." He reached for the fifty thousand dollars. "I get the rest next week, right?"

"Yeah. I got you."

Jay heard those same words many times throughout his tenure on the streets and knew what was really being said. There was no need exposing what didn't need to be exposed. Feeling the vibration of his phone, Jay looked at the caller and smiled. "I'll get at you later, O'Shay. I got a couple of dollars to make."

O'Shay walked Jay out, saw him leave. Afterwards, O'Shay walked back into his office. The one hundred thousand he kept there was about to be moved to yet another location. One he was sure no one would find.

Mike and T were pulling into the shop's lot when the Audi shot past them, the driver frowning at the two as if they were in the wrong.

"Wasn't that Jay? The fuck he is doing up here?" Mike asked before climbing out of the Lexus.

"Hoe-ass nigga probably came to get something done to one of his cars or something," T said. "Come to think of it, that was Jay's Corvette in the parking lot of the motel. What the fuck was he doing there?"

"Doing where?"

"I mean,anyway, never mind. Let's go see what O'Shay got going on now," T said before they walked inside.

Cynthia was standing at the elevators on the fifth floor of the Tarrant County Municipal Building. She was dressed in a Tom Ford sweater dress, Fendi platform heels and an assortment of jewelry. Having spent hugely for the outfit, she held her own when it came to the women her circles consisted of. The projects manager and the building's directors for both districts accepted her proposals for the bidding at the next conference. So far, the lowest bid for the janitorial contract for the school district was at 3.6 million and she was hoping she could get Bee's foot in the door. This would be a lucrative move for him. She was more than sure that she'd profit from the endeavor also. The only thing that concerned her was the fact that Bee had to fulfill the obligations of the proposal she enclosed and initiated. This would require for Bee to maintain seven high schools and eight middle schools throughout the district and would commit him and his services to a four-year duty. With the right contacts on both equipment and supplies, he'd be able to budget the project and possibly renew the contract at the completion of the term. If nothing else, his name and credentials would elevate in the world he knew little about. Feeling good about the feat she was on the verge of accomplishing for him, she felt a need to celebrate.

The phone rang three times before Bee answered. "Hey, baby?"

"You busy?" Cynthia boarded the elevator, surprised that it was empty.

"Never too busy for you. What's up? How did it go?" Bee asked, referring to the meeting she attended.

"It's hard to say at the moment, but I think you might be in there."

"Girl, if you pull this off, we're going to be all right."

"Oh, really? Last time I checked, I was—"

"You know what I mean. This is a big deal for me."

She could hear the excitement in Bee's voice. She smiled. "How big of a reward do I get for at least trying?" Hearing the dig of the elevator, she changed gears. "Well, I'm going to contact you at my earliest, so you can repair the plumbing for me. I'm going to need a new pipe fitter." She could hear Bee laugh on the other end of the phone. She nodded at a few of the women that got on the elevator and continued her call. "You're going to have to stretch it really good this time." Cynthia ended her call, placed her iPhone in her clutch and smiled.

"Hey, Cynthia, couldn't help but hear about your plumbing problem. I think I need to get some pipe laid myself. My husband tried but it's still clogged up. Who's your plumber?" one of the women asked a smiling Cynthia.

"Well, I only deal with the best, but sometimes you have to do it yourself, if you know what I mean." As soon as the door opened, Cynthia smiled and stepped off. Before allowing the door to close fully, she looked back at the women and winked to the blushing director, who asked her about a plumber. With several grams waiting for her and more on the way, date night with Cherry would be well worth it and after that, her late night would be also. Thinking about the events to come, Cynthia climbed into her Infiniti QX 30 and headed for the mall.

Willie and Momma were sitting on the edge of the bed when Kay walked back in from the other room. She stopped before closing the door, grabbed her nose and frowned at the two. "Y'all need to be sitting in somebody's bathtub 'cause that don't make no damn sense."

"All pussy stank when you hit it right." Willie handed Kay his stem and stood to leave. "I've got to go get some more work so we can keep it rolling."

Wanting to see if her suspicions were true, Kay suggested, "Don't go back to the east side."

"Nah, I got another lick lined up." Realizing he'd slipped, he tried to regain his innocence. "I mean, I—"

"Yeah, I know exactly what you meant," Kay cut him off. "Just hurry the hell up though, and don't forget to come back, stupid-ass nigga."

Willie checked his pocket, looked at Kay and nodded. "You damn right. I'm coming back, so get ready. Kay, you stay here. Momma, you keep that ass close by, just in case I get some more of that sex dope."

Sex dope was what many of them called the dope when it made you horny as hell instead of paranoid. Made some smokers start kissing and had others hissing. Willie was looking forward to the former, plus the possibility of another girl to go along with Momma.

"Where we headed now?" Riches asked after the breakfast they'd had. Tiffany had unsuccessfully tried to convince her to attend the party on her birthday or at least get out for a night downtown. Unlike Tiffany, Riches had to attend school the following Monday and would for the rest of the week. The weekend she spent with Tiffany was one she wouldn't forget any time soon and the fact that Yousef owned a store in her hood was the reason she'd be returning the following weekend, and if things went right, many weekends to follow.

"Let's go to the Galleria and see what they got out there," said Tiffany.

"Yeah, I want to try on one of them Constantine jumpsuits."

Tiffany asked, "For what? Them things run fifteen hundred dollars a pop."

"I just want to see how I look in one. Never know, Yousef might even buy it for me." Riches shrugged.

"Bitch, please. That nigga car didn't even cost fifteen hundred dollars."

"You think I ought to buy him a Movado watch or something?" Riches glanced Tiffany's way.

"Bitch, you trying to bait him, or are you for real?"

"I'm for real, girl. I like Yousef, he's nice to me." Riches fingered the button on her steering wheel.

"That's fucked up, Riches. That's fucked up." Tiffany shook her head.

"What? Just because I want to buy him something?"

"You fucked that nigga and didn't even tell a bitch."

"Girl, I didn't fuck him. There'd be no harm in trying to fuck him anyway. Well, buying him the watch might be a good gesture."

"Damn watches cost five and six hundred dollars. You are tripping. I could see if you were trying to bait the nigga, making him think he was just that damn special, but you on some more shit. Nigga ain't doing shit for you and you talking about buying this nigga stuff, hell nah!"

CHAPTER TWELVE

Two days had passed since the cops handcuffed Chubby to his hospital bed and filled him in on his role in the murders of three known gang members of the East Dallas Piru's and a member of the Stop-Six Blood Fraternity. Considering he was only fifteen years old, his mother had to be summoned before his interrogation.

Once they were alone in the room, Chubby's mother sat in the chair adjacent the bed he was laying in and asked him, "Where your boys at now?"

"I didn't call you, the cops did." Chubby looked away from his mom. Their strained relationship had ended when he left home to live with his boys, whom he considered to be his real family.

"I hope they lock your fat ass up forever!"

"I bet you do."

"You just like that damn daddy of yours, walking out on the people that need you and then you end up hanging with some motherfuckers that don't give a damn about ya."

"They'll be here." Chubby faced the wall and fought the lone tear that threatened to fall. He hadn't seen his mom since his departure and he used the money he made from the streets to feed, clothe, and shelter himself. The fact his mother did drugs was enough for his friends to convince him that life would be better if only he got out and did what needed to be done and make something happen for himself.

"This is the life you wanted for yourself, huh? Laid up in some medical unit, with the cops stalking outside of your door."

"It's better than watching you stalk around looking for a hit and doing all kinds of shit to get it."

"Motherfucker, it doesn't look like you are doing too much better. You out there doing God knows what for the crumbs another nigga pushes off the table for you and now you willing to die for him. Well, it looks as if that's exactly what you're going to do, with all the time they trying to give you."

"I didn't do nothing! I just—"

"I just, my ass! You did something. Your fat ass in here being held together with all this bullshit." She pointed to the brace and screws in his arm.

Chubby wiped the falling tear, faced his mom and told her, "I don't need you. If they lock me up forever, I'm good! If them niggas don't do as much as send me a greeting card, I'm still good!"

"I hope your fat ass die before you get back out there in them streets. At least I'll be able to say they killed you, instead of your fat ass killed yourself." She walked around the bed and stood by the window. She patted his arm, causing him to stare at her in silence. She nodded towards the door before continuing. "You might not have done shit but you damn sure going to pay for it." Those were the last words his mother spoke before opening the door to leave. He was lost for words. His mom always had a way of admonishing him, despite the things she did and the decisions she made.

He looked towards the door after her and mumbled, "Dope-fiend-ass." After hearing all the things the cops had said, he knew he'd be in their custody for a while. A deep sense of despair overwhelmed him, and he let out a heavy sigh.

Mike noticed that ever since the shooting, T had been distancing himself from what they routinely had going on. He'd been talking to himself and even arguing with any and everyone who questioned his actions. Mike knew he was still dealing with the loss of Pistol and gave him some space,but there was something else between them and Mike was sure of it. He walked into the apartment and found T sitting in front of the sixty-one-inch flat screen, staring at the blank TV. Seeing T subtly slide the revolver under his thigh, Mike asked him, "You all right, T?"

T never took his eyes off the screen, never said as much as a word in response to what Mike was asking, and continued to hear the words O'Shay told him once Mike was out of earshot at the shop a couple of days ago.

"Where was Mike?" O'Shay asked T, once alone in his office. O'Shay made T feel that Mike's failure to get out of the van had a hand in the whole thing. "If he had been doing his part," O'Shay had said, "at least lending a hand to our attack against Big Ced's boys, Pistol would have still been alive this day."

Now, T looked away from the TV and looked Mike square in the eye. "What gun did you use?"

"What you mean?" said Mike, looking askance at T.

"I'm talking about at the motel, which gun did you use?"

"I didn't get a chance to use any gun, nigga. The whole shit struck fast like lightning and when I looked up, you was pushing Chubby in the van and Pistol was on the ground."

"You didn't even try, nigga. You was still in the van when Chubby, Pistol and I were trying to keep everyone of us alive."

Mike moved from the front of the TV to the dining table. He pulled out the money he'd just picked up and placed it beside the keys O'Shay gave him.

"Oh, all this shit my fault? Pistol getting killed, Chubby getting shot and all the other shit that went wrong is my fault? That's what you are saying, nigga! That's what you trying to say?" Mike walked towards T. "I might have been the one that got killed if I had got out of the van, but I didn't and you mad? Fuck you, nigga!" The tears that fell from Mike's eyes told T that he was really hurt.

"I'm not saying that, Mike." T looked away. "I'm not blaming you, man. I'm just trying to find somebody to blame, I guess."

"That's why you've been walking around here like you crazy? You think I'm not tripping on that shit also? They gonna bury my cousin in a couple of days. I can't even go to the funeral and you know why."

"Yeah. Well, I saw Jay's car at the motel when we pulled into the parking lot that day. Remember, we saw him at the shop when we went to see O'Shay the other—"

"Yeah, I remember when that nigga was leaving the shop."

Feeling the need to change the subject, T stood up. "Let's go see if these hoes out there working." With the majority of their workers in school at this time of day, things were slow but they still expected a certain return, and with over five ounces swinging, they hit the cut.

Since setting up shop days before, Willie and Kay expanded their operations to the Oasis Motel several blocks away. Things had been going good and since the money was rolling in and the customers continually had to travel out of their way for the product, it was in their best interest to do so. Willie was reluctant at first, but after seeing Kay handle her business the way he would, he had confidence in her and proceeded to rent two rooms for her to operate her side of the biz. But, Kay had already run through two ounces and was in need of some more work that Willie didn't have, and he was insisting she wait on him before spending with someone else.

"I'm going to take care of it, damn," he told Kay for the second time in a day. Her needing to re-up on product was imperative to her because once it dried up on the spot, it would be another couple of days before the customers came back, and that was if they weren't getting something better elsewhere.

"You over there fucking off way more than you are making, Willie, and I'm not trying to wait for you to dry out my spot."

"Motherfucker, I'm the one put you up on something and now you ready to jump on the first thing?"

"I'm trying to do what should have been done years ago, nigga. We've been running these streets years before these youngsters and we ain't got shit. I'm not trying to fall off waiting on you. You know how this shit goes. You either got it or you don't. Them motherfuckers ain't going to wait until you finish getting high, before they move to the next motherfucker that's got what they need."

"I've been literally giving these hoes dope for a little of nothing, so they can wait," Willie said, before firing up his stem and inhaling the thick smoke. Kay sighed. He'd been filling both her lungs and her pockets and realized her loyalty wasn't about to wane.

"How long we got to wait, nigga?" she asked him before placing her hand on her hip. With some of the money she'd made, she was able to buy a few items of clothing, some shoes and some food for the room. The incentive she gave her workers and runners was that for every one hundred dollars' worth of work they moved, they got a twenty-piece as commission. With several runners under her in the second room she used, she offered them shelter, food, water and a place to smoke their earnings. The money they won off tricks and customers was also given to Kay and she knew she had to maintain the cycle as long as she could. Only thing that she didn't like was the fact that Willie didn't want her scoring from anyone other than him.

"Matter of fact, I'm about to bend a corner now." Telling her he was watching out a lick for the past two days would definitely give rise to questions he wasn't about to answer. With his lungs filled and his courage high, Willie pushed the .38 in his waistband and walked out of Kay's room. "I'll be back in an hour or so. Be ready."

Riches couldn't wait for the lunch bell to ring. Instead of joining the rest of the college students at the salad bar, she made her way to the parking lot. She was more than sure she had missed calls from both Tiffany and Yousef, but what she really needed to do was head to the east side. Riches looked at her Elgin watch, hoping she had enough time to complete her task.

"Um, I see you finally called back," Yousef answered his phone.

"You busy?"

"Yes. Why?"

"I'm on my way up there. I've got something for you,"

"Oh, really, and what would that be?"

"You'll find out soon enough." Riches smiled, placed the Movado back in its case and sat it in the console. She and Yousef had been talking on the phone every night since the night she got drunk, and she could tell he looked forward to hearing her voice, just as she did his.

"I might have something for you also."

"Yeah, I'm sure you do." She was feeling him and she knew he was feeling her and with Tiffany's words continually swimming through her thoughts, there was no way she was going to turn back now.

"There you go with that. I'm just going to have to give you what you really want," Yousef had been enjoying the cat-and-mouse tactics with Riches these past few days and she'd been calling his bluff.

"And what would that be?"

"You'll find out soon enough."

"Well, I'll be there shortly. I need to pick Tiffany's incoming call."

"Ok. Later."

"Yeah."

"Riches, I've been calling your ass all morning. Girl, I—"

"School, Tiffany. I do have to go to school, unlike you."

"Yeah, go ahead and rub it in. Let the whole world know I dropped out of college."

"Didn't mean to rub it in. Sorry."

"It's alright."

"So what's up?"

"I need you to pick me up later on tonight. I'm meeting Butter again."

"Why that nigga can't take you home, Tiffany? You know Byrd be tripping on me being out on school nights."

"Bitch, you forgot how to lie now? Besides, I'll give you a hundred dollars."

Riches thought about the money she spent on the watch and knew she could use the money. All she had to do was come up with a hundred-dollar lie. "Where at, Tiff?"

"The Oasis. I'll call you around eight or eight-thirty," Tiffany said before ending their call.

Riches couldn't help but laugh. One thing was for sure and that was the fact that Tiffany would definitely have the money. Upon her arrival at Yousef's store, Riches saw his Maxima parked at its usual spot. Riches parked, checked her watch and climbed out. She was glad she'd dressed in a pair of capri khakis, a cream-colored silk blouse and a pair of Fendi heels.

Yousef had been gazing toward the parking lot ever since the call and before Riches entered the store, he walked towards the door and opened it. Once she was inside, he grabbed her, picked her up and spun her around. "Oooh, I missed you, Riches," he said before planting his thick lips on hers, not minding the presence of customers in the store.

Riches laughed. That's it? That's all you have for me?" She pulled the watch out of her pocket and handed it to him. "Here."

"What is this?" Yousef frowned as he looked at the case. "Riches, you didn't have to buy me this."

"Well, I saw it and thought it would look good on you."

Yousef picked her up again, this time squeezing her. "You shouldn't have done this, Riches." He smiled at her, placed her down gently and moved a strand of hair from her eye.

"It's nothing," she lied. The five hundred dollars she spent on it was a dent into the money she had been saving for herself.

Standing there, they looked deep into each other's eyes, not wanting to look away. Realizing time had passed, Riches checked her watch, saw that she had minutes to return to school. "Well, let me get back to work. I'll call you later."

"You still haven't told me what you do, Riches."

"Does it matter?" With that said, Riches turned to leave.

During her ride back to school, she slot in an Ellie Goulding CD, and listened to the tracks in sequence. "Friday, hurry up, shit!" she yelled moments later as she drove into the gates of Buckbam College.

T ordered a cheeseburger, fries and a Sprite. He was enjoying his meal in the lobby of Wendy's when his boss walked through the doors. O'Shay called him earlier and told him to meet him at the location alone. Instead of driving, T walked up the street.

"What's up, nigga?" O'Shay sat across from him.

"Chilling."

O'Shay reached over and grabbed a handful of T's fries. "You alright?"

"Yeah, why wouldn't I be?" T had already wondered what this secret meeting was about and was praying like hell it didn't have anything to do with another lick.

"I mean, if I had killed one of my homies, I'd still feel sore." He smiled at T.

"That was an accident, man. I didn't mean to do that shit." T looked around them, then back to O'Shay.

O'Shay took T's Sprite, took a mouthful of the drink and finished up the remaining fries.

"Does Mike know it?"

"Naw." T lowered his head." He thinks those other niggas, did it."

"Well, keep it that way. But, you know what's going to happen if you do tell him the truth, right?"

"Yeah, I know."

"You sure?" O'Shay pulled out his phone, looked at its caller and smiled.

"Watch your back, T. Got to keep ya friends close and your enemies in the grave, ya feel me?"

"Yeah, I feel you."

T watched O'Shay cross the lot, climb into his Lexus, and drive off. It was now confirmed and that confirmation had to stay confidential. The thought of having to kill both O'Shay and

Mike entered his head, but he quickly dismissed the thoughts. It was something he couldn't do. Something he prayed he didn't have to.

CHAPTER THIRTEEN

Willie climbed the stairs two at a time. He knew he didn't have long to take care of what he came to do. He knocked on the door and listened for any signs of there being someone inside. Hearing nothing behind the door, Willie tried the handle. Locked.

"Damn." Not the one to leave a lick undone, he took a couple of steps backward and bumped the door with his shoulder. The flimsy structure gave way easily. Making his way inside, Willie went straight to the kitchen. Finding the box on top the refrigerator, he grabbed it, lifted its lid and laughed. There was no way this was happening. He started to check elsewhere, but he'd come for what he wanted. He hurried to leave, forgetting to at least pull the door up and making it look as if it was closed, just in case someone came to investigate the noise. Willie had just rounded the corner of the building when he nearly knocked over a youngster wearing a 49ers Starter jacket, black jeans, and red and white retro Jordan shoes.

"Damn, nigga!" T yelled, while straightening himself out.

Willie quickened his pace across the parking lot and jumped in the Malibu.

"Shit!" He fumbled with his keys. He'd seen the youngster leave earlier, but wasn't expecting him back any time soon, being that the lad had gone on foot.

T was walking up the stairs when he noticed the front door open and instead of going any further, he turned and ran after the guy who'd nearly knocked him down earlier.

"Motherfucker!" T said between clenched teeth. Before he cleared the corner, he pulled the revolver from his waistband, got it ready, and prayed he got the burglar. As soon as he got to the parking area, he immediately spotted the Chevy Malibu speeding off. He fired four wild shots into the backwindshield. "You son of a bitch!" he yelled. His first mind was to run and jump in the truck and chase the driver down, because there was no way he was about to take this loss. He spun around to see Mike pulling up in the Yukon and flagged him.

"Mike! Mike!"

T jumped in and pointed. "Catch that motherfucker in that Malibu!"

"What's up, nigga?" Mike asked and jammed his foot on the accelerator. Seeing T holding the revolver, he immediately thought about the guys from the shooting and was determined to catch the fleeing Chevy.

Willie cursed himself for not being hawk-eyed. At the corner of Rosedale and Miller, Willie took a sharp right, hit a side street and hit a left, the Malibu surprising him to no end. A couple of corners later, the Yukon was nowhere to be seen. Seeing this as his means of escape, Willie headed for the south side. "Young ass niggas can't fuck with Willie, you stupid bitches!" he yelled out the window.

Mike knew the culprit couldn't have gotten far, despite the speed the Malibu was capable of. The rear windshield had some bullet holes in it, so it wouldn't be hard to find. Ready to empty a few shells in something, Mike continued to drive, searching every block carefully.

"That had to be the same crackhead that got at Chubby."

"Really?"

"Yeah, that motherfucker damn near knocked me down when I was walking up the stairs. I cursed his bitch-ass out and kept moving, but when I got to the top of the stairs I saw the door wide open. I knew you wasn't there and I went after the hoe."

"What he take?"

"I don't know yet, I don't know yet, I didn't even make it in the apartment." T leaned forward in his seat to see better. "We gonna find his ass if it's the last thing we do. Punk motherfucker gonna die tonight."

Mike leaned back in the driver's seat and drove. "Yeah, we ain't got shit else to do but find this hoe."

"That motherfucker probably got the work and the money we pulled in yesterday." T hit the dashboard. "This shit crazy, ain't it?"

"Crackhead-ass think he got away again." Mike laughed. "You know a crackhead ain't going to be able to sit on no shit like that. He gonna think he is balling and shit and that's where he gonna slip."

"And that's when we gonna toast his bitch-ass!"

Yousef continually smiled when thinking about Riches. He was already wearing the watch she gave him. It was custom-made. Memories of his past life filled his thoughts and that was something he wanted to stay in the past. The watch he had removed from his wrist, in order to put on the one Riches had gifted to him, had cost him over twenty-seven thousand dollars and the watch was now in his pocket. He'd purchased the watch with the money he made from the drugs he flooded the streets with. His days in the game offered both him and his child's mother a lavish life, but the consequences of that very game landed him up a place he vowed not to return. The life he lived and the decisions he made back then were filled with regret and mistakes, many of which he'd wish upon no one. Those that knew Yousef personally, called him by his birth name and he had yet to adapt to the name he had been given in prison. Joseph Lewis was the guy many aspired to be, and there were others who hated him for his success back then. The money he made allowed him to be with the women he shouldn't have been with. Those were the days when he didn't care for the things he did or the consequences they brought, and that became a way of life for him. The money he made came pretty damn quick. The women he loved were way too young, and the things he did would forever be remembered by most. He learned from his experience and promised to use those experiences from now on.

Riches was like a breath of fresh air for Yousef. There was something about her he couldn't quite pinpoint, and was the reason he was now persistent about wanting to know her. The conversations they held in both person and on the phone, the way she used words to convey her vision, the understanding she had and the wisdom she held made him regard Riches as the one woman he could settle down with. She had things going for her and never had her hands out, wanting everything someone promised her. He could definitely see her in his future, but then too, so was the woman entering the store presently.

Yousef's smile was quickly replaced with a quizzical expression. He hadn't seen this face in a while.

"You lost or something?' he asked her. He looked her over. She still looked good, thanks to money.

"That's how you greet your child's mother now?"

"Well, when I try to get at you so I can see my son, you treat me as if I'm lost." Yousef walked from around the counter to replace a few items. She followed.

"Well, I'm more than sure you ain't got no money to spend on him, so why—"

"My relationship with my son shouldn't be based on money, and the things you feel I need to be giving him financially." Yousef turned to face her, his anger getting the best of him. "Where is he?"

"With his grandmother."

"That's sad. You don't even take care of your own son. Just throw him off on your mother, huh?"

She looked around the store. "Looks as if you have other things to worry about with this little store here. Anyway, I didn't come here to listen to you whine. I just came to pick up the money for the month."

"Oh, he got you working for him now. Next, he's going to have you selling his drugs, huh?" Yousef shook his head. Despite their not being together, he still loved her and her beauty hadn't lost its appeal. He looked into her eyes and saw what he used to love was no longer there.

"That won't be necessary." She looked him over, bit her bottom lip and continued. "I keep money, just opened a nail salon and just got a new Lincoln. I am good."

"For now. When that well runs dry, you'll be wishing you had listened to me."

"Nigga, you did a couple of years in prison and you get all self-righteous with me now? Okay, fine, but don't start acting like the shit I do is beyond you. The last time I checked, you was the one that left."

"I left because of you. I changed for you! I fucked my life off because of you!" Yousef noticed some of the people in the store watching them and to quell the tiff they were having, he walked off. The sooner he gave her the money, the sooner she'd leave. There weren't too many people that got under his skin but she was one of those who did, if any.

"I guess I'll be running back to you then. If my wells run dry," she said.

"I'll be damned."

"You don't miss my pussy?" She reached for this arm. He wanted to pull away, but couldn't. He should have let her know there would never be another time, but didn't. Once he gave her the money, he followed her to the door. "You tell him I said for him to come and get it next time."

Jay sat by the dining window, overlooking the parking lot and the intersection. He normally drove his wife's car when doing business on this side of town, because the cops had no qualms when it came to profiling. Not only did they patrol the South Lake area, but they pretty much knew who was who. But today, he was already in traffic when the call from his customer came through, and they'd agreed to meet at the Olive Park. Ever cautious because of cops, he'd placed the ounces of powder in the Styrofoam cup. Jay watched his customer park across the lot and walk towards the building. She'd been buying from him for quite some time now and was never short with money, and never once complained when he had to raise the prices. There was just something about her he admired. She would have been the perfect side chick if he did decide to cheat on his wife, and he'd told the babe that numerous times. She kept herself up, always professional in their dealings and kept it moving. Jay liked that. Once she walked through the doors, Jay stood to greet her.

"Hey, Cherry, what's up?"

"You," she smiled before sitting.

"You're looking good today."

"Thanks, Jay, I see you clad in designer outfit also."

Jay checked his phone and sat it beside his napkin. "You got a blessing coming today," he told her before sliding her the Styrofoam cup.

"You're a prophet now?"

"I wish."

"I didn't think you would be here so soon. I didn't see your car outside."

"Yeah, I was already in traffic when you called and didn't feel like going home, so I drove my Corvette." Jay smiled.

"This game doing you pretty good, huh?"

It has its perks for the most part, but then I guess it's doing good."

"I might need to change my profession then."

'If you like dodging the cops, then it is the job for you." Jay nodded in the direction of the cop cruiser that circled the lot for the third time. "I really think he's trying to find the driver of that car parked out there." He could see a sudden dullness in Cherry's expression. He could tell that this wasn't her game.

"Aww, hell."

"This what we're going to do. We're going to walk out of here and act as if we've been arguing, then you're going to storm off in one direction and I'm going in the other."

Cherry pulled her purse from the floor and opened it.

"No, no. It's free this time, Cherry. I just appreciate you showing up. But, I got a feeling I'm about to get pulled over and harassed for something."

Cherry was nervous as hell walking to her car. She did what she could to make the scene as convincing as possible and the slap she hit Jay with even made him look at her with question.

As soon as she closed the door to her car, she covered her face with both hands. "I'm never doing this shit again," she told herself.

Jay held his face with one hand and made his way to the Corvette. The cops were still hovering and he was more than certain they saw the performance themselves. He prayed it worked.

O'Shay had been in constant contact with a few people he knew and dealt with in the streets. Having been told of Big Ced's last location, he made his way. The description he used was one anyone could remember and once he was told the guy had four guys with him at all times, he knew it was a positive. He circled the block twice to get a better reading of the things he needed to know if things went wrong, the streets to take and the ones not to. O'Shay purchased the Jaguar he was driving for sixteen hundred dollars from a white guy that looked to be down on his luck. He drove it all the way from the spot where he parked his convertible. Today, there was no leaving Ced alive. The guys that ran with him were either going to kill or be killed and since he now had the drop on them, it was more in his favor.

He checked the clip in the assault rifle for the second time and scanned the area repeatedly. This was their apparent pool hall and the only people he'd seen go in or out was Ced and the four guys that rolled with him. The huge duffles they took inside had to have been of some value because they were well-guarded. Knowing this was the opportunity he couldn't let slip away, O'Shay walked in that direction.

Kay was stepping out of the room when Willie pulled into the circle, the shots in the back windshield telling her all she needed to know. She couldn't believe a pro like him could be making these mistakes in the game.

"What the fuck you come here for, nigga?"

"Told you I'll be right back." Willie walked past her into the room. She followed. "Listen, Kay. I got this."

Kay looked at Willie and nodded, she understood exactly what was going on now. These were the times when Willie fucked up beyond repair and acted as if he had things in control. She had a feeling Willie's actions, all the stupid shit he'd done, would get him damn near killed.

"I didn't say anything yet."

"Well, don't." Willie fell across the bed and pulled four and a half ounces from his pockets, threw Kay two and said, "give me sixteen hundred."

"Apiece?"

"You got the money or not? We in this shit together, right?" Willie loaded his pipe with a huge piece and smile at Kay. "Right?"

"Nigga, you always talking that 'we in this shit together', when you done fucked up something. Your ass running around here doing all this foul shit and expect a bitch to ride along. Who the fuck am I supposed to be looking out for, Willie? How the fuck am I going to watch my back when you do shit like this?"

"For your information, I paid for this shit." Willie blew smoke in Kay's direction, smacked his lips and inhaled a second time. "Some good shit, Kay!"

"Yo nigga ass gonna be lying like a roadkill on the curb when the niggas you offended come for your blood."

"Hating ass."

"Stupid cunt." Kay wrestled the pipe from Willie, and lit it.

With money in their pockets and smoke in their lungs, nothing else mattered. For both of them, this was the life, the moment and the way it would be forever.

O'Shay was ten steps from the door when it opened. The first guy, caught off guard, opened his mouth in attempt to alert the rest of his crew, but was silenced by the deafening sound of automatic gunfire. "Speak of the devil, motherfucker, I show up!" O'Shay screamed, pushing his way into the building. He gunned down two more guys, who were making an attempt to escape to a back room. Big Ced was the only one who returned fire, to no avail. Seeing that he was without exit, Ced threw his hands up in surrender.

"Yo, yo, yo! Alright!" Big Ced pleaded.

"What you got in here for me?" O'Shay looked around for the fourth guy. The game had taught him years ago to be extra sensitive in situations such as this and that was the reason he pointed the gun at Ced's face. "Tell him to come out, fat-ass!"

"Who? Ain't no one else here."

"You got three seconds before I blow your fucking brains out of your goddamned skull!" Like a cyborg, O'Shay's eyes scanned the room.

Big Ced closed his eyes. He'd heard enough about O'Shay and witnessed a bit more, but he was now alone with the devil and their encounters hadn't been right from the start. "What the fuck are you tripping on, nigga? I'm good at business and I've never done anything else but that."

"To hell with you!" O'Shay closed the distance between them while looking from corner to corner. Seeing the duffels, he opened one, then the other. "Oh, you about to go to war, huh?" he said immediately when he saw all the weaponry.

"Nah, nigga, that's just some shit I was buying."

"Yeah, yeah. Where the money at then?" O'Shay held up a Mini-14 and shook his head. "You was going to fuck up something with this, huh?"

Big Ced watched O'Shay with contempt. He knew he was about to die and knew there was nothing he could do about it. "Fuck all that dragging, nigga. Do what you came to do."

"I know you got to have some money up in here." O'Shay checked the pockets of the two guys between the pool tables and the bar, yet kept his eyes fixed on Ced. After pulling the wads of cash from their pockets, he redirected his attention to the big guy. "You mean to tell me everyone else has some money but you?" He walked towards Ced.

"Find it, bitch-ass nigga! Find…"

Before Ced could finish his statement, O'Shay pumped some shots into him, firing into the big guy's stomach and pelvic area. He watched Big Ced drop and went to stand over him. O'Shay aimed the gun at Ced's face and squeezed the trigger, the gun vomiting bullets until Ced's face was nothing but a mish-mash of tissue and blood. O'Shay smiled as a pool of blood formed around Ced's body. After emptying one duffle into the other, O'Shay made his way out of the room.

With a duffle filled with guns over his right shoulder, O'Shay left. He'd just have to catch up with that other guy later, if he even showed his face again. And O'Shay wasn't so sure of it.

The red and blue lights began their dance the moment Jay pulled out of the parking spot. "Bitch!" He checked his rearview mirror, decided against blowing through the intersection and pulled over, leaving his hands on the steering wheel. The pistol he kept was registered to him, so there was no worry there and having given Cherry the powder he had, he was straight, he thought.

When both officers climbed out of the car and approached the Corvette with caution, even that thought faded.

"You from around here?" The heavy-set cop held his hand loosely over the butt of his service weapon.

"I was just meeting with a friend of mine." Jay shrugged.

"A friend, huh?"

"Yes, sir."

"Well, the reason we pulled you over is because a description of a car similar to this one, has a bulletin out for area cops to look for."

Jay saw where this was going and instead of being the duck they used for practice, he said, "That's what the other cops said until they checked me out. They said something about a shooting, right?" He looked at the cop with a questioning expression.

"Then you already know about the possibly armed and dangerous part then, right?" the cop said.

Jay laughed, "Yeah, and there's that." He shook his head. "Wrong guy. I might cheat on the wifey every once in a while, but hey, who doesn't?" Seeing the cop relax, Jay exhaled.

"Well, I'm not going to keep you, sir, but take care of your wifey-girlfriend problem."

Jay continued to watch the cops as they returned to the car. He pulled away from the curb and headed for the first car lot.

Kay locked the door behind Willie and began cutting the rest of the work she had. She now had over three ounces to play with and after doing a preliminary count, she figured she'd make at least three hundred dollars off each, and after treating her runners and taking care of the workers, she'd have around eighty-five hundred. Those numbers creased the ends of her mouth as well as filled the stem she lit afterwards. "Pussy ain't never been this good," she reminded herself. With a plan to put in motion and a high to chase, Kay forgot all about the problems on the other side of the door.

CHAPTER FOURTEEN

Byrd was lowering the garage on the second stall when Willie pulled into the repair shop. He immediately noticed the back windshield and started walking behind the car as Willie parked in the back of the building. It was evident he was trying to hide the Malibu because it was as if he was looking for the perfect spot and Byrd knew it.

"What the fuck!" Byrd opened the door for Willie.

"Don't even start bitching, nigga. I'm going to pay for it." Willie climbed out and walked past him.

"Yeah, I know you are."

"I need something else to move around in, Byrd. Bitch-ass nigga tried to jack me and you know how niggas get when you pull off on they ass." Willie walked into Byrd's office to get out of the hearing of the other mechanics.

"Tried to jack you?" Byrd repeated.

"Yeah, hoe-ass nigga tried to get the Willie."

"Yeah?"

"Hell, yeah."

The fact that Willie was high as high as hell wasn't lost to Byrd, and knowing the man standing in front of him personally, the conclusion had been drawn way before now, but Willie just didn't know it yet.

"Well, I may as well sit this car out front and put a for-sale sign on it."

Willie looked at everything but Byrd and in an attempt to make things right with him, he pulled out twenty-five hundred dollars. "Here, this should be enough for it."

"For what?" Byrd looked at him in disbelief.

"The windshield, nigga."

"You punk-ass nigga, you going to pay me for my car? Fuck that windshield!" Byrd watched Willie sit in his chair, behind his desk.

"I thought you said you were selling the car. Don't make no sense to pay you for it and you still sell it." Willie leaned back and closed his eyes.

"I bet you and Kay must be on some shit!"

"Don't forget, Byrd, you started this shit. This was your idea, remember?"

Byrd couldn't forget. He'd never forget about the days when he put the pipe in his friend's mouth. The weed came first, then he started lacing it to get himself higher and eventually, to get them higher.

"You got to want something better for yourself, Willie." Byrd sighed. "You've got to want something better, man."

"Like you? What, I got to find me a little dirty-ass baby to take care of?"

Byrd faced him. "Don't bring Riches into this shit, nigga."

"I will bring her in if I like."

"Get out, Willie! Get lost."

"The only difference between you and Kay is that she bitches and smokes and you just bitch." Willie stood to leave.

"Bye, Willie. Hopefully, next time I see you, you'll be sober enough to talk to,'cause right now you done dug a hole so big, ya bitch ass could stand in it and still not be seen or heard."

Byrd watched Willie walk away. As bad as he wanted to hate the man Willie had become, he couldn't. For him to do so would mean he hated himself. Willie was the mirrored image of Byrd years ago. The addiction, the drama, the burden, he would always remember. Byrd Nichols couldn't help but remember.

Riches was just about to wash her face when her phone lit up. "Hello?"

"Yeah, beautiful, whatcha doing?"

She couldn't help but smile. Yousef's voice melted her insides, to say nothing of his deep, vibrant voice. He was unlike the guys that called her from school. Those boyish mentalities of theirs failed to stimulate her mind, failed to uplift her and most importantly, failed to make her feel as if she was the only girl in their world. She liked the way she could play with Yousef, and maturity had everything to do with it.

"Oh, just shaving this pussy."

"Got jokes, I see."

"Got a little hair too."

"Yeah, okay, who don't?"

Riches walked into her room, closed the door and fell across her bed, her body itching deep inside.

"Me now and it's so pretty and smooth."

"You going to have to let me see it one of these days, you know that, right?"

Riches rolled over on her stomach, placed her phone on the bed and said, "I can send you a pic right now if you'd like."

"A picture ain't like the real thing. Besides, there's Photoshop nowadays and I'm more than sure you know how to use that."

"Photoshop? Nigga, please. Hold on." Riches pulled her panties off and lay back, holding both her ankles with one hand and her phone in the other. She sent him the pic. "You like?"

Silence.

"Helloooo?"

Silence.

"Yousef! Yousef!"

"I'm going to fuck the shit out of you, Riches, I just want you to know that."

When remembering some of the things Tiffany bragged about, she told him, "If a nigga ain't licking it, he aint sticking it."

"Ummm! I'm gonna suck yo shit 'til it swells up. Let me see your toes."

"My toes?"

"Yeah, take a pic with your feet showing."

"Nigga, I'm no damn pretzel. You're going to have to do that shit when you fuck something."

"You make a nigga dick want to bust."

Seeing Tiffany's picture in her phone, she rolled her eyes. "Let me call you when I get in the car, Yousef."

"Are you coming up here?"

She could hear the excitement in his voice. She laughed. "Not tonight. I've got to make a run right quick."

"Come up here then. I want to see you."

"Yeah, I'm sure you do."

"Just a few minutes, Riches. I just want to hug you and tell you how much I miss you."

"Yousef, that's the last thing you're going to want to do if I came up there to that store. You'd most likely try to bend me over a couple of them boxes and that's not an adventure for me."

"Well, let me take you out. Hell, I don't even know where you live."

"Patience, you've got to play with it first, Yousef. The pussy gets wetter when you play with it first."

"See, there you go. You gonna make me take something now." Yousef regretted the words as soon as they came out. That was the same mistake he made years ago. He fell silent.

Hearing the garage door opening, Riches put her panties back on. "Bye, Yousef."

Byrd walked into the kitchen, placed his keys on the counter and hung his head. Dealing with his friend was exhausting.

"What's wrong with you?" Riches asked.

He looked up and shook his head. "Nigga ran my blood pressure up."

"You take your medication yet?" she asked, now concerned about him.

"I'm good, Riches. I just need to calm myself."

"Is it Willie again?"

Byrd chuckled. He'd told her enough about Willie to last her the rest of her life. "Do you have to ask?"

"Well, stay away from him."

Byrd smiled at Riches and walked past her. "Life has a way of placing people in your path forever, regardless of what you do or where you turn."

"Well, while you're stressing over the things you feel you can't control, I need to make a run and pick Tiffany up right quick."

Byrd looked at his watch. "This late?"

"Yeah, she done went and got a job and I promised to pick her up a couple of days out of the week, until she gets a car."

"See ya when you get back." He went in this room and closed the door behind him. Her picking Tiffany up from a job site was the last thing he'd believe, because just as Willie was talked about all the time, so was the girl called Tiffany. More than likely, Riches was going out to meet some boy from school, and that was something he had to both expect and accept. He wasn't raising a nun after all.

"You need something while I'm out?" Riches asked from the outside of his door.

"Yeah, some condoms."

"Condoms?"

"And make sure you use 'em too."

"Byrd, you in there tripping."

"You just make sure you use 'em when you out there doing what comes naturally."

"Whatever, Byrd." Riches walked away with a frown. It was as if he'd been listening to her conversation of earlier. As soon as she slid on her flip-flops, her phone chimed again. She was hoping to see a smiling Yousef, but Tiffany's face showed instead.

"Hey, Tiffany. You ready?" She spoke loud enough for Byrd to hear.

"Front, bitch, front," Tiffany encouraged her.

"I'm walking out of the door now."

"Hurry up 'cause I'm standing out here with all these crackheads and shit. A nigga already pulled up on me, talking about twenty dollars."

"Whaaat?" Riches laughed, stretching the word. She knew she'd hear more.

"Well, you shouldn't have let that nigga leave you there like that."

"Fuck him. Bitch, I just won for seven hundred and fifty dollars. The only reason I ain't walking to the store is because my pussy sore as hell. Shit!"

"Spare me the details. I'll be there in a second." Riches hung up and shook her head. Tiffany was becoming a real prostitute. Getting her to see that was the only problem.

Cynthia answered the door wearing a robe and nothing else. Cherry walked in the den and saw Bee smiling as if he'd just hit on the jackpot. The white powder on the tray also confirmed the obvious.

"I'm not ever getting this shit anymore." She pulled two ounces from her purse and placed them on the table in front of Cynthia.

"Why? What happened, girl?"

"The cops were onto us."

"And what did you do?" Bee asked, while reaching for one of the ounces.

"I left, nigga. What the hell you mean?"

Cynthia laughed. Not because of the mess Cherry slipped out of, but because of Cherry's theatrics. Cherry always mocked Bee.

"I'm just glad you're okay, Cherry," said Cynthia. "I would have hated sending someone up there to bail you out."

"Well, you ain't got to worry about that anymore, because I'm done."

'You can't let a little ole mishap like that scare you," said Bee.

"Well, you just make sure a little ole mishap don't scare your bitch ass." Cherry rolled her eyes at Bee. "I'm serious, Cynt. I'm through with that shit."

"I would be too," Cynthia said. "It's not worth it." Cynthia looked at the bags of powder on her table and thought about the words she just spoke. How she wished they were true.

"I just hope they didn't run my plates. The last thing I need is for them coming to get me, talking about drugs, guns, and all that other shit out there."

Needing to get the stress off, Cherry pulled a fifty-dollar bill from her purse, grabbed the tray and snorted an entire line, a thick line for that matter. Since this was going to be her last time, she made it worth her while.

Mike and T had been riding for most of the day, in search of the black Malibu with the shot-up rear window. They rode through the east side with vigilant eyes and after coming up empty, they decided to venture outside the hood. This was something O'Shay was going to have to look over, because they were about to find the crackhead that bled them for the second time. They were just about to call off the search for the night when T spotted what looked like a battered rear windshield. "Hold up." He pointed towards the repair shop.

"Right there on the other side of that fence."

"You sure that's it?" Mike slowed the truck.

"That's that motherfucker right there, Mike. Pull around to the front of the building."

Mike pulled into the lot and looked around. The shop was closed but there was no way they were about to leave without knowing for sure. He climbed out first, his Ruger in hand. T followed suit.

"This bitch closed," Mike said. He followed T around the side of the building that allowed them a better view of the black Malibu. "Motherfucker parked in the back so we couldn't see it. Crackhead-ass niggas came all the way from the other side of town."

"You think they work here?"

"They got to have some kind of pull here 'cause the car is here, unless they trying to get it fixed. Either way, we'll find out tomorrow."

Once they were back in the truck, T laughed wickedly. "Found his hoe-ass!" Despite them being out-of-bounds on the south side, they vowed to return and the next time, questions would be answered, blood spilled.

"I bet you'd be sweeter than strawberry," Yousef said after she spoke of liking strawberry champagne on ice.

"You never can tell until you put your tongue on it."

"Hmmmmm! I like the sound of that."

"Where the hell this girl at?" Riches asked. She pulled into the Oasis Motel lot and didn't see Tiffany anywhere.

"Who?" Yousef asked.

"Let me call you later, I've got to find this girl."

Riches hung up and continued her search. The crackheads only watched her, because there was no way a person driving a customized Challenger was pulling up, trying to get some work. But then too, it was possible. Riches parked by the payphones and blew her horn. Of all the women standing around, there was one that stood out more than any. Riches watched her, just as she watched Riches. It was now that Riches prayed the woman didn't think she was stepping on her turf, short-stopping her customers. Byrd told her many stories about just that and after several minutes, she watched as the woman approached her slowly.

"You are looking for the little girl that was by the payphones?" the woman asked.

"Yeah, I guess so." Riches looked around, then back to the woman standing before her.

"Ain't that her right there?" The woman pointed at Tiffany, who was walking down the stairs in front of a short, fat Mexican guy.

Riches smiled to herself, shaking her head when she sighted Tiffany.

"Where you from, sweetheart?" the woman asked Riches.

"I live on the other side of town. I just came to pick up that friend of mine."

"She is working for you 'cause if so, she done ran through two niggas already. If you don't mind me asking, what's your name?"

"Riches."

"Riches?"

Kay stepped back and looked her over. There was no way in the world this woman standing before her was the Riches she knew. There was no way in hell this woman was her best friend's daughter. "Where you get a name like that?"

"My uncle gave me the name." Riches could tell the woman's entire demeanor changed at the mentioning of her name, as if she was familiar with it.

"You ain't talking about Byrd Nichols, are you?"

Riches looked the woman over with a stern look. "You know Byrd?"

"Do I know Byrd? Oh, my God!" Kay placed her hands over her mouth, tears falling heavily.

Tiffany was now standing beside her friend and watched the woman also. They both looked at each othe, then back to the woman, who was still crying. Riches was about to speak then suddenly the woman grabbed her and hugged her with all the strength she could muster.

"I'm Kay, I'm Kay, Kaynese." Kay wiped tears from her eyes and continued."Girl, you are the spitting image of your mother. How old are you now?"

At the mentioning of her mother and her being a spitting image, she knew this woman knew more than she was saying. It was evident that she knew her.

"I'm about to be twenty-one this weekend."

"Hell naw! Ain't no way in hell your big ass about to be twenty-one!" Kay said, causing both girls to laugh.

"What you know about my momma?" Riches asked.

"Cecelia was my best friend. That's what I know about your momma! I used to babysit your fat ass. Damn near had to breast feed you a couple times."

"Kaynese, you say?"

"Yeah, Kay. Kaynese."

Riches remembered the pictures she kept of her mother. Along with her and Byrd, there was another woman, but the woman on the photos was a dyke. Her mom's best friend was a dyke and Byrd did say that much. "Byrd said my mom's best friend was a dy—"

"A dyke?" That's me, hell! CeCe was my motherfuckin' nigga! Always gonna be my nigga too."

Realizing that time was slipping away, Riches promised Kay they'd catch up another time soon.

"Don't forget about me, Riches!" Kay yelled.

"I'm going to swing by here this weekend, we gonna make a few moves." Riches waved goodbye.

They were several blocks away when Tiffany finally broke the silence that filled the interior of the Challenger. "You are going back, for real?"

"Hell, yeah. She seems like a good person."

"Girl, that woman in a motel hustling. Good people do that?" Tiffany watched her, awaiting her response.

"Well, I did just pick my girl up from a motel and she was hustling, so you tell me." Riches looked at Tiffany and laughed.

"Now a bitch got jokes, huh?" Tiffany laughed also.

"You are coming with me next time or what?"

"Sure."

Riches turned up the volume on her stereo and the both of them fell silent, drinking in the melody of Rihanna's "Bitch Better Have My Money."

CHAPTER FIFTEEN

Chubby listened for his name to be called, along with the rest of the guys waiting to be transferred to yet another holding facility. He'd been out of pocket for a few days and still had yet to hear from either of his boys and despite the chatter and small talk amongst the other prisoners, the words of his mom rang loudly in his head. He'd never been in the system before and knew nothing of the procedures prisoners underwent, the physicals, the questions, the mental evaluations and most of all, the whispers of those that knew of his troubles.

"They gonna try to give you the death penalty," one guy told him.

"If I were you, I'd tell them what they wanted to know," said another. One that stuck with him the most was the comment about him still having a long life ahead of him. "You gonna throw your life away like that? You stupid!"

"Derrick Allen!" The guard shouted at the hold-over doors.

"Yeah!" Chubby stood and followed the guard to the desk at the central station. Seeing his property and belongings, he thought he was about to be released.

"Thank you, Lord," he sighed.

"Really?" The old school guard peered at Chubby over the rim of his glasses, the 'No Talking' sign above the entrance apparently overlooked.

Chubby watched him sort through his belongings.

"Son, there is no way you bought these items. You have a diamond watch that I'm more than sure you robbed someone for, a ring obviously costing more than any I own personally, and a Turkish-link necklace weighing at least three hundred and fifty grams." The guy pulled off his glasses before continuing, "That doesn't even include the seven thousand dollars cash."

"Seven thousand?" Chubby frowned. "I had over ten grands on me at the time I went to the hospital."

"Well, you've got seven thousand now." He looked at Chubby. "Is there going to be a problem?"

"Hell, yeah. I need my money."

"Listen, fat ass. All this shit can disappear, if you know what I mean, so I will ask you again, Is there going to be a problem?"

Reality had finally set in and it caused him to shake his head in defeat. He'd been robbed by a crackhead and a correctional officer. "No sir."

"You're a wise young man. Now, sign here."

Chubby thought about all the events that led up to this moment. There was a warning before this downward spiral and it was now flashing before thoughts he was having. If only he'd known they were signs for him. If only he'd seen the writing on the wall, he would have never been in this position in the first place and that was something he was sure of.

"They take your shit too?" a guy asked when seeing the expression Chubby wore.

"Yeah, but at least he didn't stick his finger in my ass all the way."

Byrd opened the shop earlier than he normally did, so he could talk care of a few files before the day began. As soon as he unlocked the gates and pulled into the lot, he noticed the truck pulling in behind him. At first, he thought of potential customers, but knew otherwise when he saw a youth exit the truck. The youth was holding a semi-automatic weapon. The game had taught Byrd many things but being robbed and possibly killed was something that failed to give you the date and time. In an attempt to play the part, Byrd greeted the youngster as he would anyone.

"Morning," Byrd smiled, "need something done to the truck?"

"You own this place?" T asked him.

"I do, now, what's up? What can I do for you?" Byrd stood between the truck and the garage and prayed his being visible to all that drove past, deterred the youngsters from doing anything rash.

Mike climbed out of the truck and walked towards the corner of the building, making sure the Malibu was still around back. He overlooked Byrd and told T, "This ain't him, is it?"

"You own that Malibu parked in the back?"

"Yep. I gotta replace the back windshield first, but yeah, I'm going to sell it." Byrd offered them a better view of the car. "Come on and check it out. I'll make you a good deal on it."

"Could you tell me who sold it to you?" Mike asked him.

"I paid cash for it because the guy seemed to be in a hurry. He gave me the vehicle, I gave him the cash. Deal done."

T looked over at Mike, who was walking back to the truck.

"The guy that sold you that car, does he live around here? I mean, do you see him often?" said Mike.

"So many people come in and out of here, son, it's not much of a practice to remember just one person, unless they are stealing or trying to."

"If I gave you a number to contact me, would you call if you saw him again?"

"Sure, of course."

T walked back to the truck and scribbled his number on a napkin."He gonna call me when that nigga shows his face again," he said to Mike.

"That hoe ain't coming back and that nigga ain't gonna remember to call nobody," Mike yelled in frustration.

"We shall see."

T walked into the front office space, saw Byrd behind his desk and handed him the napkin and five hundred dollars. "Just a little something to help you remember when you see the guy that sold you that car."

Byrd was still seated behind his desk when the two youngsters in the Yukon left, his hands still holding the double-barrel shotgun underneath. He suddenly realized he was shaking. Byrd knew he would have pulled the trigger in a heartbeat and that was something that scared the hell out of him. Willie had brought the game to him repeatedly, despite his pleas for him not to. "Thank you, Jesus," Byrd said, sighing deeply.

Kay was overlooking her operation when Willie walked up the way to the motel's lot.

"Guess who I saw last night?" Kay said, once Willie was close to her.

"Michael Jackson."

"Dumb-ass nigga, I'm serious."

"How the hell am I supposed to know? My head look like a crystal ball to you?"

"I saw Riches last night."

"Where?"

"She came through here looking for her little friend that was tricking."

"She came here?"

Kay just side-eyed Willie. She could see the crack through his eyes, clouding his common sense.

"Where did she come from?" Willie continued.

"Jumped off the top of the building like King Kong."

Willie leaned to one side. "The bitch jumped off the building for real?"

After deciding this was a conversation for another time, Kay lost herself in the thoughts she was having. Seeing Riches brought back memories Kay hadn't thought of in years, the many fights she and CeCe had, the many laughs they shared, as well as the many promises they made to one another. Even though Kay was lesbian, Cecelia never judged her. She never once looked down on her for liking women and Kay respected the fact that CeCe was straight and therefore, never tried to cross any visible or unseen lines when it came to them. Cecelia was the sister she always wanted and became the very one she'd forever miss.

"You hear me, Kay?"

"What, nigga. What!" Willie's voice yanked Kay from her thoughts.

"We need to get another car."

"Yo stupid ass better buy some more shoes, nigga."

"You the cheapest bitch I know. Give a nigga a couple of hundred on it at least."

"How about a couple of hundred kicks in your ass? Think you can drive that?"

After a hearty laugh, Willie pulled out a nice sized piece of crack and pushed it deep into the stem he was holding. There was no place he'd rather be and Kay knew it. Once he'd filled his lungs, he passed it to her. She refused it, so he pushed it to her a second time. This time he mumbled, "Huh?"

Kay took the pipe, held it between her fingers, rolling it as she always did. With an escape from the thoughts that tormented her, she put the pipe to good use, and the crack she took in-vaded her nerves. She closed her eyes, making the sensation last forever.

O'Shay was seated on the couch with his head down when Mike and T entered the apartment. He looked up at the two of them. "Find him?"

"We found the car," T began, "but—"

"Bitch-ass crackhead sold it to a guy that owned a repair shop, but he didn't remember who sold it to him," Mike cut in.

"He didn't remember who sold it to him?" O'Shay asked.

Mike replied. "He said he bought it cash,'cause the nigga was trying to hurry up and get rid of it or something O'Shay stood. "And you believed that shit? Who the fuck gonna buy a car with the windows shot out of it, and not remember shit about the person they bought it from? Fuck that! Who the fuck buys a shot-up car in the first place?"

"He said—" Mike began.

O'Shay yelled."Fuck what a nigga said, it's what you know that matters and you niggas ought to know better."

O'Shay pointed to the bag besides the couch and when he saw Mike pull out the Mini-14 sub-machine gun, he asked, "You know how to use that?"

"I'll learn."

"If you niggas can't handle business, then I'll have to find some more niggas that can. You niggas been ripping and running all night for nothing."

"We found the—" T couldn't finish his statement, because of O'Shay's retort.

"Fuck finding a bitch-ass car, nigga! What has that done for you? Huh? When you start stepping on these motherfuckers, that's when you get shit done." He pulled out a wad of cash from his pocket and threw it between the two of them. "Murder is the real deal that has to be made real, niggas!"

O'Shay walked out, closed the door behind him and smiled. It was time for them to step their game up and the threat of replacing them always had the effect he approved of. The past week had been a very lucrative one for him and it was because of murder. The money he got from the hotel and the guys at the pool hall pushed him over the three hundred-thousand-dollar mark and that was where he wanted to stay. The small arsenal he won for was about to be used, because his next move was about to be a deadly one, one he was sure some would never recover from.

"That nigga be tripping for real." Mike scooped up the cash from the floor and counted it. He handed T four thousand dollars and stuffed the rest in his pocket.

"We still might need to pay that nigga a visit again." T reached for the duffle to see what else was inside.

Jay pulled onto his street and immediately noticed the 650I parked in his driveway. His first thought was that his wife had company, but seeing the guy climb out when he parked, things changed. "Can I help you?" Jay asked him.

Seeing the expression on the guy's, face Jay smiled.

"You Jay?"

"Yeah.What's up?"

"Big Ced and his niggas are dead."

Jay looked around them. "Dead?"

"That nigga, O'Shay, came to the pool hall and left murder as his signature. I managed to escape."

Jay stood and listened to a detailed account of what happened to the guys that worked for the big guy. He wondered how O'Shay knew where Big Ced and the crew hung out.

"So, now you think he trying to find you?"

"That, or he thinks I'm trying to find him. I'll give you whatever he is sitting on, Jay. I just want to look this nigga in his eyes when I sleep him. My brother didn't have anything to do with none of this shit. He'd just come to the pool hall to see me and was leaving when that nigga gunned him down. I've got to have him, Jay."

Jay closed his eyes, trying to block the visual he was seeing of O'Shay crossing him the way he crossed Big Ced. He knew they were playing a deadly game and was the number-one rule many players didn't adhere to. "How much you willing to take to fix that nigga?"

"Nothing. I just want his blood."

"So, you're willing to walk away with nothing?"

"Let me see what I can do. I'll get back at you," said Jay, before extending his hand to seal the deal.

Jay looked towards the top of the street for any signs of the devil himself, seeing none, he headed inside.

Later that night, Byrd walked in to find Riches doing what appeared to be homework. He'd been on edge for most of the day, but seeing her lifted that dark cloud. "Need help?"

"Nah, I'm just about finished anyway," she told him without looking up.

"Test coming up or what?"

"Finals before spring break."

"If you need any help or you just want to talk, holla." Byrd walked into the foyer area's closet and pulled the worn box from the top shelf. He was caught slipping today and that could never happen again.

Riches closed her book and looked back towards the dining room entrance. She could tell something was up with Byrd, because that was the only time he tried to help with courses he knew nothing about. Hoping everything was okay with him, she walked into his room. She'd seen him handling his guns before, but this was the first time he both jumped and tried to hide it when he saw her standing at his bedroom door.

"Need help?" she asked, repeating the same thing he spoke of seconds ago.

"Nah. What's up?"

"Looks as if you're the one up to something."

"Don't worry about it, Riches. I got it."

"Got what?" Riches walked in and sat in the armchair adjacent the closet. She'd wanted to ask a few questions about the woman she met and this seemed to be the perfect time.

"I got a visit today from some youngsters Willie fucked over, and they were adamant about getting in touch with him." Byrd fell silent for a minute. "I really got a bad feeling about this one though."

"Who were they?"

"Looked to be some young dope dealers or something."

"So, the gun is for 'just in case' huh?"

Byrd felt her words slice him like a sword. "Remember when I told you that people are placed in your life for reasons, seasons and lifetimes? Well, the shit goes a little deeper than that. Not only are they put in your life, but you're put in theirs also and believe it or not, you can become that influence that turns their lives upside down. You can very well become the reason they fall and for Willie, it's as if I've become that reason and now it's coming back on me. And this is something I have to deal with."

"So, you might have to kill somebody?"

He looked away, unsure of the answer he needed to give. There was one thing he was for certain of though. "Family, Riches. I'll give my all for family."

"The same goes here, Byrd, and speaking of family, I met this woman the other night and she said she knew you."

"She wasn't pregnant, was she?" Byrd was thankful for the change of subject.

"I don't think so, but she also said she knew my mom and that they were best friends."

Byrd's forehead creased in the middle. "Where you see Kay at?"

"So, you do know her?"

"Yah, I told you about Kay before. Where you see her at?"

"She was at the store Tiffany worked at," Riches lied. Her being at some drug-infested motel wasn't about to become a subtopic for them.

"How's she looking?"

"She looked all right, I guess."

"Was she high? Was she begging for money or something? I mean, how did all this come about?"

"Well, she saw me waiting and just walked over and asked my name. Then she started talking about you and the fact that I am the spitting image of my mother."

Seeing Kay mentally, Byrd couldn't help but see Cecelia. "Stay away from her, Riches. Ain't no telling what she out there doing nowadays."

"She said y'all were friends."

"We were, but right now, she's not living a life either of us needs to be involved in."

"Well, all right." She exited his room.

Byrd sighed. Once his door closed behind her, he closed his eyes and exhaled. "Shit."

CHAPTER SIXTEEN

It had been three days since Willie went to visit Kay at the Oasis Motel and she was starting to think the worst. As soon as she did her count, she put a pause on things and decided to make a stop to check on him. With over three thousand dollars made in a week, she was feeling pretty damn good about herself and the way she was handling things. She hadn't robbed anyone, stolen anything, or even sucked any dick, something she hated stooping to for the sake of the high. The top of her to-do list included finding a supplier for the ounces she would need shortly. Her mind was made up. If Willie wasn't going to provide, then she'd go elsewhere. Her spot had been rolling well enough and she wanted to keep it that way.

Kay walked to the room Willie rented for the runners and workers. That door was locked. She then looked upstairs.

"You got something?"

Kay spun around to a face she hadn't seen before and the bells in her mind went off. "Nah, I'm looking myself," she lied to the guy. Kay had been around too long for some undercover clown to get the drop on her and she was sure he owned a badge of some kind. Wanting to at least warn Willie of the infiltrator, she climbed the stairs and walked straight inside. The inside of the room was packed with both men and women. Smoke filled the air and seeped through the cracks of the bathroom and staying area. She stepped over a guy that looked to have been sleeping, then crossed the room and opened the bathroom door. Willie was sitting on the edge of the tub, with some stringy-haired white girl kneeling between his legs. "What the fuck is this shit, nigga?" Kay went off. She'd seen her friend fall off many times, but this was one time she was hoping he'd get something going other than what he was doing now. "What the fuck you got all these motherfuckers in here for, Willie?"

"Close the door, bitch!"

Neither of them stopped. The white girl continued earning her pay and Willie continued getting high. Kay went to the bedroom and asked one of the women sitting on the bed, "Is Willie treating y'all right?"

"Hell, yeah. We've been partying for two days straight and the nigga blessing everybody's game. Willie ballin', bitch!"

The woman fired her stem up, inhaled and stood up. She lifted her dingy skirt, exposed one of the happiest coochies Kay ever seen, and did her dance. "Who want some of this pussaaahhh?" the woman yelled. No one moved and Kay realized she was the only one paying her any attention.

"Gimme that stem, you nappy-pussy ass." After she inhaled the same smoke the woman did seconds ago, Kay reached between the woman's legs. "You need to shave some of this shit or else you'll have a bitch eating dirt and grass."

O'Shay was feeling himself in the worst way and Shannon was loving every minute of it. He showed up early that morning, with duffles containing guns and money. Her plans were to hit up a few boutiques and then stop by her new salon, but those plans were changed the moment he walked into her apartment and began showering her with cash. Literally.

"Take that shit off, bitch. Let me see that ass." O'Shay had snorted two grams on the way to her place and was chopping up another couple of grams now. The money was pouring in and there wasn't a care in the world.

"I see you feeling good," Shannon said before spinning and twirling out of skirt and panties.

"Shake that ass, hoe! Shake that ass, shake that ass!" he sang while throwing stacks and stacks of bills above her, causing them to cascade onto the floor. He watched as she did her striptease, moving her thick thighs, small waist and round ass. She sat on the thick carpet and twirled her legs in front of him, opening, closing, exposing a perfectly manicured vagina and hiding it at the same time. When she stood and bent over at the waist, he was on his knees, burying his face between her thighs.

"How much this pussy gonna cost today?" he asked, inhaling her fragrance.

"How does ten thousand sound?" She pushed him away, faced him, grabbed him by the hair. "You suck this pussy like you're supposed to, I might knock the cost down a little." She pulled his head into her with both hands, smothering him. He reached around, grabbed both her cheeks and encouraged her grinding. The feel of her wetness excited him and the scent of her engulfed him. He needed her now, wanted her now.

Bee couldn't believe what he was hearing. She spoke of heaving good news for him, but he wasn't expecting this, hearing of the 3.3 million-dollar bid Cynthia won for him. "I love you, Cynthia!" He picked her up and spun her around-her squealing in delight. "How did you do it?"

"Well, the lowest bid was for three point six, so I did a little averaging and felt you could work with the budget I put together. It has its ups and down though," she explained. "But, for the most part, we're looking for the long-term of it."

Bee looked down at her, he was serious now. "Why you got them panties on?"

"I've got a meeting to attend in an hour or so." Cynthia raised her skirt, his next request being obvious to her.

"Bend over for me right quick." Bee bent her over the arm of the couch and entered her vagina from the back, his thrust powerful enough to move both her and the couch. Loving the pressure he put on her, Cynthia braced herself, looked over her shoulder at him and spread her legs wider. "Make me feel it, Bee!"

Riches watched her friend pull a wad of money from her purse. She handed Riches two-hundred dollars. "What's this for?"

"Whatever you use it for. I do break bread, Riches."

"Yeah, when you up to something."

"Well, you might want to buy a new outfit for this weekend. Your birthday is tomorrow and I want you looking good enough to eat when we go to the lake."

"The lake?"

"Yeah, we not staying cooped up in no house on your twenty-first birthday. Hell, nah,"

"And what is two hundred going to buy me?"

"Better put some gas in this bitch or something." Tiffany laughed. "It's the thought that counts, Riches."

"Yeah."

"Before we head out to the lake, I would love to swing by the Oasis and see if Kay is still there." Riches had been thinking all week of the woman she met and now that spring break was upon them, she felt this was a perfect time to spend with her.

"That woman just seemed hard to me. Before you showed up, she was going off on some of the other women and was even looking at me like she wanted to kill me."

"She probably thought you were taking her customers or something. I saw her selling when I showed up and she looked at me the same way," Riches told her.

"You asked Byrd about her yet?"

"Yeah, he told me to stay away from her though."

"He might have told you that for a reason, Riches."

"I just got a couple of questions for her and since she was my mother's best friend, she should have some answers."

Byrd thanked the guy for doing business and was walking back into his building, when the Lexus convertible pulled into the lot. He recognized the two youngsters but couldn't place the third guy. Today, not only did he have the entire shop alert to possibilities, but he was strapped. If this was going to happen, then Byrd Nichols was as ready as he'd ever be.

"You guys come back for the car?"

"Not exactly." O'Shay walked up and extended his hand. "How's it going for you?"

"I'm good. Can't complain."

"My boys here said you bought a car from a guy the other day." O'Shay pointed to Mike and T, who were standing there with hands in pockets, a sign Byrd didn't like.

"What is it about that damn car? Was it yours or something?" Byrd was growing agitated.

"The guy that sold it to you broke in my apartment and took some valuable items and I am going to find him."

"Then I suggest you start looking elsewhere, 'cause he ain't here. He doesn't have shit to do with what's going on here, so I would appreciate it if we not go farther than this."

"I think you know him, 'cause only a friend or a damn fool would take that car off his hands, knowing little about the events leading up to it being shot up."

"I'm Byrd. And you are?" Byrd tried rewinding the introduction.

"O'Shay."

"O'Shay?" Byrd didn't know the guy personally, but knew of him. He'd heard more than enough to know the guy was trouble with a capital "T".

"Yeah, you speak of the devil, I show up." O'Shay smiled.

"Like I was saying, I saw a small profit so I bought the car. I'm more than sure you can understand that."

"Check this out, Byrd. I'm not buying it. You know more than you're telling us and I believe that."

"I really don't give a damn what you believe, nigga. You pull up in my shop with some bullshit, and think I'm supposed to bow down and suck your dick or something!" Byrd was already gripping the handle to his pig sticker. "I'm through talking about shit. If you want to talk business, we'll talk business, but I'm done with this bullshit here."

"I am talking business and I'm also making promises. I'm going to find the motherfuckers that hit my spot and if they as much as mention you, I will be coming back here, and I will burn this bitch down with you or without you in it."

"Bring it on, nigga, then you'll see what I dish out in return." Byrd's nostrils flared, his eyes blazed as if he were a cobra on the verge of spitting venom.

O'Shay backed away, never taking his eyes off Byrd. When push came to shove, O'Shay knew he would have to kill him and that day was definitely coming.

Once he was alone in his office, Byrd closed the door and thought about the life he was living. He'd done pretty good for himself and for that, he had no regrets. He'd provided Riches with a life neither of them were ashamed of and he planned on keeping it that way. The threat at his door was one he knew would eventually come, but his dealing with it the only way he knew how was what he feared the most. In Byrd's mind, there was no way around it. O'Shay had to be taken care of and Willie too, being that he would only continue to bring the same dangers to his doorsteps. For the first time in what seemed his new life, Byrd felt he might kill or get killed eventually.

The deal Jay got for the Vette was one not even he could refuse. Jay pecked his two kids on the foreheads, hugged his wife and was out the door, wanting to get across town before the traffic hemmed him up. In his anticipation, he'd pulled out sixty thousand dollars from the safe he kept in his game room and was about to take it along with him to the dealership, but after receiving the call from the dealer and hearing there was a buyer at the lot waiting, he wasn't thinking of anything else. He was so lost in his thoughts that he failed to see the black Dodge Magnum parked on the other side of the street.

T lowered himself, seeing Jay head in their direction. Hefirst thought Jay would be alone in the house, but seeing him leave brought a form of relief for him. He didn't have anything against Jay, but when hearing O'Shay speak about him and his association with Big Ced, it was understoodthey'd check his pockets a bit. Not knowing where Jay was headed and how long it would take, offered a small window to get in and out and that was the plan now.

O'Shay gave orders. "Mike, you check the master bedroom and make sure to look in the closets and box spring. Jay is not a shoe box nigga, so don't bother. T, you make sure you check the drawers in the kitchen, the fridge and the deep freezer. Ain't no telling where this nigga got his money."

"How long we got?" Mike asked, while pulling the ski mask over his head.

"Five minutes."

"What if that nigga come back while we in there?" T asked.

"Then he was at the right place at the wrong time." O'Shay wiped his nose and looked towards the back seat at Mike. "You ready for this?"

"Yeah."

The three of them walked around to the patio, checked the door there but found it locked. Mike looked towards O'Shay.

"Break the lock, nigga," O'Shay whispered. "We ain't got time to be standing here smiling at each other."

Once inside, Mike headed straight for the master's bedroom. He had just rounded the corner from the living area when he walked right into Jay's wife, who was going to investigate the noise she heard. "Oh shit!" Mike screamed.

Not knowing what to do he turned, aborting the mission and was stopped when facing the devil himself. O'Shay grabbed Jay's wife by the hair and pushed her into the kitchen and onto the marble floor. "Where the money at?"

"What money?" She was panic-stricken.

"Stupid bitches get stupid shit done to them, you know that, right?"

"On the bed. He left it on the bed."

Just as she completed her sentence T darted off in that direction. It took him thirty seconds to return with the sixty thousand dollars from that location. He held the bag above his head. "I got it, let's go."

"He got more than that up in here. Where is it at?"

"We got what we came for, let's go!" Mike was looking from T to O'Shay, who was standing over the woman with a handful of her hair. Before any of them could move, Jay's four-year-old son ran and grabbed O'Shay's leg, his little body pulling O'Shay away from his mom.

O'Shay lifted the butt of his rifle and told her, "You'd better get this punk-ass baby before I kill him."

Mike knelt down and grabbed the toddler before O'Shay ended his days.

"Come on, little man, come on." There was no way he'd even be ready for that.

"You tell your husband that we know he set up Ced and we'll be back for the rest of that money," O'Shay told her before backing out of the house.

T pushed the Magnum as hard as he could. The need to get as far as he could from Jay's place caused him to run two red lights and not give a damn about the sign he'd just passed.

"Slow this motherfucker down, nigga!" O'Shay spilled the contents of the bag across the seats, finding each stack perfectly blocked. Twelve blocks of hundred-dollar bundles. "Sixty grand, motherfucker!"

T laughed. "Five minutes'worth of work. If I knew it was like this, I would have been robbing."

"No, you wouldn't. Your ass scared to drop a bitch, how in the hell you gonna do some robbing?"

"She wasn't even supposed to be there."

"That's the shit you got to roll over when it pops up. When shit go wrong, you got to know how to improvise."

"I needed that lick. We still gonna split it three ways, right?" T watched his boss.

"I'm gonna give you niggas ten apiece. We got to put something up, so we can cop that new Rolls Royce in the morning. I'm going to show you niggas how to pull it off the lot."

Mike rode and just listened to the two of them go on about the lick and the money they won. Seeing O'Shay about to cash in on Jay's baby, Mike had been taken aback. A guy had beat his mother years ago and he and Pistol had intervened. Mike still wore the scar he was given that night, to this day. The entire scene pushed Mike to a place he'd forgotten about.

"Take that damn mask off, nigga!" O'Shay yelled at Mike. He threw two stacks back to Mike, gave two to T and left the rest in the bag. "In the morning, we going to get that Royce."

CHAPTER SEVENTEEN

The Cadillac wasn't as loaded as Jay liked, but with a few additions here and there, he was sure it would do just fine, and was glad he'd bartered his Corvette, only adding some extra cash to the deal, for the Cadillac. Turning onto his street it shocked him to see so many police cars in front of his house. They'd come for him because of the very car he'd just traded, he was sure. He climbed out and walked towards the cops questioning his wife.

"Is there a problem, officers?" he asked, while approaching the group.

His wife rushed him, burying her face in his chest. "They came in our house, Jay."

"What happened?" It was apparent it wasn't about him.

"There was a break-in, sir," the cop began.

"A break-in?" Jay looked towards the front of his home, a neighbor holding his kids on his porch.

"Some guys broke in and shook up your wife and kids a little," the cop informed him.

Jay grabbed his wife, held her at arm's length and asked her, "You and the kids alright? They didn't hurt you, did they?"

"They could have killed us, Jay!" He pulled her to him.

"It's okay, baby. It's okay." Jay held his wife tighter, looking at both the cops and those standing around him. Jay knew he'd planted some proverbial seeds, but he never thought they would grow into a monster of this magnitude. "Did anybody see anything?" he asked the cop.

"We're still investigating, sir but as of now, no one saw anything."

Jay led his wife inside. He was here now and when his four-year-old son ran and grabbed his leg, Jay felt glad no harm had befallen his family.

The sound of the garage door opening and closing awoke Riches earlier than usual. Today was her birthday and she was sure Byrd was up, trying to surprise her in some way. She rolled over, squinted at the huge balloons on her dresser and couldn't help but smile. "What the hell am I going to do with these big-ass balloons?" Riches climbed out of bed, walked to her dresser and shook her head. She opened the envelope. "Damn!" she exclaimed when counting the twenty-five hundred dollars her aunt enclosed with a short, but sweet letter. Riches read it.

Riches,

Happy birthday and many happy returns! I hope you know that I'm here for you.

Twenty-one, huh? Well, those days don't last and you can never get 'em back, so ENJOY them!!!!!

Cynthia.

She put two thousand in her stash spot, placed the remaining five hundred in her clutch and went to see what Byrd was doing.

"Byrd!" she yelled through the hallway. "Byrd!" She moved to the garage and found that his truck was gone. Inside the kitchen she at least thought she'd find something cooked, but he'd left without doing so. She grabbed her phone, saw birthday wishes from both Tiffany and Yousef, and speed-dialed Byrd.

"Happy birthday, nappy head," Byrd greeted her.

"Where you at?"

"I've got some rounds to make and if I don't get them out of the way early, I'm not going to. What's up?" Byrd wasn't going to worry her with the fact that he was on a mission and the sooner he found Willie or O'Shay, the sooner it would be done with.

"Well, me and Tiffany going to the lake later on. But, right now, we're going to hit the Galleria."

"Money burning a hole in your pockets already, huh?"

She could hear the smile in Byrd's voice. "Not at all. I'm saving my money."

"All right then. Call me if you need anything." Byrd hung up.

Riches frowned. He did say happy birthday, but he didn't say anything about a gift he left for her or anything. She laughed.

Riches went to the JVC in the den and once the tunes of Mary J. Blige's newest disc filled the entire house, she dialed Tiffany.

"What's up, giiirrrllll?" Tiffany answered her phone.

"You already know what it is, bitch." Riches laughed. The day had finally come.

"When you coming?"

"Give me an hour or so. A bitch gotta get cleaned up right quick."

Byrd had driven to some of the old spots, hoping to run across Willie, but hadn't seen or heard of his whereabouts. The thought of O'Shay and his boys catching up with him first did cross his mind, but someone would have heard or seen something, and word didn't take long to spread in the streets. With a full day ahead of him, Byrd headed for the shop to take care of the few things he could while there.

Willie had been up for two days straight and it was showing. He wore the same clothes and was peeking out of the same windows of his motel room. The manager had come twice in attempt to get more money from him, but Willie was so wasted, he thought the manager was the cop that continually placed them under surveillance. Seeing that Willie was not in a reasonable frame of mind and neither was the stringy-haired white girl and the rest of the users, who were sprawled around the room, the manager left.

Since the Oasis Motel was on the way to Tiffany's house, Riches pulled in there first, hoping to see Kay.

"Hey, have you seen Kay around?" she asked a guy, who appeared to be in search for his next high.

"What, are you holding?" he asked and approached her car.

"No, no, no. I'm looking for Kay!"

"Get your bitch-ass away from her!" Kay yelled before descending the stairs. She'd been watching the cut on a daily and seeing Riches pull into the lot, she made her way downstairs. "Probably ain't got no money anyway."

"I got six dollars, Kay. Can I get something?" he asked, handing her the bills.

"You can get a foot in your ass. That's what you gonna get."

"Come on, Kay. You know I'm good for it."

Kay snatched the bills from his hands and told him, "Yo punk ass might as well get a wake up, 'cause you running today."

"I got you, Kay. You know I got you!"

Kay gave the guy a blessing and he headed up the stairs. Once he reached the top, he yelled down at Kay, "I'm going to make you rich today, Kay!"

"Yeah, fuck you, punk ass!" Kay had heard that promise many times.

"What's up, Riches?"

When Kay climbed into the Challenger, Riches was humming the tune of Sandy Posey's song, Single Girl, an old school she'd gotten off Byrd's playlist.

"How's Byrd doing? I haven't talked to him in forever."

"He's doing good. Blood pressure messing with him though, but other than that, he's good."

Kay noticed a box on the floorboard and bent over. "This must have fallen when I climbed in." Kay handed Riches the small box. Byrd's name was engraved across the front.

"He probably put it in here before he left this morning." Riches opened the box with one hand.

They both looked at the diamond bracelet Riches held. It had to have been worth a fortune and they both knew it.

Kay grabbed the multi-carat diamond bracelet and said, "Wow! This is fucking awesome." She placed it back in the box.

Since it was still a bit early and Tiffany's grandmother's car was still parked out front, Riches put her own car in park and climbed out. "Let me go and get this girl."

As soon as Kay watched Riches walk inside the house, she looked down at the glove compartment, where Riches put the small box containing the diamond bracelet.

"A bitch can only be tempted so much," Kay said to herself while opening the box for the second time. After replacing the box and closing the glove compartment, Kay climbed out.

"Tiff, you ready?"

"I am ready." Tiffany grabbed her purse, snapped her fingers and started for the door.

"Hurry up, 'cause I got Kay in the car."

"You'd better make sure your car is still out there."

"Just hurry up." Hearing those words, Riches looked out the living room window. "Where did she go?" she asked herself, not seeing Kay in the passenger's seat.

Mike had completed four stages of the Street Fighter game when his phone rang. He ignored the vibrating Galaxy as long as he could and seeing the "Unknown Caller" flash across the screen, he frowned. The only people with his number were those he hustled with or the person he hustled for. He answered the call. "Yeah?"

"Punk-ass nigga, where y'all at?'

The sound of Chubby's voice brought a smile to his face. "Been waiting on you to call."

"These hoes been dragging me everywhere. Took my shit and everything." Chubby filled Mike in with the things he was dealing with and the talk of the town. He even told him he would need a hell of a lawyer, and that he needed to get at O'Shay to see what could be done as far as that was concerned. After hearing of the licks they'd been hitting, Chubby was more than sure O'Shay would advance him the cash he needed.

"Them hoes ain't playing, huh?"

"Hell naw! These niggas in here talking about I should turn y'all in and shit like that."

"Bitch-ass nigga, you better not be setting me up," Mike chuckled.

"Fuck you! Just holla at the nigga for me. I'm going to get back at y'all later."

"Bet."

Mike sat his phone beside him and nodded. Hell, they could budget at least sixty grands. He wasn't sure a lawyer could cost that much. Anyway, it's O'Shay's call to make as to getting Chubbs a lawyer.

Tiffany had closed her door and was checking herself in the mirror, when she noticed a figure materialize by her door. "Oh, you scared the shit out me," she told Kay.

"Sorry," Kay said.

"Where the hell did you go?" said Riches. Kay had opened the backdoor this time and sat in the backseat.

"I am really sorry, Riches. I stole this from where you kept it." Kay revealed the bracelet.

Riches saw tears spring in Kay's eyes.

"I had it in mind to sell it or something. You must think badly of me now."

"No. It's okay. I forgive you."

Riches retrieved the bracelet and quickly changed the topic.

"Where y'all want to eat?" She liked the idea of treating her mom's friend to a breakfast and in return, learning a little more about her mom. "You know, I got some questions I've been wanting to ask you."

"If you don't want to know the truth, don't ask."

"I'm serious. What was my mom like?"

"Cecelia was a motherfucker. You couldn't help but love her." Kay laughed at the memories of her friend. She could see where things were headed and since she wasn't the one to sprinkle sugar on shit, she was praying the twenty-one-year-old girl would accept the facts she was about to encounter.

CHAPTER EIGHTEEN

Mike and T had been waiting on their boss for over forty-five minutes and were planning to go about their day, when the Lexus convertible hit the corner.

"You niggas ready?" he asked, before jumping out of the driver's seat.

"Been waiting on you," Mike told him.

"Well then, you drive." O'Shay climbed into the back seat of the Yukon. "Go to the dealership out there in Coppell. Let's see what those hoes talking about."

"What you got in mind this time?" T asked. He was with O'Shay when he bought the Lexus and liked how his boss handled his business like a true baller. He was going to do the same thing when he got his weight up.

"O'Shay, Chubby got at me and that nigga gonna need a lawyer," Mike told him.

"That nigga ain't got no money? What the fuck he been doing?"

"He said he got a couple of dollars, but they beat him for some. Besides, he had to buy a bundle of stuff there."

"That fat-ass nigga should have been saving his shit, instead of fucking it off on bullshit. If you niggas patch up on something, I might throw something in, but that nigga got to learn to stand on his own two feet. If I keep saving his ass, he ain't gonna ever make nothing happen."

As soon as they climbed out of the truck, O'Shay walked straight to the building. There was nothing on the outside he wanted to see.

"How are you guys doing this morning?" the salesman asked the three of them.

"Ready to spend some money, that's how we are doing." O'Shay looked around and after spotting the liquid-black Rolls Royce at the rear of the room, he pointed.

"That bitch right there."

Forty minutes later, O'Shay and T were pulling out of the lot in the Rolls Royce that cost a little over three hundred thousand dollars and Mike followed.

"This is our shit," O'Shay told them.

Jay could only stand and watch his wife pack her and the kids' belongings. They'd argued all night and the one thing she wasn't about to do was stay there.

"I don't give a damn, Jay. I'm not staying here! I'm not letting my children stay here!"

"I'm going to take care of it."

"You do that, but do it without us."

Jay reached for her.

"Don't touch me, Jason. Do not touch me!" She pointed her finger at him.

"Them niggas wasn't trying to do nothing."

"The son of a bitch talked about killing our son, Jay. He was going to kill my son, because of some foul shit you did to one of their people. Does that sound like they ain't trying to do anything?"

Seeing his wife drag his kids out of the door crushed Jay. He had moved them out of the neighborhood of Grand Prairie into the more reserved class in the Crowley area to avoid things of this nature.

During their meal, Riches asked Kay a million questions about the life she lived and the reasons she chose to do so. The things that led up to her drug addiction had Tiffany feeling some type of way and Riches could tell.

"Me and Cecelia started off just like you, Tiffany. We were some of the baddest bitches in the hood and we knew it. We started hanging out and just having fun, but you know how that shit goes."

"Did my mom curse like you?"

"She was the motherfucking captain of curse words."

"Was she a crackhead?"

"Hell, you a crackhead. You was a crack baby."

"A crack baby!" Tiffany frowned.

"Goddamn right. Byrd and Cynthia pulled you out of that shit though."

"I didn't know my mom was out there like that." Riches watched Kay through her rear-view mirror. She could see the woman wasn't lying. Hell, Byrd always told her that her mom was a force to be reckoned with.

"We all used to smoke our asses off. We stole, fucked, sucked, and I lied and did anything for the high." Kay fell silent, her thoughts consuming her. "I miss that girl too."

"Did she ever say who my dad was?"

"We always thought it was a Mexican guy named Trade. Well, we wasn't really sure." Kay shook her head.

"Whatever happened to him?" Tiffany said.

"Byrd and Willie killed his bitch ass, but they said they didn't. Me and ya momma had that feeling because Byrd didn't like him. When he hit ya momma one day, we told Byrd and Willie and we never saw the nigga again."

"Maybe he just left and didn't come back," Riches surmised.

"Hell, naw. That nigga was so in love with Cecelia, he worshipped the ground she walked on."

"Why would they kill him then?" Tiffany wanted to know.

"Byrd worshiped her ass also. Besides, that damn Mexican was getting too possessive with CeCe. I was about to smoke his bitch ass for hitting her before Byrd and Willie found out, but . . ."

"But what?" said Riches.

"We found out she was pregnant and I didn't want to be the reason that baby didn't know his or her no-good-ass-daddy."

Riches and Tiffany burst out laughing at the same time.

By the time they'd made it back to the motel, Riches had learned more about her mother and about herself than she had ever known

"Let me get my ass out of this car." Kay climbed out and looked at the two of them and with tears in her eyes, told them, "Don't end up like we did, y'all. I regret this shit every day, and feel like I can't do shit about it."

"You got my number, Kay, call me if you need anything," Riches yelled after her.

"Yeah, fuck you too," Kay yelled back, a smile on her face. She before climbed the stairs and walked back into the life she'd been living for the last twenty years of her life.

Tiffany grabbed Riches' hand while they were driving out of the motel's lot. "Bitch, you'd better not ever let me fall off like Kay did."

"Like she said, you'll be the reason you do."

"Kay might smoke crack, but she's a real motherfucker. She's gonna give it to you raw and uncut."

"Yeah." Riches wiped a tear from her face. Despite the things her mom did and the way she lived, Riches still found that her mom had principles to be proud of.

Willie was standing at the top of the stairs when Kay walked up and seeing the look on her face, he laughed. "What the fuck you crying for?"

"The girls got me all the way fucked up. They took me out for breakfast and rattled my shit, for real."

"Well, you got something or what?"

"Motherfucker, didn't I just tell you I'm fucked up?" Kay walked past him and he followed.

"Soft ass should have known they wanted something. Fire something up, bitch."

For one of the few times in their history of dealing with each other, Kay lied to him. "I gave them two thousand so they could get a laptop or something."

"What the fuck you tripping on? Them hoes just played your bitch-ass. Got you feeling all guilty and then you went all soft for them!" Willie stood and watched Kay. "Bitch, we need that money!"

"What happened to the money you had, hoe-ass nigga?"

Willie sat in the chair beside the table and pulled out the small wad of cash he still had. "This ain't shit."

Kay handed Willie a quarter of an ounce. "Here, nigga, you'd better bounce back off that."

Willie looked at her with raised brows. "What the fuck am I going to do with this?"

"Get your punk ass out of here, man. I've got to shit real bad!"

When Kay closed herself in the bathroom, Willie pinched a chunk off the work she gave him, then sat on the bed. After his first puff, he called to Kay. "You let them hoes wrap you in some game with yo dumb ass!"

Jay had been doing his own investigation and was about to leave the matter for the cops, but decided to knock on a few more doors. Presently, he was approaching one of his neighbors' houses that he really didn't know, or had never tried to get acquainted with. Seeing the white guy open the door, Jay half-smiled "How are you doing, sir? I'd like to ask you a couple of questions, if you have the time."

"Of course, what's on your mind?" The guy shut the door behind him and stepped outside.

Jay wasn't in the least offended that the guy didn't invite him inside. He hoped the man could help.

"Did you see anything out of the ordinary happen around here last night?"

"You mean, like people being around that wouldn't normally be?"

By the way the man was talking Jay knew he had something more for him. "You know what I'm talking about, don't you?"

"Well, I did wonder why they parked the car in front of my home, but—"

"What kind of car? What did it look like?"

"It was a black Dodge Magnum with tinted windows and huge black wheels on it."

"Okay. Did you see the guys that got out of it?"

"Well, not really, 'cause by this time I was arming myself."

"You didn't tell the cops?"

"For what? I can kill a son of a bitch right here and not get as much as a citation. What the hell I'm going to call the police for?"

Jay thought about grabbing the guy and killing him himself. Here was a guy that could have prevented the entire thing, but chose not to for the sake of wanting to kill, only if they came to his house. "Thanks for your time, sir." Jay walked away, doing his damnedest not to disrespect his neighbor.

"Racist prick," Jay mumbled under his breath.

O'Shay lowered his phone and smiled. He'd been awaiting that call for most of the week and now that he had a green light, it was time for his next move. "Mike, I need for you to go with me on this next run. T, you make sure we heated up, just in case something goes wrong."

"What's up now?" Mike asked.

"Nigga trying to sell me some work and I'm going to buy it, then we going to break their ass for everything. We are going in soft and coming out hard, if need be."

"When we going to put something together for Chubbs?"

"That nigga gonna have to wait until we make a couple more moves. Hell, if his ass hadn't gotten shot, he wouldn't be in that mess."

"How much we getting off this one?" Mike asked O'Shay.

"Why do you ask?"

"Coz, I'm gonna give some of mine to my boy, Chubby. Mike checked the clip in his Ruger.

"Let's see what it looks like first," O'Shay said. The deal was in play for ten kilos of the same work they'd been having, and as long as O'Shay was the only one that knew, it would be his secret to keep. "If everything go right, I might be able to give you niggas half a thang apiece."

Hearing that kind of possibility, T rubbed his hands with anticipation. He'd do whatever to make sure they got the wind.

Jay pulled a hundred and twenty thousand from his safe, jumped in the Cadillac and hit the streets. There were a few places he knew people would be, and once he got to spreading word about the bounty he had for the guys who violated his home, he was sure he'd be pointed in the right direction before the sun went down. His first stop. The Prairie.

CHAPTER NINETEEN

Tiffany pointed to the Maxima when they pulled into the store's lot. Since they were going to the lake later, they felt it would be in their best interest to get a few beverages while they were still in the area. Yousef being there was the plus, thought Tiffany as she pointed him out to Riches. She was trying to make Riches see that Yousef would bend over backward for her for a few promises and nothing more.

"I'm telling you, girl, just make up something."

"Tiffany, I'm not going to start playing with that man like that. Once you get people thinking one thing and showing them differently, then the problems come and I don't do games."

"Well, just make sure you get us something to use for the night, 'cause we ain't coming back out this way until our night is over." Tiffany said.

Riches was met at the door by Yousef. He picked her up. "I've been waiting on you all morning." He kissed her lips, not minding the presence of customers in the store.

"Boy, put me down. You've got all these people in here looking at me like I'm weird."

"Mmm. Well, I posted that pic you sent me and everyone is just admiring—"

"Nigga, you'd better be lying because if you posted that pic, I would have to kill you and I'd hate to have to get my nails dirty."

"Only kidding. But, you really look so ripe."

"So, you plan on plucking the ripe fruit?"

"It's on my to-do list."

"Goodluck with the plucking."

"Mmmmm. Is that Tiffany in the car?" Yousef looked through the windows to the parking lot.

"Yeah, we had breakfast earlier."

"And now you ready to get drunk?" He watched her.

"We're just getting something light for tonight. Nothing heavy or dark."

"What's up with tonight?" Yousef led her to the beverage isle.

"The Lake. Arlington Lake. You want to meet us out there or what?"

"Nope."

Riches pulled a six-pack of Bartles & Jaymes coolers out of the fridge. "I'll be out there by myself and you need to be looking out for me, remember?"

"So, I'm supposed to be some chaperone or something now?" He grabbed her arm, turned her to him and grabbed her chin.

"You're supposed to be my friend and that's what friends do, right?"

"Oh, so all your friends get pics like the one you sent me?" He kissed her again.

Riches pressed her body against his. She felt the bulge behind the apron he wore.

"Um, seems like things are getting hard for you." She smiled.

Yousef bent down and whispered in her ear, "You make me this way, Riches."

Hoping no one paid them any attention, Riches squeezed his throbbing erection, her eyes widening. "What the hell is that?"

"Come on in the back right quick and I'll show you."

For the first time in a while, Riches was nervous. She'd squeezed a few guys before, but they were boys her age. Neither of them had nowhere near the girth she'd just palmed. For the first time since their flirting, Riches realized Yousef was a man, a big man at that.

"Boy, whatever." She looked around them, looking for an apparent way out of the hole she'd dug for herself.

"Come on." Yousef gently pulled her towards the back of the store. He had to have her.

Not wanting to be the reason things soured between them, Riches reluctantly followed him to the back. Hearing Tiffany talk about not delivering when it was time proved you were all talk and no action, and the last thing she wanted Yousef to think was that she was all talk and tease.

"I've been dying to give you your birthday present," he told her after closing the office door behind them. He took the six-pack she was carrying, placed it on the desk and stood in front of her.

Riches' body trembled. Half of her wanted to run and the other half wanted him. The feeling deep in her pussy had her anticipating the things he spoke of and wanted to do to her, but since this was her first time, she didn't know what to expect. When he began lifting her short skirt, she grabbed his wrist. "I thought you said something about a birthday present."

He ignored her and kept pushing her skirt upwards. He inhaled deeply, the Lancôme Sagamore fragrance wafted from her skin. Yousef knelt in front of her. "Ohhh, Riches," he moaned. The thong she wore accentuated her small waist and thick thighs. Wanting her to know he was serious about the promises he'd made, he pulled at the waist of her thong and swallowed the lump of lust forming in his throat. He could feel her shaking, he could see her hesitance. "Let me taste it, Riches. I just want to taste it."

Riches was stuck between a rock and a hard place and she was the reason. She and Tiffany had talked about this very moment many times. Having heard Tiffany describe the experience she'd had, Riches was hoping for something similar. Telling Yousef no was something she felt she couldn't do. She'd teased him for so long and now that they were together, there was only one thing she could do. She stepped out of her thong.

"Wait . . ." she began, but the instant she felt his tongue between her legs, she fell silent. "Ooohhhhh." Riches closed her eyes and shook her head. The actual feeling was nothing like the words her friend had used to describe it.

Yousef moaned as the sour-sweet core of Riches' pussy settled its flavor on his taste buds. Feeling Yousef suck her pussy while squeezing her thighs at the same time, made her react a way she couldn't control. She began grinding and spreading her legs more, wanting him to taste her more and more.

"Turn around." Yousef spun her and remained on his knees. Once she was leaning over his desk, he licked around her asshole three times and pushed his tongue inside of her. Hearing Riches moan, he penetrated her repeatedly with his tongue and slid two fingers into her vagina.

"Ooooooooooooooh," Riches' moan issued forth. She never once opened her eyes, because Yousef's tongue seemed to have been sent from heaven, making her feel like he was feeding her with honey. His tongue was back to her pussy now, making her feel electrified, especially as he accompanied his tonguing with dexterous fingering. Instead of reacting like the virgin she was, she let it flow and wished in her heart that this moment was eternity.

"That's just a little something for you to think about," Yousef said, before placing her legs back into her thong.

Riches opened her eyes, disappointment lining her features. "That's it?" She wanted more, needed more. For her this had to happen now, she wanted it to happen now.

"Next time, Riches . . ."

By the time Riches made it back to the car, Tiffany had already smoked half the blunt they rolled. Seeing her friend speechless, Tiffany questioned her. "What did he give you?" She began looking through the bag Riches handed her.

"The coolers were free," said Riches.

"I bet they were, as long as you were in there. I thought the nigga dragged you to the back for a minute."

"He did."

"Hmmmm. It takes longer than that to get served." Tiffany smacked her lips and added. "Unless, you sucking some dick."

"Giirrrllll, that nigga sucked the shit out of my pussy!" Riches shook her head from side to side slowly. "Gosh!"

"Bitch, whatever." Tiffany watched her for any sign of a lie, finding none.

"Licked my asshole and everything." Riches backed out of the parking spot and drove off. That was by far the best part of her birthday morning. She couldn't wait for the next time.

When Kay walked out of the bathroom, Willie was standing at the window, peeping through the blinds.

"Don't start that shit, nigga. Get your bitch-ass out and stop acting like your ancestors are coming to take you to the land of the dead!"

"Chill out, Kay, damn! A nigga ain't tripping. I'm watching this nigga roll through here," Willie told her.

"Who?"

"Byrd."

"Byrd?" What the hell are you hiding for?" Kay started walking toward the door. She wanted to see Byrd anyway.

"Hold up, hold up right quick. I'm not fixing to fight with that nigga right now. I'll go get at him later. Right now, we need to hit this lick."

"What lick?"

"The white girl got some people she be scoring from and she is putting us on half of what we get."

"I don't know about that shit, Willie. You just met that bitch and now she is talking about robbing some nigga. The bitch might be trying to set your bitch-ass up."

"Trust me, she's straight. Her dad owns a couple of hardware stores. All we got to do is front it, Kay. Them niggas ain't going to know any different."

"I'll tell you what. You do it! Motherfuckers already shooting at your black ass, so you ain't got nothing to lose." Kay walked back to the other side of the room. There was nothing else to talk about as far as that was concerned.

"Scary ass ain't going to ever have any money like that, Kay. We need this lick."

"Yeah, we needed all the other licks you fucked off too, didn't we? You might just start using your head for something other than sticking it in that white bitch's ass."

"Yo bitch ass always talking about making something happen and when a nigga put something together, ya ass start tripping. This is easy money, Kay. Real easy."

Kay lowered her hand. It was something about the way Willie looked that convinced her to at least hear him out. It wasn't always Willie came talking about something he wasn't willing to get out there, and seeing him hell-bent on the issue, she asked him,"What you need me to do?"

"I just need you to give me some front money. The white bitch got a copier and everything. We're going to make it look as if we have seventy-five hundred for the quarter and when we exchange the shit, we going."

"You really believe them niggas ain't going to count that money? This ain't no ten-dollar rock you are scoring, Willie."

"She's done this shit with them before and they ain't suspecting her to do nothing shady." Willie sat back in the chair at the table. "Trust me, Kay."

"Ain't that a bitch don't trust you." Kay put her pipe to her lips and lit it up. If she was going to make a fucked-up decision like the one she was about to make, she'd at least be able to blame it on the fact that she was high as hell.

"I want my money back, man. If you fuck me out of my shit, I'm going to kill yo hoe ass."

As soon as Byrd got word that Willie was seen at the Oasis, he made that his destination. After pulling out of the motel's lot, Byrd made a right and headed for the nearest gas station. If Willie did leave the motel from that entrance, then the tables would definitely turn.

O'Shay ran over his plan more times than any of them could count. As simple as he made it sound, it was a wonder why he hadn't done it himself.

"So, what's the M-14 for?" T asked after hearing the simple plan for the umpteenth time.

"Just in case." O'Shay, made sure the money was presentable and looked back at Mike. Keep ya eyes open."

Inside the textile building, people were going about their duties at the workplace. Surprised at the fact that the textile workers were in the building in the first place, Mike and T looked at each other. From what O'Shay had told them repeatedly, they would be in and out in no time. Seeing their boss being called to the rear of the building, they followed. The duffle Mike carried held the money they'd use to purchase the work, and the duffle T carried held the M-14 they might use to ensure they left with both money and drugs. The rear of the building offered no exit, as it did in O'Shay's outline of the building, and required them to walk past the same staff they'd seen when coming in. Mike hoped O'Shay wasn't leading them to the kind of situation that ended putting Pistol, Chubby and all of them between a rock and a hard place. When they got to an office on the second floor, they met a guy carrying a shotgun and guarding the entrance to the office. The guy and O'Shay exchanged nods by way of greeting. Mike and T maintained a business-like look.

"Is he inside?" O'Shay asked the guy, who replied in the affirmative.

O'Shay led Mike and T inside.

The white guy they met in the office rose from a chair behind a mahogany desk. "I have been expecting you, O'Shay."

"Yeah. Let's cut to the chase," said O'Shay.

"I'll tell you what, O'Shay, the deal was for ten, but I'm going to throw in an extra two for waiting," the white guy said.

"If we like what we came for, we should be back in a month or so for subsequent deals and I hope you feel the same way."

The guy laughed. "Of course." As soon as he placed the packages on the desk, O'Shay scratched his head, the cue Mike was supposed to wait for before doing the same with the cash.

"The weight on all the same?" O'Shay asked in a bid to make small talk.

"Some are a thousand and eight and a few are a little over, but nothing under."

"Well, this should be quick." O'Shay pulled out four bundles of cash and told the white guy, "Twenty thousand apiece." He'd wrapped it in bundles to deter the count and seeing the guy transferring them to yet another case, O'Shay nodded. "You could have kept the bag we brought the money in. That's why we brought two."

Hearing his cue, T sat the duffle he was carrying on the chair besides him and instead of pulling the M-14 out of the bag fully, he gripped its handle, spread the bag open and showed the whole thing to the white guy. "Don't trip out, man." T's eyes widened.

O'Shay watched the white guy's facial expression change.

"We don't have to do it this way, O'Shay. We don't—"

"Where's the rest of the shit at?"

"This is all I have at this location, man."

"Well, then I guess this is going to have to be enough," O'Shay told him.

"You know you won't make it out of here alive, don't you?" he told O'Shay.

"That makes two of us." O'Shay reached over and grabbed the case and the duffle containing the money. He slung the duffle over his shoulder and started for the door.

The white guy rested the palms of his hands on his desk and continued. "I'm a cop, O'Shay. How do you think this is going to turn out, you robbing me?"

"We're about to find out." O'Shay drew a silencer-tipped gun from his jacket pocket, pointed it at the white guy and fired some bullets that sank into the guy's chest, knocking him backward into the recliner behind his desk. O'Shay then faced Mike. "Hey, nigga, go to the guy at the door. Tell him his boss is having an epileptic seizure. Ask him to come immediately. Make sure panic is written on your face as you tell him that."

Mike did what O'Shay asked him to do. As soon as the guy at the door walked in with Mike and realized that his boss had been shot, he threw his arms up. "God dammit, O'Shay, that was a cop, man!"

"Doesn't matter. You knew that before you set this shit up, didn't you?"

"Robbing him wasn't a part of the plan, nigga. What the fuck are you tripping on?"

"Are you having second thoughts or something?" O'Shay aimed the silencer-tipped gun at his friend.

"Oh, you going to kill me too? Nigga, I put this shit together for your benefit and mine. What the fuck wrong with you, nigga?"

"Shit like this happens when you make deals with the devil." O'Shay smiled at him.

"You're a son of a—"

O'Shay opened fire, the bullets hit the guy in the stomach and he crumpled to the floor. Blood wet the guy's white jacket like menses reddening a tampon.

"Niggas, let's roll." O'Shay, Mike and T left the office and headed downstairs. Mike was glad there had been no need to use the Ruger or the submachine gun, the report of the gun would have been heard by everyone in and around the building. The trio walked out of the front door, got in the truck and left.

CHAPTER TWENTY

On the way to the place Willie and Kay agreed to meet with the people the white girl had mentioned, Kay sat in the backseat of the stringy-haired girl's SUV. The money the white woman had printed up sat beside her in the plastic bag they got from the Chevron station earlier.

"He's already here," the white girl told them, pulling into the huge Walmart parking lot.

"You got a knife or something, dumb-ass nigga?" Kay asked Willie.

"I've got this, Kay, you just chill."

Willie climbed out of the SUV and jumped into the Escalade with the guy. "Hey, man, what's up?"

"I'm good. Let's take a spin."

Before pulling off, Willie gave Kay a thumbs-up. He was sure about himself and he wanted her to know that.

"Where they are going?" Kay asked the white girl.

"More than likely, they're just going around the block."

"So, who are these guys we dealing with?" Kay wanted to at least know who she'd have to look out for and whether they even stayed in the Worth. Willie leaving her in the blind was bad enough and if nothing else, she wanted to know who she could deal with once she had to step out on her own.

"These guys work for Murphy. He's a friend of my father's," said the white girl.

Kay couldn't believe her ears. "Melvin Murphy? The Melvin Murphy?" The name alone had Kay looking out of the windows around them. Melvin Murphy had been in the game ever since they were Riches' age. And everyone knew that although Murphy had enough connections with the fabric of the streets they ran, he still employed a team of guys that made sure the old man stayed relevant in the game. The guy that just drove off with Willie could have very well been the old man's grandson, Michael.

"You know Mr. Murphy?" The white girl turned in her seat with a smile that told Kay even she didn't know the man.

"Hell, yeah, I know Murphy. Did you tell Willie this before this shit got put in play?' Kay asked.

"Yeah. Willie knows exactly who we're dealing with, because I told him personally."

The world Kay was living in had just gotten smaller than it already was. Willie was not only putting himself in the furnace of fire, but he was making sure she wore a pair of gasoline boots aswell. I might well kill that nigga as soon as we get away from here, that's if they don't kill him first.

The guy driving the Escalade drove a couple of blocks away before looking over at Willie. "So, you're really trying to make something happen, uh?"

"Yeah." Willie shifted with unease in his seat. He felt as though he had no long spoon and yet was dining with the devil.

"When I told the old man that it was you, he couldn't believe it. He told me to make sure I kept my eyes on you." Michael laughed. "He told me all about you and a partner of yours back in the day."

"Yeah, I was a real kickass back then."

"Well, here's the nine you are paying for and the other nine is the front that come with it. So, now you owe me another seventy-five hundred."

"That sounds about right. Here's the money." Willie, at first, fumbled with the plastic bag before handing it to Michael. "I'll be back at you in about two and a half weeks, Michael."

With over five hundred and fifty grams in his possession, Willie climbed back into the SUV with Kay and the white girl and lied. "He only gave me four for the front."

"What front? You ain't said shit about no front, and you damn sure didn't say shit about it being Old Man Murphy and them." Kay went on. "Where my money at, bitch-ass nigga?"

"Chill, Kay. We good. Damn!" Willie gave her a look she was all too familiar with. She tended to give him that very look when she held a few cards up her sleeve also.

Willie pulled four ounces from his pocket and handed them to the white woman. Is this good enough?" He could tell by the look in her eyes and the way she was smacking her lips that she was more than good with the win.

"Yeah, yeah, that's good, that's good enough," she nodded quickly.

"I gave you my money, Willie, because you said I would get it back. I'm broke now," Kay lied. "It's about time you paid up what you owe me, Willie."

"Here, you keep nine of them and don't say I don't look out for you." He gave Kay nine ounces and kept the remaining five. "Just make sure you give me half of the seventy-five."

"Get your ugly ass out of here. I've got things to do and people to see." She walked to the door and opened it.

"Damn, you ain't even going to smoke nothing with a nigga?"

"Get your bitch ass out, nigga. That's your damn problem now."

As soon as she closed the door behind Willie, Kay was heating her blade at the tip. She placed a huge rock on her Brillo and pushed it a quarter of the way inside. 'Mmmmmmmmm!" She'd never had this much dope before. The fire that sizzled the crack did its dance with the perfect rhythm, melting the hardened cocaine and filling her lungs with the fuel it took to make her feel as if she was floating in the air. Kay kicked her shoes off, closed her eyes and her soul took flight. "I am in heaven," she muttered under her breath.

Willie was making his way to the Southside Motel and was feeling damn good about what just went down. He was so caught up in his moment, he never noticed the Dodge Ram that was slowly pacing alongside him. By the time he did look over at the driver, it was too late. "Let's go for a ride, Willie!" Byrd yelled from the driver's seat.

"I've got shit to do, Byrd! I'm going to catch up with you later, man!" Willie tried to wave him off.

Byrd turned the truck, abruptly stopping it inches in front of Willie and before Willie could react, Byrd was pointing his Desert Eagle at him. "Get your ass in the truck!"

Willie exhaled fully, looked around them and climbed into the Dodge. Hell, this wasn't the first time either of them pulled a pistol on the other and he was sure it wouldn't be the last.

Little did O'Shay know that the cop he'd shot in the chest wore a vest and hadn't died, it only knocked him out. Mike had gotten a call, much to his astonishment, from the cop in the evening of that sameday. He'd put the phone on speaker, so T could hear everything. The words of promise to both of them were enough for the secret they now shared. "Just make sure O'Shay doesn't know I didn't die," the white cop had said. "O'Shay is going to burn and you guys have a chance of a lifetime. I'll make sure each of you get ten kilos apiece. The only way to win in this game is to look out for yourselves. You see what O'Shay's doing. I will call you again, so I can arrange for you boys to meet with me."

Mike thought about those very words and he was now satisfied that he'd made the right decision for himself and his friend. The time for working for O'Shay was coming to an end and they both knew it. With enough product to flood their hood and three other hoods, it was time for them to step up and step out. Knowing it was only a matter of time before O'Shay was buried under the same bodies he'd buried, Mike set out to recruit his own workers.

Ever since winning the janitorial bid, Cynthia had been meeting with equipment companies, chemical plants and several used-truck dealerships. Bee would need to revamp not only his crew, but the supplies and equipment they used to perform the new duties he was obligated to do. He wasn't trying to negotiate or compromise in the least, it was his drug use. He and his staff being subject to random drug testing came with the stipulations and when looking at the fact that they'd be working around kids of all ages, drug use would not be tolerated at all. Alcohol was frowned upon, but having drugs, doing drugs and being influenced by drugs around kids, was the sole reasons companies and executives tanked and Cynthia wasn't about to be shunned in that fashion. "Why didn't you tell me about that shit before you did it, Cynthia?" Bee asked after hearing he wasn't about to get high.

"We are not having this conversation, Bee. You wanted me to do what I could so you could secure that bid and I did. Now you are tripping on the fact that you can't get high, are you serious?" Cynthia was completing a call when Bee walked in her office with his grievance and to hear something so asinine, had her standing behind her desk with both hands on her hips.

"I told you that nigga was strung out," Cherry said.

"Ain't nobody even talking to you, woman." Bee defended himself.

"Cherry, I got this." Cynthia returned her focus to Bee. "Do you want this or not because there are over a dozen of established custodial firms waiting for you to back out for whatever reason. Three plus million dollars is the reason they wait, need I remind you?"

"Is there any way around that shit?"

"Bee, no, there's not. Do you want it or not?" Cynthia was stern in her reasoning. "I'm not going to allow you to burn my name for the sake of a high."

"That nigga don't want no money," Cherry cut in again.

"Cherry, how long of a break are you going to take?" Cynthia nodded for her friend to leave.

Cherry then reluctantly took the hint and stood up. "Well, I guess I need to get back, so I'll let you two battle it out without me." Cherry walked over to Cynthia and looked at her neck, arms and breasts.

"Girl, what are you doing?"

"Just making sure you don't pop up with any new bruises," she told her while looking at Bee.

"Cherry, get out of here." Cynthia pushed her out of the door and closed it. Seeing Bee in such a languished state, she walked towards him. "Bee, you know how you get when you're high." Cynthia sucked his bottom lip and continued. "You get horny as hell and you get abusive. What do you think's going to happen when some of them young chocolate pussies run past you when you're dying for me, dying for some of this head, wanting to suck on these titties, huh? What are you going to do with this?" She squeezed his dick. "You're going to eventually fuck up, Bee, and I can't have that. The way I got things set up for you, you'll pocket over three hundred and seventy-five thousand dollars a year and I can use some of that."

Bee reciprocated her actions. Cynthia was his vice, his muse. The cocaine was just his addiction. "You got me between a rock and a hard place, Cynthia, but I like it. We'll talk about this some more tonight, right?"

"If that's what you want to waste time doing." Cynthia eyed him seductively.

"I'm going to beat you like you stole something, you know that, right?" Bee pinched her nipples, causing her to moan.

"Hmmmmm."

"I got a little surprise for you too. I'm bringing company and I'm not talking about that white girl either."

"Guess I've got to go out and buy me something sexy then. I'd hate to disappoint." Cynthia looked across the lobby outside her office door and seeing others head their way, she told him, "I want it done just like you always do it."

Loving the games Cynthia played, Bee smiled, nodded at the rest of the staff and exited the building.

Both Willie and Byrd remained silent for most of the ride but when they approached Cobb Park. Willie broke that silence. "What's out here?"

"I got something I need for you to see," Byrd told him.

"Like what?" Willie looked around the area, then at Byrd.

"Some nigga named O'Shay came to my shop, making a bunch of threats because of some shit you did to one of his spots. You know anything about that?"

"Man, that nigga ain't talking about nothing."

"You think so?" Byrd pulled to the curb on the darker side of the park. There was no traffic whatsoever.

"You know how niggas be talking." Willie shifted in his seat.

Byrd pulled the money from his pocket. "Those niggas paid this for anything that leads to you. Still sound like they ain't trying to do nothing?"

Willie picked up the money and counted five hundred dollar bills. "I got it, man. I got it."

"I saw you earlier with one of Murphy's boys. What were you doing, Willie?"

"Don't even worry about that, Byrd. I'm straight on that end." Willie's lying was something both Byrd and Kay were used to hearing. Byrd recalled the white girl he'd seen earlier. He had a feeling if he mentioned stuff about the white girl, Willie would deny it.

"That's not what the white girl said earlier."

"That bitch don't know shit. All she did was set up the lick. I gave her her cut and that was it."

"You are jacking Murphy for a white bitch now?"

"Man, they ain't worried about us. The nigga didn't even count the money. We good."

"You still out here fucking up, Willie." Byrd cut the truck off and opened his door. "Get out."

"What?"

"Get your ass out, I want to show you something."

Willie followed Byrd to a secluded area of the park, where an uneasy feeling greeted him.

"I should leave your strung-out ass with ya dick in the dirt and be done with it, but that ain't going to keep these niggas you fucking over from knocking on my door." Byrd pulled the Desert Eagle from its holster and held it to his side. He needed Willie to know the seriousness of their talk.

"You killing family now, Byrd?" Willie eyed the huge pistol.

"Family? You don't know what family is, what family do for each other and the shit you don't do to each other." Byrd tapped the barrel against his thigh.

If Willie didn't know anything else about the man standing in front of him, he knew these actions and instead of the disadvantage he saw himself with, he told Byrd, "Put the gun up, Byrd. You want to scratch, we'll scratch. Just put the gun up."

"See? That's the problem now, you think niggas just want to scratch. Motherfuckers come and threaten to burn my shop down because of some foul shit you did, and you think I came here to scratch with your stupid ass?" Byrd raised the gun to Willie's face. "I came to burn your—"

Before Byrd was could finish his sentence, Willie rushed him. They both wrestled for control of the weapon and as soon as Willie wrapped his fingers around the gun, two shots rang out, echoing through the silence around them. Seeing Byrd fall, Willie stumbled backwards. "I couldn't go out like that, Byrd," Willie panted. "I wasn't going out like that, nigga."

Since visiting Yousef, Riches had been dealing with the fact that things were getting serious between them.

"He just makes me feel like it's real, Tiffany, like..." Riches paused. "Like, I'm all that matters."

"Bitch, please. That nigga licks you in the ass and you think you the only motherfucker he is thinking about? You crazy," Tiffany scoffed.

"Oooooh, he made me feel so, so good, Tifff. I was, like, 'that's it?' "

Both of them laughed.

"I don't know whether to get my pussy ate a few more times, or get what I want from him, and move on to the next nigga willing to do the same things," Riches said.

"You see how you already ready to follow this nigga through the dark, no flashlight, no candle, no nothing?"

"So, he is using me now, getting what he gone get and gone huh?"

"Your ass jumped out of a candy-painted Challenger, bought a nigga a five hundred dollar watch and you the kind of bitch every nigga want. Hell, my tongue would be in your ass too."

CHAPTER TWENTY-ONE

By the time O'Shay made it to Shannon's apartment, she still hadn't made it home. The salon was demanding a little bit more of her time, and the duties she now had kept her busy. Knowing she'd at least question the purpose of the red oak trunk he put at the foot of her bed, he filled it with the kilos of cocaine he took from the textile building and placed a bunch of sheets and comforters on the top of them. The Louis Vuitton bag sitting on the floor contained over a hundred and seventy-five thousand dollars and that would be placed under the tire compartment in the trunk of the Lincoln he bought for her. The way he saw it, if someone did get the ups on him and hit one of his spots, they'd only get the amount there instead of all he owned. The two kilos he had swinging were broken down and ready to be sold. As a reward for the job both Mike and T did he was going to give them a chance to buy their own work at prices they wouldn't be able to get anywhere else.

He placed each ounce he cooked on the DYMO scale and debated the amount of weight he'd sell them for. He knew the numbers more than any and felt in order to get the work sold as fast as possible, he had to at least drop the price,something not even he could do without cringing at the thought. He made a call to one of his loyal customers.

"Yeah," the guy answered.

"Got something for you, you ready or what?" O'Shay sat and watched the numbers adjust on the digital scale.

"Tell me something good then."

"I'll give you sixteen softs for ten thousand right now."

There was a brief pause, then the guy said, "Where we are meeting at?"

"Stop Six, one hour," O'Shay said, but when hearing Shannon walking through the front door, he told the guy on the phone, "make that two."

O'Shay couldn't help but smile at the woman walking past him. The Chanel pant suit she wore had her looking like the executive she should be. She stepped out of her red bottom heels, sat her briefcase on the floor beside his carry-on and went to hug him. She pecked his lips. "Where are you going?" she asked, looking down at the luggage.

"Down south." O'Shay smiled.

"For what?" she asked, not catching his humor.

He reached between her legs and rubbed her. "For this."

"Um . . ." Shannon stepped back, looked him over and asked, "Do I get to shower first? I've been working all day and I'm sweaty."

He picked her up and carried her to the couch. "I like sweaty." He began undoing her belt and as soon as her pants hit the floor and she was stepping out of them, O'Shay's head was between her legs. Feeling his phone vibrate he checked the caller ID and seeing Mike's name, he sent it straight to voicemail. He'd catch up with them later. Besides his next lick, he was putting together a few more for them. "With money comes power—" he began.

"And with power comes?" Shannon questioned him while grinding her pelvic bone into his face.

"Murder."

When Jay pulled into the service area of the shop, he was hoping to see O'Shay, but was greeted by one of the guys that worked there. When discussing the things he wanted done to the Cadillac, he watched those that were around. He looked for anyone matching the descriptions of the three guys that violated his home.

"We also have the new Clarion unit that allows you to monitor things both at home and on the road," the rep told him.

"The Bose stereo would do just fine and instead of the little monitor in the dash, I'd like to upgrade it to a bigger screen. I want the tint darkened and I was thinking about getting that other grille with the mesh." Jay went through a list of upgrades and made sure it totaled around twenty-five grand, what O'Shay owed him from the deal with Big Ced.

"We have a virtual display booth that gives you a pretty good visual when it comes to concepts you'd like to see,if you'd like to view it before the final works are done to your ride."

Jay followed the guy through the respite virtual display booth. The selection of cars getting repairs and modifications done had him looking at everything from Range Rovers to Benz Wagons and from Maserati to an all-black Rolls Royce, sitting on the priority ramp at the rear of the building. Seeing the show-stopper had Jay rethinking his vision for the Cadillac because it definitely caught his eye. "Whose Royce is that over there?" he asked the rep.

"Oh, that O'Shay's new toy,bought it earlier and brought it straight here for upgrades," the rep stated proudly.

"Ain't that a bitch?" Jay said.

"Bitch bad, ain't it?"

"The twenty I'm putting into the Cadillac ain't shit now, huh?" Jay looked over the selection a second time and seeing nothing as stunning as the black Royce, he looked back at the rep, who was shrugging as if it was obvious.

"Hell, O'Shay owns the place, he should have the nicest cars."

"He should also have my money." Jay swiped the screen of his phone. He and the devil had some things to discuss. "How long is it going to take for the shit I need done?"

"Well, we have to order the grille, but everything else would be done within the hour."

Upon hearing the voicemail, Jay ended the call and as pissed as he was now, he told the rep, "Let's get it." In his anger, he turned and started back for the respite area of the building, walking right past the matte-black Dodge Magnum without noticing and without a second glance.

Byrd stood, looked around the park and then back to Willie, who was now holding his abdomen. When he'd first seen Byrd fall after the gun went off, he'd thought it was Byrd who'd got shot. It wasn't until Willie felt something wet trickling around his own belly that he looked and saw those bullets did deposit themselves in his abdomen. The reality of the situation hit him when he began to feel pain, and his hand resting against his stomach, his eyes full of horror.

"We always knew it was a matter of time before you killed your damned self," Byrd told him, seeing the huge hole Willie unsuccessfully tried to cover. When Willie fell, Byrd went to stand over him. "I loved you, nigga!" He pushed the Desert Eagle to Willie's head. "I loved you, nigga!" Tears found their way onto Byrd's cheek. This was his best friend, his brother.

Willie feebly watched Byrd, the pain raw and biting, pushing him into the arms of death. "How could you do this to me!" he managed. "The way I turned out to be wasn't my doing. It was you who…" Willie's words faded, as did the lights above him and the life within him. Finally, his body was still. Even though his eyes were open, he was dead.

Byrd quietly walked across the park to his truck. He climbed inside, with no eyes following his every move and no sirens alarming him of the thing that just happened. He checked the burning sensation on his left arm, praying he wouldn't have to make a trip to the ER and seeing he was only given a huge flesh burn from the fire of the blast, he wrapped it with a rag he kept in the glove compartment.

Arlington Lake.

Riches and Tiffany had been debating on where to park, and with Tiffany wanting to at least be where the crowd was and where the action was sure to happen, Riches relented.

"Girl, I'm telling you, just pull in behind that truck right there," Tiffany told her while pointing to the burgundy and platinum Chevy.

"Your ass just want to be seen, bitch."

"Keep your lamp burning. Ain't that what the Bible says?" Tiffany checked her appearance in the mirror, making sure her lips were glossed to perfection.

"Shut up, Tiffany, and no, it doesn't say anything like that. You just need to keep your ass from getting burned." Riches shook her head and watched the sky-blue Avalanche slowly passing them.

"That's one of them plywood niggas," said Tiffany. "They on money too."

"And how would you know that?"

"Mona used to fuck a couple of them niggas."

"Hmm."

"See, this where you find a nigga pushing something nice. If a nigga got something worth riding in and a ride worth a bad bitch's approval, then he's going to bring it here."

Riches nodded at a few more cars and trucks, giving her approval. She loved the fact that Byrd kept her in something of her own because if she didn't have a ride, she'd more than likely be one of the many women walking back and forth trying to be seen and wanting to be picked. Realizing how things could have been, Riches sighed. If it wasn't for Byrd and her aunt Cynthia, there was no telling how she would have ended up.

"I love nice things, Tiff, I just feel there are other ways to get them instead of selling yourself short, and letting all these niggas test drive your engine, don't mean they gonna buy it."

"That's why I charge their ass for the ride. I get mine off the top. I get on and I get off, can't beat that, Riches."

Riches leaned away from Tiffany and smiled. "You know I pray for you, don't you?"

"I hope you're praying I get rich quick, 'cause I want to." Satisfied with her appearance, Tiffany untied the sheer shawl around her waist and climbed out.

"Come on, bitch, let me show you how to get it."

Knowing her friend was about to perform, Riches grabbed a wine cooler, half of the blunt she rolled and opened her door also. "I'm just going to sit on the hood and enjoy the show, Tiff. You go ahead and do your thang."

"See, niggas going to pull up on you because of this car alone, but me, I've got to do some trappin'." Tiffany spun around, snapped her fingers above head and told Riches, "The real trap queen, bitch!"

Riches was passing the blunt to Tiffany when a Cadillac Escalade pulled up, vibrating everything that wasn't bolted down. Hearing Ed Sheeran's song playing, "The Shape of You," Tiffany sang along.

"Who is that?" Riches asked her, really admiring the car.

"That's that chick, Nicole. I heard she just got out of the feds and ain't looked back," Tiff told her, before inhaling another stream of smoke from the blunt.

"She a dope girl or what?"

"Nah, she used to fuck with them checks, but now she has her own publishing thing going on." Tiffany nodded at the driver. "I've got to step my game up, huh?"

"Yeah, you'd better start writing about the shit you be doing."

"Nah, I'm going to let these niggas write about the shit I do."

Riches could only shake her head at her friend. The logic in that response was lost on her. Hoping the blunt they were smoking wasn't the cause of her lack of understanding Tiffany, Riches held it out and looked at it, took two pulls and looked at it again. "This has got to be some good shit we are smoking, Tiff."

Jay was overseeing the modifications of his car when O'Shay's convertible Lexus pulled into the lot, with the champagne colored Sierra in tow. With a few things to discuss, he stood and met him at the entrance.

"Hey, Jay, what brings you by today?" O'Shay grinned.

"You got that money ready for me or what?" Jay got straight to the point.

"Things are slow at the moment, but I'm making something happen as we speak."

O'Shay could see the attitude in Jay's demeanor and instead of addressing this openly blatant disrespect, he pointed him in the direction of the office.

"Let's step in there for a minute."

Since the three of them had plans for the rest of the night, Mike and T walked around to the back of the shop with thoughts of their own, paying no attention to the way Jay was eyeing them contemptuously.

"What's on your mind, Jay?"

"I need that issue, O'Shay. Got to pay for the shit I'm getting done to the Cadillac I just got."

O'Shay looked out of his office window into the service area.

Jay felt as though O'Shay wasn't really paying him attention. "You got me or what?"

"Like I said, things are slow at the moment, Jay. You that hard up for sixty, I mean, twenty-five G's?"

O'Shay acted as if he was looking over a few papers, hoping Jay didn't hear the slip.

"Sixty what?"

"I meant to say twenty." O'Shay looked up at him.

Jay closed his eyes and exhaled. "You and your little boys ran up in my house, nigga?"

"What are you talking about?" O'Shay asked him with raised brows.

"You threaten my wife and my kids, O'Shay?"

"I don't know what the fuck you're talking about, nigga, and I would appreciate it if you toned that shit down."

"That sixty you took wasn't so painful, nigga, but putting your hands of my wife and threatening my son! Man, that was taking things too far! You got me fucked up, bitch-ass nigga!"

The people in the lobby had begun to notice the heated conversation going on in the office and were making their way for the door. Mike and T hurried towards the front of the building after hearing a couple of the techs talk about what was taking place, and to make a good showing for their boss, they entered the office with their pistols drawn.

"Jay! Jay! Jay! Come on, man. Let's walk it off." T tried to grab Jay's arm.

Jay jerked away. "What the fuck you are putting your hands on me for, dumb-ass nigga!" He grabbed T by the neck and pushed the youngster against the office door.

"Get out! Go get in your shit and get out!" O'Shay told him in a low, menacing tone.

When Jay turned to face the devil himself, the barrel of Mike's Ruger halted Jay in his tracks.

"If I run up in your shit, you'll be the first to know, Jay." O'Shay pulled twenty-five thousand from his office safe and threw it on the desk. We're through, Jay. That's it, nigga."

Before Jay could respond, the technician walked into the office and held out his keys to him. "Your car is ready, sir. It's ready to go."

Jay snatched his keys and grabbed the stack of money on the desk. He laughed, "You might as well enjoy that shit, 'cause you earned everything that come with it, buddy. You earned that." Jay threw the money at O'Shay's chest, pointed at him and chuckled. He walked past both T and Mike, saying, "I don't know which of you niggas it was, but thanks for grabbing my son."

It wasn't until Jay had left that Mike concealed the Ruger he'd been holding, and helped T up off the ground. He sympathized with the guy whose son was nearly taken by the devil, and knew that the time was growing nearer when the devil himself got what he had coming.

CHAPTER TWENTY-TWO

As soon as Bee walked into the house, Cynthia began undoing his belt buckle. She'd done a couple of lines earlier and had been waiting on his arrival for the past hour and a half. She smiled when she saw the overnight bag he carried on his shoulder, because the last time he brought it, their night was one she hadn't forgotten yet. With an itch she needed scratched in the worst way and a fetish that pushed her past paradise, she pulled him into her room.

"What you got in here for me?" she asked, pointing at the bag he carried.

"I told you I was bringing company." Bee looked down at the see-through nightie she wore and whistled. "Your black ass be fucking me up. You know that, right?"

"That's because you be fucking me right." Cynthia pulled his belt completely off and handed it to him. She opened her nightie and let it fall to the floor, exposing the three-piece stringed set with crotch-less panties. "You take that pill yet?"

"Took that over thirty minutes ago."

She smiled. "Good, 'cause I need you to stay hard tonight."

"Them damn blue pills ain't nothing like that white girl, though."

When Bee's pants fell to the floor, she pushed herself back onto the bed. "Show me what's in that bag you got."

Bee pulled out a long wire that was attached to a small remote. The second item he pulled out was a paddle, then a leather flogger, which she pushed from his hands.

"Um, a clit spanker." She rubbed it between her legs. "I might like it."

"You're going to like that, but you're going to love this," he told her and pulled the lubricant from the bag. After squeezing a small amount on his fingers, he coated the cylinder-like bullet and told her, "Lift your legs up right quick." Seeing her comply without protest or even question, he added, "You are the freakiest woman I have ever seen in my life, Cynthia." He pulled her thong to the side and inserted the small bullet in her ass, until half his finger disappeared also.

"Hmmmmmm." Cynthia squirmed under him.

Bee kissed her inner thighs and licked around her pussy, teasing her in the very ways she liked. Before she could pull her leg through the thong, he rolled her onto her stomach and began tying her hands to the two posts of the headboard. He kissed her back, sucked her neck and began massaging her ass, oiling her flesh and slipping off her thong. "Time for your spanking."

"Let's go with it," she said eagerly. Knowing how Bee liked to see her, Cynthia arched her back and spread her legs. "What you—"

Whack!

"Oowwww!"

Whack! Whack!

With her arch giving him the perfect target, Bee pressed the second speed on the vibrator he'd pushed in her ass.

Cynthia screamed.

Whack! Whack! Whack!

'Oohh, Shit, yes! Beeeee!"

Loving the feeling of both pain and pleasure, Cynthia felt herself bursting repeatedly. She could feel the juices flowing, she could feel the sting of the paddle and the splat of the leather clit-spanker. It was times like this that made her grip the sheets and cry in the pillows and it was times like these when Bee could get anything he wanted.

"Put it on high, Beeeee! Put it on hiiiggghhhhh!" she cried.

Riches and Tiffany had been approached by guys both riding and walking and it was beginning to be something that irked Riches and encouraged Tiffany. It wasn't until a car with a dyke pulled up on them that Tiffany showed anything other than disgust.

"Sorry, hon, but I like the sticky, sticky, not the licky, licky," Tiffany told the dyke.

"I'm more than sure I can make that happen too," the woman told her.

Tiffany looked over at Riches and rolled her eyes. "She must be talking to you, 'cause I don't do that. I might fuck with some spandex and some elastics, but no plas-dicks!"

"Well, when you want to give that ass a good massage, give me a call, baby." The woman threw a napkin out of the window towards both of them and drove off.

"She looks like she got a little money, Tiff. The bitch pulled up on you in a 550 Benz, rimmed up and bang in the trunk. You never know, Tiff, she might be the one for you," Riches laughed.

Tiffany only watced the pearl-colored Benz pull away. When she was sure no one was looking, Tiffany walked over and picked up the napkin. "Bitch wrote all her numbers on here, she laughed also. "Pussy-eating ass!

Seeing Riches eye her suspiciously, Tiffany shrugged, "What?"

Riches shook her head and continued smiling.

Tiffany thought it over a second and went off. "Hell naawww!" She threw the napkin across the park. "I'm tripping for real now, huh?"

"Hey, don't do it because of me, bitch."

"A bitch damn near tripped out." Tiffany held the blunt she was smoking at arm's length to examine it. "Did you roll this shit, Riches?"

They both laughed.

"Hey, ladies. What's up?"

Riches turned to find a smiling Yousef standing behind her. She leaped off the car and jumped into his arms. "Hey, baby, I thought you weren't coming."

"Well, I had to sit back and be sure one of your other friendsdidn't show up." He hugged her.

Riches kissed his lips.

"A room ain't nothing but ten dollars," Tiffany reminded them.

Riches glanced back at her friend. “Jealousy don’t match that outfit you wearing, Tiff.”

“Bitch, please,” Tiffany said. “I’m going for a walk right quick, I’ll be back.”

Yousef watched Tiffany. “What the hell she got on?” He frowned.”Hell, she may as well have that off too.”

He looked down at the attire Riches wore. “Why you not dressed like that?”

“Because my man told me I didn’t need to.”

“Your man?”

“Friends don’t do the shit you did to me at the back of your store. You are definitely beyond the friend zone now.” Riches smiled at him.

“Oh, really?”

“Yeah.”

“You know I’ve got more than that to give you, right?”

Hearing those words, Riches dug into her pocket and fished out a ten-dollar bill. “Who are we waiting on?”

Yousef laughed so hard, he bent at the waist. “In good time, girl.”

She pushed him back on the hood of the Challenger and stood between his legs.

“Where you park at?” she asked, not seeing his Maxima around.

“Right over there.” He pointed. “I rode my bike tonight.”

“Bike?”

Yousef laughed at her. He could see she was actually looking for a bicycle, so he grabbed her face and directed her to its location.

“Ohhh, motorcycle,” she said, seeing the white, green, and chrome Kawasaki Ninja. “I’ve got to ride that.”

“That might be a little too big for you.”

Riches faced him. “I was talking about the bike.”

“I was too and when thinking about earlier, I don’t think you’d have a problem riding anything.”

"Guess we'll just have to see about that, because you are holding something, for real." Riches looked down at Yousef's crotch, grabbed his belt and pushed herself to him.

He turned her, made her lean her back against his chest, and wrapped his arms around her bosom.

"Yousef?"

"What's up. Riches?"

"I need to tell you something Promise you're not going to get mad at me for any reason."

"I promise."

"Tell me, what are deal breakers for you in a relationship?"

"I thought you was about to tell me something."

"I'm just trying to see what you consider to be deal breakers. That way, I'll know if I can tell you."

"Well, I can say that one of the deal breakers would be if you tried to kill me."

"What else?"

"If you cheated on me."

"What else?"

"If you stole from me."

"And?"

"And I would say the most important one would be if you lied to me about something you shouldn't have. Like, lying that child is mine when it's not, or it's not mine when it is. Stuff like that."

"So, I take it you've been lied to in the past?"

"You wouldn't believe me if I told you."

"Try me."

Yousef exhaled. He hadn't been truthful with her and that was something he was about to change. "I not too long got out of prison for a statutory rape charge, something I didn't do. But being that me and the girl was having a child, there was no other way I could tell them otherwise."

Riches pulled away from him. "A rape charge?"

"Can I finish?" Yousef looked at her with nothing but sincerity. "I was twenty-three years old and I was involved with a woman,well, a girl that was sixteen but told me she was older. Things got serious and she got pregnant and when her mom found out, she was hot. Despite the relationship we had and the baby she was having, I still got sent away and did time. I had some money put up from the game and used damn near all of it to get back in the courts, and my lawyers got my time reduced."

"So, that's what you meant when you talked about not making the same mistakes twice?"

"That and the fact that I was out in them streets in the worst way."

"So, you was a hoe?"

"Naw, naw, nothing like that, girl. I was in the game. I was plugged in with some heavyweights and money wasn't shit, women weren't shit, hell, my life wasn't shit to be proud of."

"That's why you quit the game and got the store?"

"Partly. Well, I had to borrow some money from my brother so I could make something happen when I got out. He's out there in them streets now and he's just as fucked- up as I was, if not worse."

"Riches! Riches!" Tiffany yelled, while walking towards the pair. "Guess who just pulled up."

Both Yousef and Riches looked in the direction Tiffany was looking, the same direction everyone was looking.

O'Shay could see the eyes were on him and his guys as soon as they pulled up at the park. Now that it was dark outside, the Royce's interior lights being on and the headlights being off had the luxury car looking as if it was floating. The custom paint and rims sparkled when passing the lights of those cars parked on the side of the street, and the panoramic roof caused the interior light to create a halo- like display above it. "The dark angel," someone yelled as they passed.

O'Shay addressed Mike and T. "You see these motherfuckers, nigga? This is how you pull something out on a bitch! No music, no announcements, no nothing, only silence, nigga. Silence." Mike and T sat back and reveled in the moment. The atmosphere, the drinks and the fact that they were the center of attention lifted them higher than the seats they sat on. As they passed, people waved as if they were celebrities. Seeing the familiar Cadillac Escalade parked on the side of the street, O'Shay slowed then stopped. "What's up, Nicole?"

"What you want to be up, O'Shay?"

O'Shay smiled."That ass." Before she was able to respond, he drove off. He made a mental note to catch up with Nicole later.

They continued up the strip and once they came within view of the burnt orange Challenger, Mike pointed." That's that bitch I've been waiting to catch up with right there." O'Shay pulled alongside the Challenger and nodded at the trio, Riches, Tiffany and Yousef. He'd been waiting to catch up with them himself.

"You know that girl that drives the Challenger?" he asked Mike.

"Naw, me and Chubby pulled up on her at the light one day, and the bitch pulled off on me like I had leprosy or something."

O'Shay laughed. "You is broke, nigga. If you ain't sitting on a quarter mil and you fucking around out here, then you broke."

"Bitch seem to have a little money herself," Mike added.

"Yeah, something about rich people in her family," he told them, really thinking of other things.

"What the fuck she up here standing in front of Yousef for?" T asked, seeing the store owner.

O'Shay licked his lips. "That nigga ain't gonna change." He watched them through his rear-view. It was then he promised to get at the driver of the Challenger. "Riches, that's her name. Riches."

CHAPTER TWENTY-THREE

Kay had separated herself from both the work and everyone in it. The knocks on her door went unanswered and after cracking her pipe because of the continual use, she decided to venture outside. Kay knew how to get high, knew the high personally. She knew how long a good high would last and if nothing else, she knew she was higher than she'd ever been.

With over eight ounces stuffed in the vent and the remaining twenty-four grams in her pocket, Kay walked towards the room door and stopped. She listened intently to the noise beyond it. Hearing what sounded like people standing outside, she took a quick peek out of the window and seeing no one, she called out, "Punk-ass motherfuckers, I got a gun!"

Silence.

"You hear me! When I open this door, I'm going to bust somebody in the ass!"

More silence.

She unlocked the door, turned the knob and yanked the door opened.

No one, only the morning light greeted her and her paranoia.

"Bitch ass better run!" She told no one in particular. Kay was crossing the parking lot when she was approached by a familiar face.

"Kay! Motherfuckers been coming through here all night. Where the fuck you been, bitch?"

"On the moon." Kay walked past her, slid on the imitation sunglasses she stole days before and said, "Why y'all ain't out here working?"

"For what? Your ass been gone all night and we dried out."

Kay hated hearing those two words and as high as she was now, she still couldn't allow that to happen. "You tell the rest of these motherfuckers we are going rock for rock." She did a quick count in her head and told her, "Two grams for seventy-five."

"Two grams for seventy-give dollars?"

"Are your ears under your ass or what, bitch? We gonna blow this bitch up!" Kay pulled three nice-sized rocks from her pocket and handed them to the woman. "Here, go break bread, bitch!"

The woman briskly walked off in the direction of the strip and before rounding the corner, she called back to Kay.

"Hey, you heard about Willie, didn't you?"

"Willie? What about him," Kay asked, concern now replacing the courage and paranoia, pushing aside the perfect high.

"They found him at Cobb Park this morning."

"What the fuck he doing way out there?" Kay frowned.

"Whatever he was doing got his ass stepped on. Them niggas out here that found him got a bunch of work off of him and they partied like a bunch of bitches. They found him dead, you know." The woman walked off.

"Dead?" Kay questioned herself. "I told that stupid-ass nigga!" Of all the people she knew, the only person she felt she needed to tell was Byrd. Being that he was no longer in the game they played, she knew he'd be the last to know and that news was about to crush him. "Byrd ain't going to believe this shit."

Riches had awakened and was able to catch him just before heading out.

"Byrd!" she called from the hallway

"Yeah?"

"My brakes were squeaking last night and I need to get them looked at ASAP."

"Where your keys at? You just drive the truck today. I—"

"You know I can't drive that big ole truck, Byrd, I can barely see over the dash in that thing." Riches pouted.

"Well, what you want me to do, Riches?"

Riches looked down, noticed the fresh bandage on his left arm and pointed. "What happened to you?"

"Oh, um, burned it on a pipe yesterday."

"I'm going to need some wheels, Byrd. It's spring break and you know I can't just sit around this house."

"Tell that boyfriend you be sneaking around with to come pick you up. I want to meet him anyway."

"What boyfriend?"

"Pretense from you can't score a goal with me, girl," he said with his brows raised.

"Byrd, you are tripping." Riches shifted her stance.

Byrd smiled and shook his head.

Anyway, I'm going to need some wheels."

"Call your aunt and ask her if you can drive her car that's at the shop, because you're getting your brakes looked at. Tell her it's going to take a couple of days, if not longer." Byrd started back for the door.

"I'll call you later and let you know something." The thought of pulling up on both Tiffany and Yousef in a Mercedes Benz brought a smile to her face and despite it not being hers, she'd been told plenty of times that she was welcome to it anytime.

Byrd closed the door behind him, climbed into his Dodge and headed for the shop. The gun he loved so much, the Desert Eagle, was sitting readily under the armrest next to him. He knew he had a date with the devil and actually looked forward to it. Nothing good would become of that meeting and in Byrd's mind, the sooner the music began, the quicker the dance would be over.

The combined aromas of coffee, eggs, toasted bread and bacon greeted Cynthia, just as the dull pain between her ribs did. The welts around her wrist weren't visible, but she sensed the pain, the swelling of both her thighs and legs caused her to grimace. She rolled onto her back. "Uuummmm, my ass," she mumbled, before squirming between the satin sheets.

"Rise and shine, baby." Bee entered her room wearing only a pair of silk boxers, his heavily muscled thighs, toned abs and sculpted chest, creating yet another spark in the flames deep in her loins. "Breakfast is served," he told her, before sitting the breakfast tray on the nightstand beside her.

Cynthia pushed herself up slowly, resting on her elbows. "Can I have the dessert first?" She reached for the rim of his boxers.

"I didn't make all this so it could get cold, so eat up and if you still feeling that way, we'll make something happen."

"Um, sounds good to me." She took a sip of the freshly squeezed juice. "You need to bring company over more often, Bee."

He sat on the edge of the bed besides her. "Drink up. You were coming up so hard and so long, I had to place a bath towel under you."

"I am so, so sore, Bee. That shit felt so good to me." She closed her eyes in emphasis of her statement. "Where the fuck did you get that vibrating thing from? Shit, you tried to kill me!"

Cynthia's phone rang. She told Bee, "If it's Cherry, don't answer it."

"It's Riches."

"Give it here." She reached for the iPhone. "Hey, Riches, what's up?"

"I need a small favor."

"What's up?" Cynthia forked some eggs, bit a piece of toast and sipped her juice hungrily.

"Byrd wants me to leave my car at the shop until he gets a chance to check my brakes, and he wanted me to ask if I could use your Benz for a couple of days, until I'm straightened out."

"Girl, you didn't have to call me for that. Hell, I barely even drive that car." Cynthia continued to chew, in an attempt to hurry her meal so she could have time for Bee.

"Okay, thanks."

"Hey, you be careful out there, Riches. Bye." Cynthia ended her call, grabbed the napkin from the tray and wiped her mouth. "You ready?"

Bee laughed, caressed her thigh and leaned in to kiss her full lips. "You know, I have a couple of things to do this morning, Cynthia."

"Well, you need to hurry up or something." Her shift in positions caused her to grimace again.

"I might have time for a quickie though." He pulled the sheets from around her and climbed into the bed.

Cynthia smiled mischievously. "Where that vibrator at?"

As soon as she ended her call with her aunt, Riches dialed Tiffany's number. Knowing her friend, she'd been up and was more than likely about to step out.

"Hey, Riches, what are you doing up this early?" Tiffany answered.

"Had to catch Byrd before he put it in the wind. My brakes need to get looked at, I guess."

"So, what happened last night?" Tiffany inquired.

"Nothing."

"Bitch, please. The way you and Yousef was feeling each other, something happened when I left."

"He went his way and I went mine. Besides, you know I'm not about to let that nigga know where I live. Byrd would kill his ass if he even pulled up over here."

"Yeah, you right about that."

"Where did you go last night?"

"Girl, that nigga was trying to stick his dick in my ass and everything, but I told his ass no."

"Whhaaaat, you told somebody no?" Riches found humor in those words.

"Hell yeah. Nigga pulled out like a hundred and twenty or some shit."

"So, what happened?"

"I let the nigga suck on the pussy before he dropped me off, so he was good."

"You sick, Tiff."

"Yeah, sick of these cheap-ass niggas thinking a bitch selling herself short for some dick."

"Well, bye, Tiffany. Later."

Riches was standing under the jetting shower head, lost in thoughts of the conversation she had with Yousef the night before. When hearing him talk about family values and the fact that family was supposed to come first despite all, she was feeling him all the more. After washing and conditioning her hair with the Pantene Moisture Booster, her phone began vibrating on the bathroom counter. She stepped out and hit the speaker. "Yeah."

"Hey, beautiful, what are you doing?"

"Feeling myself."

"Feeling yourself?"

"Yeah, in the worst way, and you?"

"Getting ready to start my day. I was just calling to give you a wake-up and to tell you that I love you and can't wait to see you."

"Awww, that's so sweet. At first, I thought you were calling this early to make sure I wasn't with company."

"I'm too cool to be sweating, Riches."

"What time do you want to do lunch?" Riches stepped out of the shower and wrapped her hair with a towel.

"Whenever you get here, we'll do lunch."

"I've got a taste for some of them chili cheese nachos you'll be making."

"Done deal then."

Mike and T had been anticipating the call they received and now that the meeting was set, uncertainty created doubt.

"I hope these motherfuckers ain't bullshittin', nigga."

"I just hope they don't try to arrest a motherfucker. These crooked ass cops will do anything," T said, while looking around the lot of the textile plant.

"I'm going to see if these hoes can do something for Chubby's fat ass while we are doing business, might as well get all we can from their ass."

After tucking his .40 cal in the waistband of his jeans, T climbed out of the Sierra. Mike followed suit.

Once inside the textile building, they were led to the exact same office as the last time,the only difference now was that security was everywhere. At the bottom of the stairs, both of them were frisked and despite having guns on their persons, they were still escorted up.

"How are you two doing today?" the white cop asked the two of them upon entering.

"We good," Mike said.

"How about you?" T asked, seeing the big guy stand.

"Got a couple of cracked ribs, but for the most part, I'm good. So, let's get down to it, shall we?"

Both of them took seats across the desk and after the security guys stepped out, the officer leaned forward on his desk. "You guys made the right decision."

"Where is our work?" T asked, getting straight to the point.

"It will be given to you before you leave here today, but there's something I need for you guys to do for me."

Mike and T looked at each other. This was what they were anticipating.

"And what will that be?"

"I'm going to need for you guys to sit on the product I give you until I give word. I had to pull some strings in the evidence department and I don't need these drugs surfacing anytime soon."

"Yeah, that's cool. How long?"

"Um, about ninety days or so."

Mike looked as if he was mulling over the idea and said, "I'm going to need for you to do something for me also."

"You name it."

"I have a friend named Derrick Allen that's locked up and I need to get some of that shit off of him."

"Allen, Allen, the name doesn't ring any bells."

"He's in a juvenile facility for a couple of murders." Mike was about to continue when he was told something that halted his spiel.

"Forty thousand. If I grease the right palms with the right amount, I'm more than sure I can make a few things disappear." The white guy smiled at the two of them.

Mike could tell by the way T hesitated, he had no intentions of splitting the bill and this bothered him. "Imagine that! Forty thousand!" T said on their way back to the vehicle.

Once they were inside the cabin of the Sierra and the twenty kilos of cocaine rested on the seats behind them, Mike picked up where they left off.

"What is there to imagine, T? Chubby need some help."

"We need to flip something first, Mike. If we pay that money right now and them hoes didn't do shit, then we get fucked," T tried reasoning.

"Nigga, this shit was free. It ain't costing us nothing."

Instead of arguing with Mike, T pulled out of the lot and headed for the spot. O'Shay had told them he was going to come through early to discuss a few things and put together their next lick. T relaxed and allowed his thoughts to take him elsewhere.

Byrd parked in his usual spot and climbed out. Not only was there work that needed to be done, he had plenty of it to do. He'd gotten out early this morning, in hopes of finding out more about the ghost of a man he'd come to know as O'Shay, and after hearing that he only came around every so often, Byrd was sure he had to do a little stalking. With that being the top of his agenda, he walked into the shop and headed straight for his office to make a few calls that would definitely place him within inches of the devil they called O'Shay.

Riches pulled up minutes after Byrd and parked the Challenger on the side of the building facing the intersection. As soon as she stepped out of the car, the technician handed her the keys to the gray C-320 parked in front of the service center. "Here you go, Riches."

"Thanks." Riches handed him her keys and went inside to find Byrd.

"Aunt Cynthia already call you?"

"Yeah, she sent a text right after she got off the phone with you." Byrd walked around his desk, pulled some papers from the file cabinet and faced her.

"Where you headed anyway?"

"You already know I'm going to pick up Tiffany and—"

"I thought that girl just got a new job?" Byrd asked, knowing better.

Riches smiled, shook her head and said, "I did say that, didn't I?"

"Sounded like it." Byrd pointed to the chair. "Sit down right quick."

Riches rolled her eyes and fell into the chair. "Here we go."

"Who is this guy you're involved with, Riches? It's about time you said it, once and for all. He got you running around here lying to me and God knows what else." Riches saw the grave look on Byrd's face.

She sighed. "His name is Yousef."

"Yousef?"

"Yeah, he lives on the east side, I think, and he owns a corner store out there."

"You both fucking?"

"What?"

"You heard me."

"No, we're not having sex, Byrd."

"I didn't say shit about having sex, I said fucking."

"No Byrd, we haven't done anything."

Byrd scoffed, "So, why is it so hard to detach from this nigga?"

"I don't know." She pouted.

"Is he licking on you?"

"Byrd!"

"I'm human just like you and the shit you are doing, I've done it. I know how it feels to be wanted, Riches. I know what it feels like to get horny, Riches. I know—"

"Okay, I hear you."

"You don't have to rush into anything, Riches, and if the nigga is pressuring you, then stay away from him. These perverted-ass niggas out here doing every and anything to get some pussy."

"Byrd!"

"I just want my words to find you, Riches. When you let motherfuckers sugarcoat shit, that's when the same motherfuckers start trying to feed it to you."

"I know, Byrd. I'm going to be careful."

Satisfied that he'd gotten across to her, he smiled. "I know how easy it is to get caught up with someone you shouldn't and I know the prices we both pay in the process."

Byrd stood.

Riches followed suit.

"Let me get one of the guys to look at them brakes."

She followed him to the service area before leaving. "I'll be home around midnight, Byrd."

"Take care of your business, Riches. I'm serious."

Riches climbed into her aunt's Mercedes and adjusted the seat. "Damn, it smells good in this bitch!"

After setting the A/C, Riches hit the horn and pulled out. There were a couple of stops she needed to make and a woman she needed to drop in on, and being that it was on the way to Tiffany's, Riches headed for the Oasis Motel.

CHAPTER TWENTY-FOUR

As soon as they made it back to the Windsongs, Mike took his ten kilos and climbed into the Yukon. No words had been shared between them for most of the ride and therefore, it was already understood—no help would come from T.

"Fuck them niggas," he told himself before firing up the truck. The ninety days the cops asked for was about to be shortened. With a little over nine grands to his name, Mike pulled out and headed for the south side.

After making a couple of calls and a few stops, Jay found himself on the southside of Fort Worth in the Pilgrim Valley Apartment complex, meeting with the only survivor from Big Ced's crew.

"How much we are talking?" Jay asked, hearing about the number of drivers it would require for him to have some work moved to Nevada.

"Each of them want at least five apiece," Cain told him.

"Five apiece?"

"You know how the game go, Jay."

"Shit, I'm going to have to pause on that shit for a while. I'm really out there already as far as work is concerned. I'm not hurting at all, but that doesn't mean I'm not trying to make something happen elsewhere."

Jay watched Cain sort out his thoughts. His making a piece of change off the deal was something he needed, because ever since O'Shay robbed and killed Big Ced, Cain had been trying to put the pieces back together for himself.

"How long you think it's going to take before we knock that nigga off?"

Before he got a chance to guess, Jay recognized the Yukon that just passed him. "Let me get right back at you. That just might be happening sooner than either of us expects."

Cain climbed out and Jay pulled off. There weren't too many people Jay felt he needed to catch up with, but the driver of the Yukon was definitely a person of interest.

Mike was conducting a call as he pulled into the eatery and with a little time to spend, he decided to do the drive-through. As he sat, he thumbed through the duffle and looked over the work he had there. The guy walking up beside the truck wasn't seen until he was opening the passenger's side door of the Yukon. "What the fuck?" Mike yelled. He pulled the Ruger from under his thigh, but before he could point it, Jay grabbed his arm.

"Whoa, whoa, whoa, youngster, I'm not tripping on you like that."

Mike paused, acknowledging the fact that he was on the bottom end of the ordealpushed the Ruger back under his thigh and looked around the area.

"What do you want, Jay?"

"I just want to holla at you for a second. I'm not tripping with you."

Mike watched Jay eye the duffle and the contents of it. There was no use in hiding it now and Mike was feeling the error in his ways.

"Who you done robbed now?" Jay smiled at the youngster.

"Didn't rob anybody. I'm trying to help my nigga out. Why?"

"Check this out. I already know your niggas ran up in my shit and I owe one of your niggas, so I'm just going to say, that's you. Me and you both know you could have been dead right now if that's what I wanted, but I have other concerns. I want O'Shay and if you're smart, you'll stay out of the way. I see you got a little something to work with and by the looks of it, O'Shay don't know shit about it."

Jay paused. "Money talks, right?"

"We say that!" Mike continued to watch the area around him.

"How much is it going to take for me to get close to this nigga?"

"I'm not in the game like that, Jay. You got issues with that nigga. I've got my own shit to worry about. I—"

"Fifty thousand?"

Mike fell silent,hearing those numbers. The first thought that came to mind was Chubby. That would be more than enough to cover the cost and since the cops were already making the same moves against his boss, it wasn't going to change much. Adding another player to the game wouldn't hurt. Besides, once O'Shay was out of the way and Chubby was back on the streets, they'd be able to make some major moves with the work he now had and in no time, they'd be rich. "You drop them numbers and I'll out a nigga in your lap," Mike told him.

To his surprise, Jay climbed out of the truck. "Hold on."

Mike smiled to himself as soon as he saw Jay retrieve a bag from his car and walked back to the Yukon.

"Here's fifty, whatcha say?"

"You know where Copper Creek is?" Mike asked, while looking through the stacks of hundred-dollar bills.

"Are you talking about Woodhaven?"

"Yep."

"Yeah, I know where you at."

"His bitch, Shannon, lives out there. You trap that bitch, you trap the devil."

With that said, Jay climbed out of the truck and walked in the other direction.

Seeing no need to rush, Mike locked both of the doors and waited his time in line. There was a time when doing something of that nature was against everything he believed, but where his boy, Chubby, was concerned there was nothing left to think about. Seeing as how both T and O'Shay felt Chubby was to be thrown to the curb after all he'd done for the set, he knew where they stood. Before he could place his order, his phone chimed and seeing the unfamiliar number, he smiled. "Fat-ass nigga," he answered.

"What's up, bitch?"

"You couldn't have called at a better time," Mike told Chubby.

"Why, what's up?"

"I've been going through hell for your fat ass, nigga. You owe me."

"What the hell are you talking about?"

Mike could hear the cheer in his friend's voice and after whispering in Chubby's ears, to avoid others listening in, telling him about what he was now sitting on, and that he was about to pay the cops to get some of the charges dropped, Chubby screamed. "Fuck you, bitch-ass nigga. Lying ass!"

"You think I'm making this shit up, nigga? We on, bitch. I'm rubbing fifty grands on my balls right now. You want me to send you a selfie?"

"You know I'm on this hoe-ass building phone, nigga," Chubby laughed.

"Just sit tight, nigga. I'm coming. Fuck these niggas. Fuck O'Shay, fuck T and fuck everybody that ain't standing by us."

"Bitch-ass nigga, if you lying, I'm going to screw you!" Chubby continued, "I've got to go, these hoes calling lunch."

"Alright, nigga, go eat a dick then." Mike pulled out of the drive-thru and headed back to the textile building. After dropping off the forty for Chubby and pocketing ten, he'd sit back for a while and watch the game from the other side of the street.

Kay was posted by the pay phones when the gray Benz pulled into the motel lot. Knowing it had to be a potential customer, she nudged the guy standing beside her and nodded, "Get to work, trifling-ass nigga." Since putting out both word and some good work, the spot had been rolling non-stop and the smokers had gone from crackheads to casual smokers, to hustlers. The only problem she had now was finding a potential plug to score from. The white girl hadn't come around and getting at the Murphy boys was becoming a distant thought for her. What Kay needed now was a ride.

"Kay! Kay! This bitch said she's looking for you," the runner told her after pulling up on the Benz.

"Yeah, I bet she is," Kay yelled back.

"Riches, she said her name is."

Kay pushed herself from the pay phone and bent to see the driver of the foreign car. "Get your punk ass away from that car!"

"You told me to see what she—"

"I told you to do a bunch of shit, nigga. Get your drunk ass on somewhere." Kay squatted down and smiled at Riches. "What you got going on, girl?"

"I was in the area and decided to drop in on you, see what you had going on."

"You already know a bitch hustling. Looks like you are doing a little something yourself." Kay looked over the Benz and said, "You are pulling up on a bitch in sports cars and Benzes and shit, got a motherfucker out here looking real dry, Riches. Well, now that you're here, I need a favor?"

"What's up?"

"I need for you to take me to Byrd. I've got to tell him that Willie got killed."

"What?"

"Yeah, the nigga done some fucked-up shit and got stepped on." Kay relayed the message the way it was given to her and after hearing about it happening last night, Riches began to worry about Byrd. He'd been carrying his gun more often and just this morning, he claimed to have gotten burned at work.

"Get in."

Kay looked around at the traffic and movement. Now was not the time to leave things, but she had no choice. Hoping that things would still be conducted on her behalf, she called over the guy she just cursed minutes ago. "James! I got to make a run a right quick and I need you to make sure things run just like they are now."

James' eyes widened, "You're going to leave me with some work, right?"

"Naw, I'm going to leave your bitch ass stankin' if you fuck off my shit."

"You know I got you, Kay. You can trust me."

Kay looked from James to Riches. He could have said anything besides that, and that was the reason she looked back at Riches and said, "Let me go lock my shit up. Dick-sucking-ass nigga can't wait 'til I bend a corner."

Not wanting James to think or feel as if he wasn't to be trusted, Kay reached into her pocket and pulled out over twelve grams. "Here, nigga. You fuck off my shit, my boots going to be so far up your ass, you'll be belching rubber for a month."

"Man, ain't nobody going to fuck over you," James said, snatching the drugs.

After stashing some work and locking up the room, Kay climbed into the car, reclined her seat and told Riches, "Stupid motherfucker gonna smoke that up and swear he got robbed or some shit. Watch."

O'Shay looked around the room and seeing T alone, he asked him,"Where that nigga, Mike, at?"

"The hell if I know! He was talking about putting some bread together forChubby's fat ass."

"What about him?"

"Nigga going to need a lawyer."

"What happen to that nigga money? That nigga gonna break y'all while he sits on his shit."

"Yeah, I guess," T agreed.

"You've got to learn how to keep stepping, T. Nigga's going to try to play both ends when they feel they are winning, so you've got to make sure you win, regardless of if they are playing a game or not. We ain't in this shit to pay for another motherfucker's mistakes. Nigga get caught slipping, so let his ass fall. You hear me, nigga?"

"Yeah, I hear you."

"We are throwing a party in the jet this weekend, so make sure you get the homies together and move something. Be ready by Friday," O'Shay told him before heading out of the door. "And make sure y'all invite a bunch of hoes this time."

T closed the door behind his boss and pulled out his phone. He walked across the living room and looked down at the two hundred and fifty-two grams of dope O'Shay left. T laughed. This bullshit ain't going to work no more, O'Shay. T knew exactly what he was going to with the quarter kilo.

"You want me to come back and get you or what?" Riches asked Kay, before she turned in behind her Challenger.

"Naw, I'm going to have Byrd's blind ass drop me back off. We haven't talked in a while and we'll most likely be fighting shortly. You be careful out there."

Kay stood in the middle of the lot and just looked at the building. It had been years since she'd been with Byrd. The thrill of the high was all she, Willie, and Byrd once lived for, and when Byrd told her not to come around anymore until she got herself together, that was enough for her to walk away and never come back. Before she could reach for the door, Byrd came out through the number-two stall and walked slowly towards her. "You lost or something, Kay?"

"Do I look lost, fishbowl-head-ass nigga?"

Byrd smiled before shaking his head. "Actually, you look much better, Kay. He stood inches in front of her, neither of them wanting to be the first to break.

"So, you just going to stand there and smell a bitch?" Kay opened her arms.

They embraced.

"I see you doing all you said you were going to do." Kay didn't want to let go of the embrace. To step back and look at Byrd would definitely open the many wounds she thought healed. These were the best of friends at one time and that was something neither of them could deny.

"Didn't have a choice, Kay."

"Yeah, you had a choice. You just made the better one."

"Come on in, Kay. Don't want too many people seeing me out here wrapped up with a crackhead."

"How about they see you with a foot in your ass, nigga?" Kay laughed.

"You hungry?" Byrd led Kay through the shop and into his office.

"If I was hungry, I would have asked for food already."

"I was just being thoughtful."

Kay dropped into the chair in front of Byrd's desk and got serious for the moment. She looked Byrd straight on and told him, "Willie got stepped on last night."

"What you mean?"

"He was snuffed out, nigga."

"Who did it?"

"The hell if I know. All I know is that the nigga was getting out there, Byrd. The nigga was pulling up on me with work all the time and just recently, he hit up some youngsters on the east and gave Murphy some fake money some white girl printed up for him."

"Ain't no telling who fucked Willie off." He looked Kay over. "You in on it or what?"

"I smoke crack, nigga, but I'm not the stupidest bitch that ever done it. I been telling that nigga to slow down, but you know how Willie was. He always believed he had everything under control." Kay's gaze paused on the walls behind Byrd, lost in the thoughts she was having.

"You know that nigga got my car shot up, don't you?"

"Yeah, he came straight to my spot with his heat-drawing ass."

"Well, not only did the nigga run his ass here, he brought them niggas here with him. Particularly, a nigga called O'Shay. You know him?"

"Yeah, I head of the nigga before. A real mad, motherfucking son of a bitch." Kay crossed her legs.

"Nigga came through here threatening to burn my shit down and everything."

"Really?"

"Yeah he did. Him and two of his angels."

"He didn't know who the fuck he was fucking with." Kay smiled, remembering the man Byrd used to be.

With a few things to catch up on and more to sort out, Kay told him all the things she knew, as well as the things she thought.

With two voice messages and a text for Yousef, Riches waited until she was halfway to the east side before calling him back, and one of those reasons was that she wanted to talk in person, instead of over the phone.

She knew he was most likely looking at her photo and hearing her ring tone at the exact moment but acting as if he was busy or away from his phone,which she was sure wasn't the case at all. After the eighth ring, he finally answered."Hey, Riches."

"Yeah, right, nigga. You are acting like a real bitch now."

"Excuse me?"

"You been looking at that phone, acting like you busy and shit." Riches adjusted her Bluetooth before continuing. "Now you are acting like you crazy."

She could hear him laughing away from the mic. She knew she was right.

"Well, whatever, Riches. I might have just been making sure you were really wanting to talk, 'cause I've been calling you also."

"I was busy."

"Well, I'm busy, but I'm never too busy that I can't at least tell you that, or send you a text explaining that," he told her.

"I hear you, Yousef."

"So, where you at?"

"On my way to the store now."

"Well, I'm across town at the moment with a few vendors. I should be back that way in a couple of hours though."

Riches twisted her lips."Well, we'll just have to finish our talk when I catch up with you."

"Talk, what's up?"

"I'll talk when we are face-to-face, Yousef, unless you just want me to make some shit up."

"Naw, ain't even going to start dragging each other, so let me hurry up and get things finished here. I really should be back that way in a couple of hours."

"We need to talk, Yousef, I'm serious."

"Okay, okay."

Riches ended her call, pulled up to Tiffany's house and hit the horn.

Tiffany stepped out of the house. She gave the Benz the once-over. "Bitch, you out here blowing the horn like we about to be late for church or something." Tiffany smiled as soon as she sat in the passenger's seat. "Spoil-ass tramp."

"You like?" Riches smiled back, knowing Tiffany was talking about her driving the Benz.

"Almost jealous. Hell yeah, I like."

"I think Aunt Cynthia is going to give it to me," Riches told her, just as she pulled off.

"Why you say that?" Tiffany frowned. "You just got the Challenger, Riches."

"Well, she told me to get used to it, because I need to retire my car."

"What Byrd say about it?" Tiffany knew there had to be something else to factor in.

"Nothing." Riches shrugged. "He seemed cool with it."

"Well, we need to pull up on some niggas anyway." Tiffany adjusted her seat and checked herself in the compartments mirror. "You run that nigga off or what?"

"Naw, I haven't had a chance to tell him yet."

"Well, that's on you but if it was me, I wouldn't tell his ass shit."

"I should let him choose if he wants to be with me, instead of me making that choice for him."

"Well, you already know how I feel about it." Tiffany shrugged.

"So, where we headed?"

"Just ride, something gonna come up."

CHAPTER TWENTY-FIVE

Byrd thought about the life he once lived, and he regretted turning his back on someone that meant so much to him at one time. When hearing about the way things turned out for Kay, he couldn't help but think about the fact that if it wasn't for Riches, he'd have been in the same situation or worse. Having something to live for gave him both a different perspective, as well as scope of the way things should be. Not only did he understand Kay's reasons for walking away, but he understood the reasons she felt she couldn't come back.

"I thank God for her every day, Kay. Cecelia left me with something I'll cherish the rest of my life." Byrd nodded. "And I love her for that."

"In the short time I've been around her," said Kay, "she's been fucking with my mind. Got me feeling some type of way and shit." Kay smiled. "CeCe would have been proud of her."

"Yeah, I know."

"She's been making me look at things differently also, Byrd, talking about opening up a bakery with me." Kay began tapping the corner of the chair, losing herself in the memory. "Kaynese's."

"Mmmmmm."

She looked up at Byrd. "Yeah, nigga, that's what we're going to call it."

"Sounds as if she's got you believing in something you don't even—"

"What are you driving at, nigga?"

"Don't get mad at me, I'm just telling you the truth." Byrd held both his hands up, surrendering.

"You ain't telling shit, nigga. I can see me getting it together and doing a hell of a lot better than what I'm doing now."

"It sounds better than it looks though. You know how many times me and Willie been through this same shit, talked about the same things over and over and over? Soon as you motherfuckers find something to smoke, you're off to do some shit that set you back even farther than you were. You've got to get tired of that shit, Kay. Not only that, but you've got to hate it." Byrd leaned forward, rested his elbows on his desk and continued. "But, that's not going to happen because your punk ass doesn't want it. I've always been there for the both of you always, but you continually shit on me because of the bullshit you do. But guess what, Kay? I never went nowhere, I was always here."

"You're right, Byrd. A bitch be trying to make something happen and the only way I know to do so, is by conduct of the game, by taking it from the streets. This the same shit you taught us, man." Kay pulled at the seams of her shirt in attempt to distract her emotions.

"I've been trying to show you differently for years now, but it's something you got to want to do, Kay. Something you have to do for you, not me, not the people you lock yourself in them rooms with, but for you."

"You sound like one of them con artists that be selling them DVD's at the rec center or something." Kay laughed.

"I'm serious, bitch!"

"Yeah, I see that, ya lips and shit shaking like you about to blast off. Hell, you might still be smoking, what with the way you acting."

"I get like that when it's something I'm passionate about, something worth putting my voice behind."

Byrd knew he was striking a chord with Kay, because she always had the habit of trying to at least bring humor to the situation, instead of dealing with the seriousness of it. They were all just alike in so many ways and that was something they were able to identify in each other.

Yousef was ecstatic. He had just signed several vendors as well as spoke with contractors about adding space for both an arcade and billiards, for the building two blocks over from his store. Now that he'd gotten his business out of the way, all he could think about was Riches. She had continually spoken of wanting to talk about something and with thoughts of his own. The idea of an engagement swam freely.

Yousef was heading back to the east side when he passed the mechanic's shop, and was more than certain he saw Riches' Challenger parked out front. It was just minutes ago when she told him she was on the east side. Hoping that things were alright with her ride, he made the U-turn and pulled into the lot.

Yousef circled the Challenger and was heading for the door when the tech approached him.

"How's it going today, sir? You need the Maxima looked at or what?"

Yousef looked back at the Maxima. "No, I'm actually here to see what's up with my girl's ride."

"Which ride would that be?" the tech asked him.

"The Challenger," Yousef said proudly.

"What Challenger?"

Yousef half-turned and pointed to Riches' car. "That one."

"Um, Riches' Challenger?"

"Yeah, you know her?"

The tech laughed. "Yeah."

"Well, what's the problem with it? If nothing else, I'd like to pay the balance." Yousef began digging into his pockets. "Is she still here?"

"Well, I think you're going to have to speak with the owner. I'll be right back."

Byrd and Kay had been together for over an hour and it was like old times for them both. He even agreed to loan her a ride until she got on her feet.

"Here's fifteen hundred for a hire on the ride. I—"

"I don't need your money, Kay."

"And I don't need your handout, Byrd."

"It's just a Mazda that I put a lien on."

Kay sat the money on the desk in front of him. "And this is just fifteen hundred I made last week."

Instead of arguing with Kay, he put the cash into his desk and reached for the key to the small car.

"Byrd! Byrd!" the tech yelled from the service area.

"What the fuck this nigga out there yelling for?" Byrd opened his bottom drawer and pulled out the Desert Eagle he was so fond of. "Motherfucker sound like we are getting robbed or something."

Seeing the familiar piece, Kay smiled. "I see you still got that eight shots with B.N. engraved on the cask."

"Yeah. I always have it, just in case."

"Mm."

"Byrd, some nigga out there has questions about the Challenger."

"Tell him it's not for sale." Byrd began to sit back down, seeing as there was no emergency.

"Naw, he is talking about Riches being his girl and he wants to pay her bill or something."

"What bill? Who is the boy?"

"He ain't no boy, Byrd."

Byrd immediately thought about the guy Riches had discussed with him. Both he and Kay went to meet him. Byrd looked Yousef over and frowned. The guy was several inches taller than Byrd and looked to have been an athlete in his day.

"How can I help you, sir?" Byrd asked.

Yousef smiled, "My girl brought her car here and I just wanted to surprise her by paying the balance."

"Yousef, right?"

"Excuse me?" Yousef frowned.

"Your name is Yousef, right?"

"Yes, but how did you get to know my name?"

Hearing the name for the umpteenth time, Kay looked towards the ground and shook her head.

"Riches has no bills here," said Byrd, cutting Yousef off. "As a matter of fact, this is her building."

"Really?"

"Yeah, really."

"Well, I was just stopping by to see if there was anything I could do for her."

"Come to think of it, there is something you can do for her and yourself for that matter."

"And what would that be?"

"Stay away from her." Byrd walked closer.

"Excuse me?"

"Stay the hell away from her."

"I can't. I love Riches."

"She's not for you, man, so leave her alone before you find yourself weighed down. You're probably just like one of them niggas, who just eat a girl like a banana and throw away the peels."

"I'm not that kind of guy. Besides, Riches is woman enough to decide who she wants to be with. It's not your place to say."

Byrd laughedand the laugh spoke volumes that only Kay understood.

"Mister," said Kay, addressing Yousef, "if I were you, I'd leave right now. A living mouse is better than a dead cat, if you ask me."

Seeing things going in a direction he was sure to be downhill, Yousef backed away, climbed in the Nissan Maxima and left. He didn't know what all the drama was about, but Riches had some explaining to do.

Jay had to wait at the entrance of the Copper Creek Apartment complex for a resident to either enter or exit and once the gates opened, he pulled in and slowly drove around the complex, looking around for either of the cars O'Shay drove. Knowing what kind of guy O'Shay was, Jay bypassed the front sections of the complex and went straight to the back. Even before turning the corner towards the rear of the apartments, Jay recognized the front of the ghost white Lincoln that had delivered his drugs to the Great Western the day Big Ced got robbed. He looked around for the Lexus Coupe. Being an old-timer in the game, Jay knew

O'Shay would keep the Royce at the shop, at least to showcase it to the customers that wanted some things done to their rides. Hoping that his target would be returning soon, Jay found a parking spot adjacent the building he was watching and settled in for however long it would take. The thought of running up in his spot creased the corners of his mouth, but this was bigger than the money he felt he had or even the money he could have summoned. This was about the devil's demise.

Mike walked into the apartment and the aroma of burned crack rushed his senses. His mom smoked, her friends smoked and all the crackheads that scored from him smoked, so the smell in the air wasn't new to him.

"What the fuck you in here doing, nigga?" he addressed T, who was standing by the patio window overlooking the parking lot.

"Minding my motherfuckin' business, nigga." T pulled on the blunt he was smoking and dumped the ashes in the ashtray on the speaker besides him.

"Primo-smoking-ass faggot." Mike walked past him and into the back room. As soon as he got his bread right, he was leaving but until then, he would be about the game that needed to be played.

"That nigga, O'Shay, said we are throwing a party this weekend, so we got to get out money right."

"Fuck you, fuck that nigga and fuck that party!" Mike yelled from the back.

T yelled, feeling the effect of the crack, as well as the need to say the words he spoke. "Naw, nigga, fuck you and the shit you got going. You can't get mad because a nigga trying to make something happen with what he got."

"We always promised to help make something happen for the people who couldn't do it for themselves. You forgot that though. A nigga need your help and you turn your back on him.

We started this shit together and now you letting that nigga rub off on you and letting this money come between us."

T looked over his shoulder and shrugged. "Whatever, nigga. I might just be tired of breaking myself for your niggas and not having shit. I'm tired of paying for the mistakes of those around me. From now on, I hustle for me." T blew a thick stream of smoke into the air.

Mike watched his friend. Seeing him smoke a primo wasn't the factor that now had him gripping the handle of his Ruger, it was the words that came because of it. "I guess you got to do what you got to do, bitch-ass."

"Just make sure you invite some hoes this time, nigga," T said.

O'Shay treated Shannon to a shopping spree and a new phone. Knowing he was about to be rewarded for the outing, he even let her drive the convertible. Entering the complex to the Copper Creek Apartments, O'Shay ended his call.

"I'm going to have to make a trip this weekend," he told her.

"When you are coming back?"

"Ain't no telling. However long it takes me to get money. You know how the game go."

"Well, I'm pretty sure you're going to make it happen, so I'm not trippin' on you." Shannon leaned over to kiss him before climbing out. Before walking to the stairs, O'Shay subtly monitored his surroundings.Once he was satisfied things were as they should be, he walked in behind Shannon and closed the door.

"You know you've got to take care of me, right?" Shannon stepped out of her shoes and walked her bags into the room. "Take that shit off, nigga. You know what it is."

O'Shay smiled. He loved the way Shannon took charge and made sure she got what she wanted. That was the difference between her and the many women he accosted. Shannon took charge both inside and outside of the bedroom.

"This pussy been itching all morning," she told him while coming out of the Diablo sundress she wore.

Jay lowered himself in his seat as soon as he saw the convertible Lexus around the corner. The fifty grand he gave Mike had paid off faster than he expected. Now that he knew where the devil himself holed up more often than not, Jay made a mental note of the apartment he and Shannon entered. Afterwards, he slowly drove off. The time for O'Shay was coming. "Bitch ass would see it coming," Jay whispered to himself.

Tiffany both nodded and smiled at every syllable that escaped Mona's mouth and no matter how outlandish the suggestion, Tiffany praised the ideology her cousin lived by.

"I told her she needs to play the game like they play it," Tiffany added, after Mona advised Riches to let things take their course.

"Pussy meets dick, then pussy and dick become familiar with each other and if dick fucks pussy well, then why can't pussy and dick live happily ever after?" Mona snapped her fingers and went on. "Riches, the point I am trying to make is, let things take their course. Having said that, don't you find it kind of odd that the nigga never even tried to find out where you live, where you work or who your people are? That's because the nigga doesn't give a damn."

Mona filled both Riches and Tiffany in on the way things were for her, and the reasons she felt the way she did about men. The game was meant to be played and for those that played stupid, stupid shit happened to them.

"Well, if he didn't give a damn about not knowing, he shouldn't give a damn about knowing," Riches said to Mona.

"I see."

Riches looked at Tiffany and stuck her tongue out.
"Whatever, bitch," Tiffany mumbled.

CHAPTER TWENTY-SIX

As ecstatic as he'd been moments before he'd gone to the repair shop, Yousef found his picture of things drastically changing. There were things Riches failed to mention when it came to the things she should have. Her having another guy in her life was something he never thought about.

As soon as he was away from Byrd's threat, he dialed her number.

The phone was answered on the second ring. "Hey, baby, what's up?" said Riches.

"Where you at?" Yousef's tone was cold.

"What's wrong with you?"

Yousef laughed. "Really, Riches? I should be the one asking you that."

"Well, I really don't know what's up with this attitude, but find me when you lose it." She hung up.

Yousef hit his steering wheel and dialed her again.

Riches frowned. The call she just received was not from the man she'd come to know and as bad as she wanted to talk with him, she wasn't about to sweat issues he had that was beyond her control. Seeing her phone light up repeatedly, she relented. "Yeah?"

"Meet me at the store in about thirty minutes," he told her and hung up.

"I told you, bitch. Them niggas get what they want and they start trying to get shitty, I told you."

"Shut up, Tiffany. He wants me to meet him at the store in a few."

"So, now you going to run after him and shit? Tiffany rolled her eyes and twisted her lips. "You're a better bitch than me."

"Are you coming or what?" Riches was heading out of the door, hoping that Tiffany would follow."

"Now you got me sweating some nigga and he ain't did shit for me." Tiffany grabbed her purse and they were out of the door.

Byrd stood watching until Yousef was out of sight. Out of habit, he tapped the Desert Eagle against his right thigh, consumed by thoughts he did not like.

"Nigga, you just going to stand there looking like you stupid?" Kay asked, snapping him out of the daydream holding his head captive. They went back to his office.

"Can you believe that motherfucker, Kay?"

"If you haven't noticed, she's not a little girl anymore, Byrd. She's got wings and—"

"Kay, I get that, but damn." Byrd turned and started back for the shot.

"At some point, you're going to have to understand that niggas are bound to be pulling up on her left and right, Byrd. Niggas see her and they dick get hard and—"

"Kay, shut the fuck up! You ain't had a dick inside you since you crawled out of you daddy's ass!"

"Get mad then, nigga. If some nigga doesn't fuck her, then who will? You? If you go on acting like that, one would think you're amenable to incest or something. I'd hate to see what you do when you walk in the house and she's got her ass in the air or with a dick in her mou—"

"Get the fuck out, Kay! Get your bitch ass out of my office and get the hell away from my shop!" Byrd slammed his pistol on his desk and fell back into his desk recliner. And seeing Kay sit back and cross her legs, he knew the problem would linger.

"When you take that dick out of your ass and start acting like the man I know, we'll talk.But until then, I guess I'm going to sit here and watch you keep fucking yourself." Kay grabbed a magazine from Byrd's desk and began thumbing through it. "Byrd, you acting like you ain't never preyed on no bitch. He might be having genuine feelings for Riches after all, and it may well be a mutual thing."

Riches pulled into the store's lot, just as Yousef was parking and seeing him exit his vehicle, she blew her horn. "Let me see what this nigga tripping on right quick, Tiff."

"Remember, bitch, we cash checks."

Riches crossed the lot and followed Yousef through the doors of the store and he ushered her to the back office. Once they were in the office and the door closed, Riches faced him, crossed her arms and just looked at him.

"Where's your car?"

"In the shop, why?"

"I just so happened to be driving around when I spotted your car. I thought you were there, so I went to see if there was something I could do for you. But, guess what happened?" He waited for her response. Seeing that Riches wasn't willing to speak yet, he went on. "Ya sugar daddy charged me up, had his gun out and everything. He was with some dyke bitch."

Riches smiled. "Are you serious?"

"And this is funny to you? Really, I—"

"Nigga, that was Byrd, and he ain't my sugar daddy." Riches imagined the meeting she was hearing about. "He pulled a gun on you?"

"Hell, he might as well had. The nigga told me to stay away from you and his laugh was menacing."

Riches pulled out her phone and dialed Byrd's number. She wanted Yousef to know Byrd wasn't her sugardaddy or even her daddy for that matter.

"Riches?" came Byrd's voice.

"What's up, Byrd. What you doing?" Riches asked, allowing Yousef to hear the voice of the man he'd been suspicious of.

"Over here tripping with Kay's sick ass."

"Any excitement over that way or what?" Riches looked up at Yousef, who was calming himself.

"Matter of fact that man pulled up over here, talking about he loves you and some more shit."

"Well, I'm about to go and meet him myself. I was just calling to see what you were doing. Oh, yeah, ask Kay if she need me to come get her."

"Naw, I gave her something to ride around in."

"Well, I'm going to get at you later, Byrd."

"Call me if you need anything. Oh, how's your new car working out?"

"Bye, Byrd." Riches ended her call and asked Yousef, "That sound like a sugar daddy to you?"

"Well, I might have been wrong about that."

Riches sighed, sat her purse in the chair besides the one she sat in and told him,"I don't want to lose you."

Youssef walked around his desk, removed her purse from the chair and sat beside her. "You're not going to lose me, Riches. I'm not going anywhere." He reached for her chin, lifting it. "I do love you, Riches." He kissed her lips. "What I feel for you ain't a nine-days wonder kind of thing. It's real, true, deep and strong."

"Byrd thinks you're just gonna get it on with me and dump me. That's why he doesn't want me around you. Let me get at him, so there won't be any bloodshed."

"Yeah, you do that, 'cause I'd hate for the blood to be his." Yousef walked back around to his desk, opened the drawer and pulled out a huge, pearl-handled Bowie knife. "My signature pieces."

"Nigga, what's that going to do? You can't take a knife to a gunfight." She laughed.

"You just have to know when to use it, Riches."

"Well, let me get out of here so you can run your store. I've got things to do today." Riches began gathering her purse and phone.

"What you got up for later?"

"Tiffany said something about a party in The Jets, so we might stop by there for a few minutes."

"The Jets?" Yousef frowned. "You know what kind of parties they throw in The Jets, don't you?"

"I'm just going with Tiffany's crazy ass. If I don't like it, I know how to find my keys."

Later that night, the party came into full swing. O'Shay had paid guys to smoke meats on the huge trailer smokers they pulled behind their trucks. Two women even allowed their apartments to be used to cool all the drinks people would come for. Plates were made at either of the store trucks parked in the square and the weed they smoked was passed all around for people to both enjoy and test. Mike and T's workers passed around everything from Hydro's to Oxycotin and from Xanax to Roxy's. The E-pills were what the big players were using. The feel-good was in the air and everyone was feeling themselves in some type of way. O'Shay'sconvertible, along with his Sierra and Yukon sat lavishly in the middle of the square and people had to either drive or walk around the area.

"I see you boys did pretty good on the invites," O'Shay told T,seeing the sea of young girls walking around. The skimpy clothing they wore had the guys showing wads of money, as well as paying for small favors. The booty-hugging shorts, the low-cut tops, the short skirts and the catsuits the women wore had older guys filling their phones with numbers and promises. O'Shay swallowed hard when saw a woman twerking to some raunchy song. The way she rolled her ass and dropped it with a timing that synchronized with the beat of the song, had him imagining sexual acts he was sure she couldn't handle. "Who is that right there?" He asked T.

"Bitch named Melody. They call her Mel though."

"See if that bitch trying to make some money." O'Shay winked at the woman. She winked back at him before he continued his rounds. He was going to make sure everyone remembered this night as one of his legacies. For weeks to come, people would be talking about O'Shay and the party he threw in The Jets. And with money on his mind he had several guys walking through The Jets, recording any and everything in the hope of having the footage edited and sold.

Jay and Cain had been circling the projects for the past thirty minutes, and knew there was no way they'd be able to get at O'Shay, without a million people knowing and seeing what was going on. What Jay did like was the fact that he'd put together a pretty good picture,showing Cain that he was about his business when it came to making sure they got the devil when he least expected it. The surprise he had for O'Shay was even surprising to him.

"This nigga going to burn, Jay."

"Yeah, and everything around him will also."

Tiffany had been telling Riches about the party and the prospects that were sure to be there and after giving Riches the rules of The Jets, she stepped out of the Benz. "Everything should be free so if a nigga tries to sell you anything you cuss his ass out."

"Girl, please, I'm good." Riches watched the plethora of women around them. The ones that were with a man or a boy and the women trying to attract them all had one thing in common, everybody was high.

"Hey, you want to try one of these Xanax?" a guy asked as she passed him.

"Naw, I'm cool, thanks though."

Riches followed Tiffany through cars and people and as big as The Jets were, people were actually bumping into each other in passing. Of one thing She was sure of one thing, everyone was having good time.

"Riches! Riches!" someone yelled.

"Girl, that's that nigga, O'Shay," Tiffany told her, now excited that the man himself was approaching them.

"Hey, O'Shay, what's up?" Riches smiled.

"You're looking good." He looked Tiffany over. "And you too," he said to Tiff. "What y'all got up for the night?"

"Just mingling, waiting for some of that brisket to get done," Tiffany said.

"Well, eat all you can and let me worry about the rest." O'Shay looked around and found T and the woman that winked at him earlier walking their way. And knowing it was about to be more to their intro, he excused himself. "Well, I'll see you later and if you two need anything, just get it. It's all on me tonight." O'Shay walked past Riches and turned to see if her ass was still as plump as it was weeks ago. Seeing her ass bounce in the Constantine mini she wore, he squeezed his crotch. "Aw yeah! Got to have me some of that tonight," he told himself before greeting T and Mel.

T introduced Mel to O'Shay and left them to themselves. He pushed through the crowd until he got close to Riches and Tiffany."Hey, hold up right quick."

Riches stopped and spun around to see who the caller was, because she didn't allow guys to approach her in that fashion. To her surprise, he looked past her to a smiling Tiffany.

"Hey, what's your name?" he asked.

"I'm Tiffany. Don't I know you from somewhere?"

"Yeah, I ran into you couple of times or more, but didn't really get the chance to make something happen." T looked down at the camel toe between Tiffany's legs. He licked his lips.

"Well, it was nice meeting you, T. Hopefully, we'll get to get at each other later." Tiffany had no intentions of ending the conversation and was just exercising the game she'd been given. And seeing Riches twist her lips, Tiffany smiled.

"Hold up, hold up, what's wrong with you now?" T said to Riches.

"Well, me and my girl were just mingling, trying to see where everything at, until you came along to disrupt our—"

T cut her off with a wave of his hand. "I put this shit together. Let me show you two where everything at. Come on."

"Hold up," said Tiffany, stopping him. "O'Shay said he was the one put this together."

"We put this shit together. Hell, who you think run these jets?" he said, before leading the way.

Knowing she'd scored a few points with the game she played, Tiffany looked back and smiled at Riches, who was already frowning.

O'Shay walked through the apartment belonging to one of the women he paid to keep the beverages cold and led Mel straight to the bathroom. There was no use in wasting time, when they both knew what they wanted.

"You were popping that ass like you knew what you were doing," he told her once they were alone in the tiny room.

"And you were acting like you knew what to do with it," was her response.

Before she could say anything else, O'Shay spun her around, bent her over the sink and pulled her booty shorts down. Seeing her eagerly step out of her shorts and panties only fueled his intentions more and seeing her nude flesh, he bent down and licked up her thigh before sucking her. "Ass taste like some puddin'."

"You going to give me five hundred dollars?" she asked before spreading her legs, allowing him a view of her vulva and when feeling him spread her, she looked back at him.

"That's all you want? I'll give you five hundred dollars for some of this asshole. You cool with that?" O'Shay pulled a condom from his pocket and tore the package.

"See if they got some baby oil in here first."

Instead of leaving the moment to search for something that would not be found, O'Shay spat down the crack of her buttocks twice, licked around her anus and pushed deep inside of her. Her protests and grunts encouraged him and her pleas for him to stop pushed him over the edge. When he pulled out, he discarded the condom and spun her around. "Let me see what this pussy feels like."

Knowing she was about to be hundreds of dollars richer, Mel, just like many of the girls that sold themselves short, lifted her legs, held on to the devil and rode him for all he was worth.

CHAPTER TWENTY-SEVEN

Seeing Tiffany smile at every word that fell from T's mouth, Riches grew tired of the act her friend was performing and decided to do a little venturing of her own. She'd seen a couple girls she'd met previously and then, there was the Nicole chick she'd seen at the lake and there were a few questions she wanted to ask her about possibly publishing a book for Tiffany. The way Riches saw it, if she at least gave Tiffany another way out, she'd have other things to consider when thinking about selling herself short for whatever reasons. Riches had walked from her aunt's car twice and both times, she noticed the emerald green Cadillac CTS-V coupe parked at various spots around the complex. She prayed they weren't here to cause any trouble and made a mental note to herself to point it out to O'Shay the next time she saw him, but decided against it when considering the fact that the driver of the car was most likely eyeing a girlfriend or a wife. When thinking about it from that perspective, she felt the need to keep her business to herself.

"Hey, beautiful, where you from?" a guy with the recorder asked her.

Riches smiled. "Does it matter?"

"Yeah, I mean, niggas are going to want to hear about where you from, so they at least know where to look when they see you on this DVD."

"DVD?"

"Yeah, we are filming the whole night and we're going to put it out on DVD in a couple of weeks. We are putting The Jets on the map. 'O'Shay's Love' is the title of the shoot." Almost immediately, he went running after a girl that had half her butt hanging out of her tights.

"Nigga crazy." Riches pulled an already-rolled blunt from her purse and fired it up. With some fire of her own, Riches continued her walk.

O'Shay cleaned himself up and handed the woman seven hundred dollars. "I'm going to have to keep your number in my phone." After promising her more than that the next time, he found his way to the front of the apartment, picked up a wine cooler and walked out. He was just about to make his way back to the square when he saw Riches alone. This was the chance he'd been waiting for. "Hey, hey, hey," he called after the youngster that was passing out the E and Xanax pills. "Give me a couple of them." Then he called out, "Riches, Riches."

Riches half turned and smiled widely. She could use the company. "Hey what's up?"

"I saw you walking by yourself and thought you might want something to drink, but didn't know where to get any." Riches had been smoking and her throat was dry and against her better judgment and Byrd's words of wisdom, she took the cold beverage. She thanked him when he helped her open the drink.

"I see you, you're getting your smoke on and your drink on so you're straight, right?" O'Shay smiled while looking her over, her thighs creating a fire in him he was sure to quench.

"Yeah, yeah, I'm just going to walk around and vibe, I guess." Riches looked across the lot at the Cadillac as it was pulling away from the curb.

"I'll tell you what, I'm not busy so I'll just keep you company for a while, make sure you stay out of trouble."

"Sounds good to me."

Both Cain and Jay had been watching O'Shay so close, they saw when he slipped back into the apartment and came out screwing the top back on the cooler he had. And after seeing him take a couple of what appeared to be some kind of pills from the youngster, they couldn't help but think the obvious and Cain let it be known.

"Sick-ass nigga is going to end up date-raping that girl."

"Hate to say it, but that's her business. These hoes got to learn the hard way out here in these streets."

"Yeah, you're right."

Yousef smiled every five minutes it seemed and Rodney noticed. "Did you see what you just did?" Rodney asked him. "What's making you smile like you posing for a camera?"

"I was just thinking something, is all."

"Something or someone?"

He thought about just that and a smile creased the corners of his mouth again. "That girl is something else, man."

"Riches?"

"Yeah."

"Well, take good care of her."

Yousef thought of the conversation he and Riches had earlier, and did remember her saying that she and Tiffany were going to a party in The Jets tonight. He was going to surprise her if he could. Tonight, he was going to make love to Riches and it was going to be a night she wouldn't forget. Tonight was the night he'd take Riches home and make her a woman and thinking of all the things he was going to do to her, he told Rodney, "Can you close tonight? I've got some things I need to do."

"Yeah, we good. Take care of your business."

Yousef walked back to his office, hung his apron on the hanger and pulled his Bowie and sheath from his drawer, just in case. After strapping on the knife, he made his way to the parking lot. "I'll get at you tomorrow, Rod." And with that, he was on his way. "I've got a nice surprise for you tonight, Riches. A niiiiiiice surprise!"

Byrd had no choice but to listen to Kay's words and realized she was right in many ways. He'd gotten used to people choosing the words they used, but with Kay, she was without filter and that was something Byrd was reacquainting himself with now.

"Remember that time we kicked that nigga's ass by the school, 'cause he was acting like we was the laws and shit?"

"Naw, we were all kissing and you started playing like you the law, so he'd give you the rest of the dope he had. Your bitch ass pulled out a wallet or something, like you really had a badge." Byrd laughed at the memory.

"Punk-ass nigga ran harder than a bitch too."

"Yeah, you were stupid as hell, Kay. You and Cecelia used to do all kinds of shit that had a nigga whopping for nothing."

"CeCe had us robbing them niggas by the library, talking about they had a whole bunch of money and shit."

"You did the same shit with that nigga that had on all that damn silver shit on under them street lights. You had us thinking the nigga had on a bunch of gold necklaces. We got all the way to the spot and found out we had a bunch of bullshit."

Kay laughed hard.

"We should have kicked you in your ass," Byrd reminded her. They'd gone from one conversation to the next and so much time had passed,Byrd couldn't believe they weren't high or even getting high. Looking at the time, Byrd suddenly remembered the mission he planned for the night. And hoping Kay could at least offer some kind of information, he subtly asked her. "What my boy, O'Shay, out there doing?"

"Who?"

"O'Shay." Byrd played with the word as if it was a common and casual inquiry.

"That nigga be out there on the east side."

"He out on the east side now?" he asked, hoping she wouldn't read too far into his act.

"That nigga been running Stop Six." Kay stood because she'd been watching the clock also.

"Look at you, ya punk ass can't wait. That's a damn shame, Kay." Byrd hated seeing his friends like this ,but this was her reality and it was also one he was glad he escaped.

"Fuck you, skinny-leg-ass nigga. I wasn't even thinking about smoking shit."

"Well, you over there squirming, looking at the clock every five minutes, like your pussy on fire and you looking for something to quench it."

"Naw, nigga, if i need to quench any fire on my pussy, I know where to get a tongue. Or, I might as well have a quickie with my fingers."

"Mm."

"Actually, I'm just thinking about the money I could be making, instead of sitting here smelling your ass. Hell, I already fucked off fifteen on the car you sold me."

Byrd, as bad as he wanted to believe her, knew how the drug called them and hoping it would paint a different picture for her, he pulled the money from his desk and sat it in front of her. For a crack head, fifteen hundred dollars was the beginning of a dream and the work they could get for it, started the rocket it would take for their travels. "What you gonna do? You gonna—"

"Fuck you, nigga. This shit out here don't make me. If your ugly ass can kick the dope habit, I know I can."

"Yeah, we say shit like that all the time, Kay."

Byrd walked Kay to the Mazda and opened the driver's side door, his chivalry not going unnoticed by Kay.

"Nigga, don't be rushing a bitch like that. Got a motherfucker feeling all tricky and shit."

"I ain't said nothing about you being no trick." Byrd slammed the door as soon as her leg was inside. "Tear your nasty ass, Kay."

Once she was out of sight, Byrd went inside, grabbed his Desert Eagle and headed for the east side. "The projects, huh? Then, the projects it is then."

O'Shay and Riches had made rounds from one end of The Jets to the other, and he could tell she was starting to feel the effects of the drug he'd slipped in her drink. The way she now looked at him, the slurring of her words and the fact that she'd stumbled against him more than a couple of times already, said it all. She was just minutes away from where he needed her and that was the reason he was escorting her back towards the apartments he had available for such moments as this.

"Girl, you need to slow down on the drink before you pass out," he told her when catching her yet again.

Riches laughed. "My head spinning like hell, O'Shay, but I'm good."

"Yeah, I can see." O'Shay looked around to see who might have been looking at them. While placing his arm under her for the support, he sneaked a hand around her breast that was closest to him. He caressed the breasts, warming to their softness, feeling each nipple harden. He smiled. "Oh, I'm sorry, Riches. My bad."

"That feels good," she mumbled. Riches closed her eyes a little longer this time, an apparent sign he identified with.

"Come on, I'm going to take you somewhere you can sit down for a minute or two." He held her tighter from behind, pressing his erection into her buttocks and grinding slowly against her. "You like that?"

No response.

Yousef drove up Rosedale towards Amanda Street and was sure he saw the gray 320 he saw Riches driving earlier; he parked behind it. He climbed out of his Maxima and nodded. He remembered those days when the money and the game allowed him and his friends this same luxury. Just under four years ago, Yousef was the guy many envied on the east side but for him, those days were to be kept in the past.

He made his way through the crowd of partygoers and even got bumped a couple of times by women that smiled at him provocatively, winked and even tried to grope him while passing. He tried to look over the crowds for one face in a pool of many and it was getting him nowhere. Thinking he'd most likely be looking for Riches all night and probably walking past her in the process, he began to inquire of her and Tiffany's whereabouts. "Excuse me, have you seen Riches?" he asked a couple of girls nursing beers and coolers.

"What kind of riches?"

"Never mind." He found himself going from one person to the next, asking about a name they either frowned at or smiled at when they heard it.

"Hey, man, I got these pills, I got weed and got a couple of condoms if you need 'em," a guy smilingly told Yousef.

"Have you seen a girl named Tiffany?" he decided to ask, knowing she'd be the more flamboyant of the two.

"Tiffany?" the guy's forehead wrinkled in an attempt to remember the name.

"Yeah, she was with a mixed-breed broad."

"A kind of short chick with a fat ass, wearing the brown cat suit?"

"Yeah, yeah, that's her. Man, the last time I saw her, she was with that nigga, T, and they were mobbing through."

Feeling hopeful, Yousef asked, "What about the mixed breed that was with her?"

"I'm sorry, homie, but I didn't see her with any girl." The guy walked away.

"Joseph?"

Yousef turned the instant he heard his name and the familiar voice. "Hey, Nicole, what's up?"

"Ain't shit. What you are doing out here?"

"I was looking for my girl," he told her, still looking over the crowd of faces.

"Well, it was nice seeing you again," she told him.

"You too, Nicole." Before she could disappear, he yelled out, "Nicole, you stay up."

"You too, Joseph."

Deciding to return to the car and wait for Riches, Yousef gave up his search and just as he was about to leave, he saw what appeared to be a guy holding up a woman that fit Riches' description. Praying it wasn't her, he made his way in that direction. It didn't even take him six steps to recognize the guy, because of the diamonds that captured the lights, even in darkness. And seeing the same mini dress Riches wore earlier, anger replaced worry and his demeanor, posture and attitude reflected as much. As soon as he neared the couple, he grabbed the guy. "What the fuck are you doing with her, nigga!"

O'Shay looked at the guy and told him, "Mind your fucking business, Joe! This ain't got shit to do with you."

Yousef pulled Riches from his hold and pushed him. "She is my business!" He could tell she'd been drugged, because she was still slurring and mumbling incoherently and the fact that this wasn't the first time he'd seen this very picture with the same guy, he pushed him even harder. "What the fuck wrong with you, O'Shay?"

Seeing people turn and beginning to noticing the scuffle, O'Shay pulled back, threw both his hands shoulder-high and said, "My bad, player."

"Riches! Riches?" Yousef called to her, holding her upright.

"Hey, babe, whhaaa—"

"Come on. I'm going to get you out of here." Yousef looked at O'Shay with both hate and disappointment in his eyes. "You still doing the same punk-ass shit."

"Me and you both." O'Shay smiled.

Yousef lifted Riches off the ground and carried her away from the devil of a man he knew personally.

"I feel sooo good, baby," Riches said, slurring the words.

"Yeah, yeah, Riches. I know."

"You can't keep saving these hoes, nigga!"

Yousef ignored the statement and kept walking. "I got you now, Riches. I got you."

Byrd laughed when he saw a guy get slapped by what appeared to be the wife or even the girlfriend. The attire she wore alone told that she wasn't a part of the crowd of partygoers and the car door being opened showed that she must have just driven up. When driving past the corner of Amanda, Byrd saw the very car that had been sitting in his shop for over a month.

"What the…" Byrd left the words unfinished, because there was no way he would be able to put in work while Riches was around. But to make sure he wasn't tripping, he backed up to check the bumper on the Mercedes. "Shit!" he said aloud when seeing the sticker that read, "A Touch of Magic Learning Center". It was now that he wished to be elsewhere and instead of hanging around, he decided to catch up with the devil at a later time.

Two blocks away, Byrd thought it would be funny to leave a note on the windshield, reminding her of the curfew he was sure she'd break and that was the reason he turned around and headed back to the projects.

Kay couldn't believe her good fortune. Not only was the motel still rolling, but she was now able to move around when she needed to. To her surprise, James even handed her a thousand dollars and when she frowned in confusion, he explained.

"I fucked off two grams with a couple of niggas that came through, but them niggas were spending a shitload of money, Kay."

Not the one to expose a soft spot, Kay hardened up. In this game, it wasn't allowed and as long as she was to maintain the reputation she had, she couldn't. She wasn't tripping with James in the least, but he'd never know that. "Ya punk ass out here trickin', nigga?"

"Ain't nobody trickin' shit," he told her, still acting as if he was waiting for his cut or at least some reciprocating drug.

"What? Why the fuck you still standing over me for, nigga?"

"Come on, Kay, give a nigga something to work with."

"Bitch-ass nigga, you ain't ate no pussy or licked no ass. What you need some work for?"

"You know I will though, I'll suck the discharge out of your shit, Kay."

Kay knew the things a crackhead would say, but that statement made even her smile. She pushed past him. "Nigga, you'd better not ever put your lips on me, with your trickin' ass. Hold up right quick." Kay unlocked her room and walked inside. Everything seemed to be in place and finding her stash still intact, she pulled out a couple of ounces and chopped it in half, with the heated blade she regularly used. And after cutting over twelve grams into even rocks, she walked back outside, finding James sitting on the stairs talking to a couple of guys. "Here, church-boot-built-ass nigga." She handed him the pack. "Let's get this shit rolling, boys!"

James and the rest of the guys seemed to come alive the minute they saw the drugs and knowing they'd most likely need wake-ups, Kay told them, "If y'all fuck off my cash, I fuck off y'all ass!" Hoping things were about to fall in place for her, Kay returned to her room, hoping she'd be able to fight the urges that awaited her and hopefully, she'd win. "If Byrd's punk ass can kick this shit, I know I can," she kept telling herself. "I know I can!"

Byrd wrote a brief note on the napkin he had and was placing it on her windshield, when the guy walked past him with a woman in his arms. It wasn't until he was climbing back into the truck that he realized the woman was Riches. He pulled the Desert Eagle from its compartment and casually approached the guy.

"Riches?" he asked, hoping that she wasn't hurt and seeing her in such a state, he reached for her. "Riches!"

"I was just try—"

Before Yousef could finish explaining things, Byrd hit Yousef as hard as he could with the barrel of the huge gun. "You motherfucker!" Byrd yelled, before hitting him a second and third time. Byrd pulled him away from Riches and pressed the barrel into Yousef's forehead. "I'll blow your fucking head off, nigga!"

"Byrd," Riches began, her words so quiet neither of them could hear her over the yells and screams of the crowd that was beginning to form.

"I didn't do it!" Yousef pleaded, just before Byrd hit him again, splitting Yousef's head above the ear. Rage replaced reasoning and before Byrd realized, Yousef was on the ground shaking.

O'Shay smiled at first when seeing the altercation between the two guys, but when the older guy raised the Desert Eagle and smashed it against Yousef's head repeatedly, he knew he had to something. Seeing the knife still seated on the side of Yousef's waist, O'Shay ran to grab it and before the older guy could turn on him. O'Shay pushed the entire blade between his ribs. And seeing it had little to no effect against the enraged man, he stabbed him three more times, dropping him. Realizing the need for something bigger than the knife, O'Shay grabbed the Desert Eagle from Byrd's grasp and pointed it at his head. But hearing the crowd and murmurs closing in on him, he backed away and blended in with the crowd of onlookers, making it look as if he was a good Samaritan that rendered help. "Call 911," he yelled. "Somebody call 911!" When seeing the attention pass him, O'Shay stuffed the Desert Eagle in his pants and disappeared.

CHAPTER TWENTY-EIGHT

Mike was the first in line for visitations at the juvenile facility off Kimball Road. He sat in the truck contemplating his next moves and was sure Chubby would agree, as well as want to get in on what was happening, even from where he was at the moment. The night before, he met with a few guys from the south side and things were looking pretty promising. After being seated on the stool behind the mesh window, he looked around at the other visitors. Seeing Chubby walk through the doors at the other end of the room, Mike stood.

"What's up, nigga?" Chubby greeted his friend before grabbing the stool he was to sit on.

Mike was still standing. "What them hoes doing about your arm, nigga?"

"Sit your dumb ass down. I got to tell you something." Chubby motioned for Mike to be quiet.

"Can you move the motherfucker or what?"

"Don't worry about my arm, nigga." Chubby smiled.

Mike could see Chubby's eyes glossed over and by the way he was acting, something had to be wrong. Mike sat and watched his friend. Not only did he feel sorry for him, but he wasn't feeling the fact that he'd got turned out on the pain medication they were giving him.

"I got the hook-up, nigga," Chubby whispered.

"You what?"

"I said I got the hook-up." Chubby adjusted his sling, causing Mike to take notice again.

"What kind of hook-up?"

"I know who need what and the prices they be spending and believe it or not, these pills are the shit, nigga."

Mike smiled. "Dope-head ass in here making moves, huh?"

"Hell, yeah. I need you to do me a favor too. You still got some work put up for me or what?"

"Yeah, what's up?" Mike just knew it was going to be an outlandish request, but Chubby surprised him.

"I need you to front a couple of niggas some work for me. I got a few niggas getting out of here in a week or so and I'm going to put them niggas on. They get a spot rolling and we supply they ass. Money come and money go our way."

Mike started to tell Chubby at first that he really wasn't on the same page as O'Shay and T, but decided against it. The things he wanted to do and spoke of didn't have anything to do with them anyway, so instead of bringing up the names of people that didn't give a damn about him, he kept his remarks to himself.

"Yeah, I need for you to give them niggas two hundred and fifty-two grams apiece. I want to see what they do with it."

"Nigga, you can do that with a couple of grams, instead of half a thang." Mike frowned.

"Just do it. I know what the hell I'm doing. I run this shit in here, nigga." Chubby pointed at himself. "I call the shots up in this bitch and if you just shut the hell up with the hoe shit, I'm going to lace you up." When Mike cocked his head to the side and stared at him, he continued. "These niggas in here got the game and the numbers wrong. They are paying a grand for an ounce and anything over that, they are taking the front. We gonna drop on these niggas with prices they can't refuse, nigga. You already know I got the whip game under my belt and I'm coming straight off the stove on they ass, plus I'm taxing the hell out of the ass for the labor. All we need is some niggas that ain't scared to go to war, 'cause the way we going to do this shit, we will be going to war with somebody."

Mike thought about the words Chubby spoke and if he was right, he knew just the people he was talking about. "You've got to get out of this bitch first."

"Oh yeah, them hoes came and talked to me yesterday and they said something about having to sit up for a minute until all this high-profile shit die down. What them niggas O'Shay and T out there doing?"

"Don't ask me shit about them. Be ready to ride against every and anything that ain't riding with us. You hear me, nigga?" Mike filled his friend in on what he had going on,what he planned on doing, and even told him when the smoke cleared, only one of them would be standing. Adding that in the game they played, it was prey and predators and the more prey, the merrier.

Riches opened her eyes and was greeted with the brightest light she'd ever seen in her young life. Something was causing her right arm to both itch and burn and before she could wipe her eyes of sleep, her aunt's voice was inches away.

"How are you feeling, Riches?"

"Aunt Cynt?" Riches was gathering her bearings as best and as fast as she could. She hadn't awakened to Cynthia's voice in forever, and that was the morning after she slept in the hospital lobby the night when Byrd had the heart scare. And for her to be there now, something had to have been wrong. Riches sat up, immediately noticing the IV in her arm and a gown on her body. Cynthia was standing at her side and looked to have been crying.

"What's wrong, Aunt Cynt? What am I doing here?" Riches looked towards the door.

"You were brought in late last night, Riches. Someone drugged you and you were dehydrated, but they say you'll be just fine." Cynthia patted her hand.

Dreading the obvious and knowing she was in trouble in the worst way, she asked,"Where's Byrd?" The last thing she did remember from last night was Byrd and Yousef arguing over her and she prayed things were well between them.

Cynthia closed her eyes and sighed, an action that made Riches ask her again, "Where's Byrd, Aunt Cynthia?"

"Byrd's down the hall, Riches."

Riches blew out hard.

"Your boyfriend's down the hall also."

"What?"

"Byrd must have called you to come get your car, huh?" Riches felt a punishment coming from both Cynthia and Byrd. She had that coming.

"As a matter of fact, Tiffany called me last night and told me I need to get up here."

"It's nothing serious, Aunt Cynthia. I drank a cooler and smoked a little weed."

"Well, the doctors found something heavier in your system, opium."

"Opium? I didn't do any drugs, Aunt Cynthia, honest to God" Riches shook her head. "I would remember doing something like that."

"I wasn't called to come here because of you, Riches. Cynthia paused before continuing, "Byrd is on life support."

"Life support? What the fuc—" Riches caught herself, shook her head and closed her eyes, doing her best to rethink last night.

"He got stabbed several times and one of his lungs collapsed. On the way to the hospital, he had a heart attack and by the time they made it here, he was unresponsive, wasn't even breathing on his own."

Riches saw her aunt's mouth moving, but she stopped listening when hearing that Byrd got stabbed. There was no way this was happening and for the first time in her life, she thought all of this was a dream and swore that if she closed her eyes for a few minutes, everything would be back to normal afterwards.

T found himself wrestling with a very familiar feeling and the closer they got to the Meddle Brook exit, the feeling was becoming one he couldn't shake. Despite being told of the plain and simple, T knew someone was about to die and he prayed it wouldn't be him.

"You hear me, nigga?" O'Shay nudged him. "Don't go up in here with all that scary shit, nigga. We in and out in ten minutes. We drop the nigga for the cash and we out."

T checked the work several times in an attempt to shake his discomfort. Even with it being the real deal and the exact amount, it was still unsettling when taking into account that there could possibly be more than one guy to deal with or kids that might be present. After going over the plan a last time, T checked the magazine of his .40 calibers and shoved it in the shoulder holster O'Shay gave him. And when seeing the new Desert EagleO'Shay placed on the armrest between them, he knew this was a moment he not only planned, but was ready for.

The palatial estates they drove past told T he was more out of place than he'd ever been, with the six-foot hedges that lined the driveways, the circular walkways and the neatly manicured lawns exhibited the prominence of the home owners. It also surprised T that people of this setting were actually dope fiends. The way O'Shay told it was that the guy named Larry was into exports and imports and wanted to finger the drug game, to see what kind of return he'd get. Being the owner of a manufacturing company allowed him to invest in areas he shouldn't and with this being the first time dealing with the devil himself, T was more than sure it would be his last. Unlike the hit on Jay, there were no masks to be used and unlike the hit on Jay they had to enter the estates by way of a security gate and monitors.

"Showtime, nigga," O'Shay told him as the gates were slowly opening inward.

Larry was a slightly older guy that looked to be in his mid-thirties and from the looks of him, did a little working out. The Meddle Brook ball club hat he wore explained just that. He waited for them on the steps besides an outdoor pool that had both a slide and fountain. And after parking behind the black 911 Porshe and the Land Rover, T's uneasy feeling came creeping back.

"Hi, guys. Come on in." Larry waved them.

O'Shay climbed out of the convertible and caught up with T and told him, "Follow my lead, nigga."

Larry ushered them through a custom tiled foyer area and around two 300-gallon fish tanks that held miniature sharks of some kind into a spacious kitchen, He led them over to an island counter, offered them seats and said, "Let me get your money."

When he did reappear, there were two guys with him and the game changed for T yet again.

"I thought it would be better for the both of us if I turned a couple more of my guys on, O'Shay, if that's all right with you?" Larry paused, awaiting his response.

"If everyone's ready to spend some money, why would I mind?" O'Shay nodded at T, who then placed the LV backpack containing five kilos on a make-shift table in front of them.

T unzipped the bottom half of the backpack and before he could pull one of the kilos out, he heard a series of shots, the deafening sounds so close he stumbled sideways and seeing O'Shay pointing the huge cannon, T knew it was kill or be killed. He pulled his Ruger and began firing also.

"Get the money, nigga! Get the money!" he barely heard O'Shay yell, despite being a few feet from him.

T ran over and grabbed the case Larry fell on and before he could pull it from under Larry, the latter pointed a small caliber pistol at him and fired. Feeling the graze of the bullet, T kicked Larry's hand and fired three consecutive shots into his face and head.

O'Shay stepped over the two guys Larry failed to introduce them to and in making sure they were dead, he fired point-blank-range shots into their temples. He walked to where T stood and looked down at Larry. "Wasn't so bad this time, huh?"

T did his best to still himself and the nerves that didn't seem to want to cooperate. He'd been shot, the burning sensation coming from his side confirming the fact. With over one hundred thousand dollars in his hand and enough adrenaline running through his veins to crank a car, he pushed himself through the foyer area. All he wanted to do now was get as far away from there as possible. Back in the pool area,O'Shay smiled and nodded.

"I've got to get me one of these hoes." He was talking about the six hundred and twenty-five square-foot- mansion before them.

T threw the case into the back of the convertible and grimaced at the sharp pain he felt. He reached for his side, blood covering his palm. He immediately felt a dizzy spell coming on and before he was able to say just that, O'Shay threw him a set of keys.

"Take the Rover and meet me back at the shop in two hours." O'Shay climbed into the Lexus and backed out, leaving T a duty of his own. "I've got to make a quick stop right quick."

Mike was starting to think the guys Chubby had him meet were no-shows, until they saw the sky-blue Caprice pull into the space in front of him. Being that there was no money to be exchanged and nothing to talk about, things were simple for Mike and he liked that. Chubby's business would be his own and if he wanted to test drive with his share of the work, then that's exactly what Mike was going to let him do.

Seeing the guy approach the Yukon, Mike unlocked the door.

"What's up, cuz?" the guy greeted him. Even though Mike was a member of the Blood gang and the guy was an apparent Crip, business would still be business and instead of being the one to trip, Mike made it known that he represented.

"I'm bloody, homie."

The guy smiled. "We ain't tripping on this end, player. Money makes the world go around, colors don't."

"We good then." Mike handed him the plastic Kroger's sack and shook his hand. The deal had been done. "I'm out."

Mike pulled off with a new sense of pride. He'd formed an alliance, well, Chubby had formed an alliance with the very guys they'd been warring against for the longest. No more tripping on a color when they were all after faces of various men and no longer was Mike tripping on the rule of not going outside of the hood. Money was about to be made and they all knew The Jets wasn't big enough.

The nightmare she thought would disappear remained. She was now seated at Byrd's bedside. The slow, rhythmic sound of the breathing machine and the steady beep of the heart monitor had Riches in a world she wished to escape, but could not.

She placed her hand on Byrd's. "I'm sorry, Byrd. I'm sorry," she cried. "I need you, Byrd, come on, man. Please!"

"Byrd's strong, Riches. If there's something left in him he's going to use every ounce of it to get back to us," Cynthia told her, while trying to manage poise herself.

"I'm sorry, Aunt Cynt, I'm sorry. I should have never done it. I shouldn't."

Cynthia pulled Riches to her, "Shhh, I know, baby, I know. We're going to be okay." Cynthia spoke the words, but felt something totally different. Despite the life her brother once lived, he was still the rock she stood on. He was the reason she continued her schooling, he was the reason for Riches' existence. Cynthia's inability to have children created a void she did her best to fill, but with helping raise Riches, that void slowly began to fill.

"I got you, Riches. I got you."

Two days had passed since her first visit and Riches had been back and forth ever since. The home she once snuck in after curfew was now a place she tried to avoid all together. With Yousef being roomed six doors down, it wasn't hard for her to hear things regarding his condition and the day of his discharge. The twenty-something stitches he received for the gash caused by the blunt trauma was nothing, compared to the pain she felt for Byrd. And hearing that Yousef would be discharged and not detained for further questioning angered Riches in a way she hadn't known. He was the reason Byrd was tied to the machine in that room because she told him how Byrd felt about them. He could have explained that to Byrd, but he chose to war in the streets. After hearing the version of the things that took place from the doctors and staff, she concluded that Yousef stabbed Byrd repeatedly.

"Byrd should have shot his ass instead of hit him," Riches told Kay as they sat on the stairs of the motel. Cynthia's words to Riches were to let the police conduct their investigation but that wasn't enough for her. She wanted Yousef dead and she needed someone to do it.

"I want you to kill him, Kay." Riches' tone was right above a whisper, but Kay knew she meant it.

"You're just upset, Riches. You need to just—"

"I want him dead, Kay. I want that motherfucker dead!" Riches stood, slammed her fist against the railing and told Kay, "Close casket on the nigga!"

"So, now you ready to have a motherfucker killed? You're ready to take a nigga's life, 'cause you feeling like you can't move on with yours?"

"He killed Byrd, Kay. That's it! I want him dead and if you won't do it, I'm going to do it, 'cause it's going to get done. The nigga's going to die one way or the other."

Kay dropped her head. "Let me make a couple of moves first, Riches, just to make sure we cross all our T's and dot all our I's, 'cause I don't need this shit falling back on me. My bitch ass is gay, but prison ain't for me, Riches." Kay pulled her stem from her pocket, thought about taking her a good hit, but became disgusted at the very thought."Ain't nobody going to prison, Kay, 'cause ain't nobody getting caught."

"The only way you can guarantee some shit like that is if we don't do the shit," Kay told her before continuing. "When you get involved with shit like this, Riches, that's the first outcome you should consider. That, and the fact that you might be the one getting stepped on. You think motherfuckers out here laying down their lives, 'cause you feel they should? Jesus gave his life so a motherfucker could be spared, but you trying to take a life so yours can be lived. It's a big difference there, Riches. A big ass difference, baby."

"You with me or not?" Riches wasn't trying to hear the sermon and she damn sure wasn't listening to the choir.

"You're going to make me cuss your bitch ass out, Riches. You know I'm with you, but wait a damn minute. Killing a motherfucker shouldn't be no spontaneous shit and a motherfucker with a motive shouldn't have shit to do with it, anyway. That nigga gets stepped on and the cops coming to fuck with Cynthia and then you."

"I don't care."

"You know how many sick motherfuckers are locked up for killing? A million." Kay spat on the pavement and popped a piece of gum in her mouth. "I just told your ass, prison ain't for a bitch like me."

"Well, somebody need to do it."

"The thing is, Riches, don't take nothing from the game that you don't want a motherfucker looking for. Nothing!"

CHAPTER TWENTY-NINE

Being that Kay would be her eyes and ears in the streets, Riches felt it would be best if she gave her the phone she'd been using. It was a direct line of communication for them and now that spring break was over and schooling had resumed, she wouldn't be able to visit Kay on a daily basis.

With Byrd still on life support, he had no need for a cell phone and Cynthia suggested as much. Kay was up earlier than usual, because there were some things she promised Riches she'd do. She hadn't taken a hit in over a day and was feeling the effects of it, but was determined to shake the monkeys that had clung to her for years. She was headed to the east side, hoping the questions and the work she had would benefit them in some kind of way. Kay began with the dope fiends and crackheads around the Stop Six Projects. When seeing the cell phone Riches gave her light up, Kay looked to find a face with the name YOUSEF under it.

"I know damn well things ain't the same, motherfucker," she said to herself before touching the screen.

"Hello?" came Yousef's voice.

"Yeah, what you want?" Kay asked a second time, knowing he didn't know her voice.

"Is Riches around?"

"Look, nigga, I don't know you, but I don't think you need to be calling this phone ever again."

"How'd you get her phone?"

"Listen, clown, she doesn't want to talk to you and I sure as hell don't." Kay ended the call and threw the phone in the passenger's seat. "Mad nigga," she told herself. Before she was able to climb out of the car, the phone lit up again. Same caller.

"Bitch-ass nigga, you need to do something different," she told him, now upset at the fact that he wasn't understanding her.

"Wait, wait, wait, hold up! I know she's upset, but I didn't do it. I didn't do what they saying I did."

"What did you do? What are you talking about?"

"She thinks I had something to do with Byrd getting stabbed and I didn't do it. You have to tell her. I've been calling her all morning. I need to talk to her."

Kay could tell in his voice that the guy was sincere, but the game she was in didn't allow her to believe shit she heard or half the things she saw, and if nothing else, she was about to find out where the guy resided.

"Where you at?"

"Excuse me?"

"I said where you at, meatball-head-ass nigga!"

"I'm at the store. I just got here right now."

"What store?"

After taking down the address and telling him she'd be there within the hour, she climbed out of the car and spoke with a few of the smokers on their early morning wake-ups.

Jay rubbed his palms together and nodded in agreement with the plan Cain planned. The only thing he didn't like, was the fact that Cain was willing to take out every and anyone that was present at the time they caught up with O'Shay. As bad as Jay wanted O'Shay, he wasn't down with stepping on people to make that happen.

"Let me walk through a couple of ideas and I'm going to get back at you on that."

With a few T's he wanted to cross himself, Jay made his way back to the projects. Knowing the freaky O'Shay, all Jay needed was a willing woman to bait him and with ten grands at his disposal, he was sure he'd pick up something amenable before the day was out.

T had waited for O'Shay at the shop all night and after patching himself up as best he could, had Mike pick him up. Sleep evaded him in the worst way and in an attempt to find rest, took a couple of leftover Oxytocin pills. He even told Mike to wake him when O'Shay did come by, because he was expecting his cut from the lick they hit days before. Moments later, T woke up, hearing the conversation beyond the door of his room. He pushed himself from the bed and headed that way.

"I'm just doing me right now," Mike told O'Shay.

"Ain't no you, this is us, we doing this shit!" O'Shay challenged him.

"Your niggas around here making moves without me! What the fuck am I supposed to do?"

"You do what the fuck I say, nigga. You ain't have shit before me. You didn't have shit. None of you motherfuckers had shit, you, T, Pistol or that fat ass nigga. I brought you niggas in, 'cause I saw potential and I wanted to see you niggas have something."

"Nah, you put us on, 'cause we the ones that was putting in the work around The Jets. We were the niggas you saw making noise."

"Bitch-ass nigga, running around here throwing colors in a nigga's face ain't making no noise. That gang banging shit had your niggas broke, getting locked up for bullshit and getting killed at the same time. I brought you niggas out of that shit and put money in your niggas' pockets. I'm the one made motherfuckers respect the shit y'all got going on in them jets." O'Shay stood over Mike while ranting. This wasn't the first rant he'd ever had, but it was the first that T took sides with O'Shay.

"He's right, Mike, we on money now because of him," T spoke, after hearing the argument for himself.

Mike didn't know if he was referring to the fact that they were sitting on something for themselves, because of the positions O'Shay continually placed them in, or the fact that he was the one fronting them the little work he was crumbing them with. Either way, T came in the conversation and decided to make that known.

Mike stood and began walking towards him. "Your bitch ass wouldn't even help Chubby, a nigga you been down with from day-one."

T frowned. "Man, I'm not about to go there with you." He was at least hoping O'Shay would side with him, but looking over at the boss, he saw he was now seated on the other side of the room, watching the two of them.

Mike walked past T and went out the front door. There was nothing here for him and if push came to shove, he knew what he was up against.

O'Shay stood, pointed his finger at T and told him, "That nigga gonna be the reason you starve, T. He burning your shit up and you can't even see the shit."

"Man, that nigga just be bumping. He ain't talking about shit."

"That nigga up to something and if you ask me, he's getting ready to cut you off all the way, if you know what I'm saying." O'Shay gathered his keys and grabbed a blunt from the kitchen table.

"What's up with that cut from our lick?" T asked, seeing O'Shay about to leave.

"I'm going to bring it through later on. I didn't want to ride with all that money on me."

T closed the door behind O'Shay and once he was sure he wasn't coming back, he hit the table. "Bitch-ass nigga trying to play me." T checked the bandage he redressed earlier and seeing only a little blood, he knew he'd be ready soon. "Fuck all them niggas!"

It took less than twenty minutes and three dimes for things to start falling in place for Kay. The people she spoke with personally, didn't know what the hell she was talking about, but when asked about the party thrown, they told her, "You need to find them youngsters that was walking around recording everything. We more than sure they saw something."

Kay figured by the time she finished her talk with Yousef, she'd come back to The Jets to further her investigation. In all of her years in the game and on the streets, this was the first time she'd ask any questions other than trying to locate some work or a lick. "Bitch got me acting like the damn police," she told herself after closing the door to the Nissan. She was just about to put the car in gear when someone tapped on the passenger's side window. She at first thought it was a head wanting a favor, but when looking up at the guy standing there that was the farthest thing from her mind. Not only was Kay out of bounds with all her detective work, but she was at a disadvantage with no weapon of any kind. Using the tools the game and streets had equipped her with, Kay unlocked the door and began her performance.

"One hundred and fifty for some head and three hundred for the ass," she told him.

Jay smiled, then laughed. "I'm not here to do no tricking. I just want to know if you wanted to make some money in another way?"

Kay looked the guy over, something about him so familiar but she couldn't place it and instead of guessing she said, "Make some money how?"

"I need you to get with this nigga, take him to the place I tell you and you walk away with ten grands."

"Ten grands? Who the nigga, where he at and when?"

Jay laughed. "Money talks, huh?"

"Hell, yeah it talks. A bitch got to re-up somehow."

"Oh, you fuck around? I might even have something better for you, if that's what you want."

The work he wanted to hire her for was something she'd done for years, but hearing the name of the person it was to be done with, made bells ring at every corner of her mind. She told Jay, "Here, put your number in here. I've got to ring a few bells and I'm going to get back at you ASAP."

"Here's a little something to help you think about it." Jay pulled two thousand from his pocket and handed it to her. "It's plenty more where that comes from."

Kay looked at the money. "Cool."

Yousef had been watching the parking lot ever since he ended the call with the woman that answered Riches' phone. He prayed she wasn't just agreeing to see him to get him off the phone and seeing the car she described to him pull up to the store, he made his way to the door.

"Kay?"

Before Kay could close the car door, a tall dark-skinned guy greeted her; the same guy she'd been looking at in the phone's screen; and, from what she saw, he and Riches were pretty fond of each other.

"So, you the nigga she is sending pussy shots to?" Kay frowned in disgust.

"Excuse me?"

"Yeah, you heard me with your freaky ass. You got that girl showing her ass."

"Come on in right quick."

After being led to the back of the store, Kay sat in the chair in front of his desk and from the way he was acting, she could tell he was a nervous wreck about something they'd done. With other things to do, she got straight to the point

Riches was hearing, but not listening to anything being said in either of her classes, and as soon as the bell rang ending their school day, she hurried to the car hoping Kay had called. Seeing the One Missed call signal, she immediately dialed her phone. She'd been waiting all day to see what Kay found out and as much as she hated it, she couldn't stop thinking about Byrd's condition and her hate for Yousef, whom she loved just days ago.

"Riches?"

"Hey, Kay. What's up?"

"I got some bad news, Riches and I think you'd rather hear it in person."

Riches was anxious. "Where you at?"

"The Oasis."

CHAPTER THIRTY

Tiffany couldn't believe what she was hearing come from Riches' mouth. Never had she seen her friend so upset and it was something that was beginning to scare her. And with her talking about murder, deceit and money, she felt she had been hanging around Kay too long.

"You can't be serious, Riches. I mean, I fuck around and do some crazy shit, but don't you think you're going a little too far?"

"Fuck all that, Tiff. My nigga only alive because of some machines and you telling me about taking shit too far. I'm already over the edge." Riches watched her. "I've got to be sure myself, Tiff and if I got to fuck a nigga to do it, then that's what I'm going to do."

"I still think you ought to go to the police with this theory, 'cause what if the nigga didn't do it, then what?"

"I'm not asking you to do shit, Tiffany. I'm just telling you what I'm going to do." Riches walked over to her bed and sat down. She rested her elbows on her knees and hid her face. "I still can't believe this shit, Tiff!"

Tiffany sat beside her, placed her arms around Riches and told her, "This gonna be my first time having anything to do with a nigga getting killed, but fuck it. If you drive, I'm going to ride, and you know this."

Kay climbed into Jay's coupe and told him, "Give me my money, nigga." She held out her hand. "All of it."

"I'm telling you, Kay, I got this end. You just make sure you deliver."

"If anything happens to that girl, I'm—"

Jay cut her off. "You think I'm throwing my money away just to be doing something? This shit is bigger than you realize."

"You know what happens if we ever see this nigga again, right?"

This level of the game wasn't beyond hers but the last thing she needed was for Riches to get caught up or even worse. But what was done was done, and instead of allowing her to do things half-ass, Kay made sure she was going all the way.

"Well, you know what it is." Kay climbed out of the Cadillac ten thousand dollars richer and much surer that things would go exactly as planned. The only thing now was getting Riches to settle down and not jump the gun, something she was very much itching to do.

O'Shay smiled when seeing the number and face of the woman across his screen. He'd been waiting for this call for weeks and after the time they spent together the night of the party, he was sure she'd contact him sooner or later. He'd been around women long enough to know that many of them only needed an excuse to come out of the shells they hid in. His giving her the Xanax and E-pills were only part of the reason she was opening up. If Yousef hadn't interfered, I would have tasted her. With that thought in mind, O' Shay answered his phone with a mischievous grin.

"It's about time."

"O'Shay, I need a favor," she told him.

"Anything for you, Riches."

"I need a nigga stepped on and these motherfuckers acting like they scared and shit."

"Whoa, whoa. Hold up now. That's some serious shit." O'Shay laughed.

"You know my people got money, so whatever you need, I'll get it."

O'Shay squeezed the erection he felt coming. He closed his eyes, envisioning himself inside of her. "Umm, I don't even need your money, Riches. I got plenty of that."

"I know, I know. I just want this nigga dealt with ASAP."

"Where do you want to meet? We'll talk about it then."

"How much I got to bring? What you want me to do?"

He checked his watch. He was supposed to meet with T shortly, but that could wait and for what he was about to do, that would wait. "All you need to bring is you, Riches. All I need is you."

His asking anything about the guy she needed stepped on didn't matter and for her, he'd close a few caskets. If murder was all it took to have her, she was good as his. "I'm going to bust that pussy wide open," he told himself before taking the 820 exit and heading for the Great Western Hotel.

Riches knew she was about to cross the line, but she needed this to happen and whoever was against her, would just have to live with that. Her friends had traded sex for money many times, but with this being her first time, she felt it would be well worth trading her sex for murder. And she was going to make it worth his while.

O'Shay parked on the side of the Benz Riches climbed out of. He pushed his gun into his waistband. The calls from T were sent straight to voicemail and the text from Shannon went unanswered and when she walked around the front of the car, he grabbed two E-pills, pulled the shirt he was wearing over the gun and climbed out. "Hey, beautiful."

"Hey."

"Where's your little friend?" he asked, striking up conversation.

Riches laughed. "She had some more shit to do and besides, my business is my business."

"Yes, it is."

O'Shay paid for the rest of the night and with intentions of his own, they entered the room.

"Damn it's cold in here," Riches complained.

"So, tell me what you trying to do."

After hearing the things she needed done, O'Shay had a pretty good idea of how he'd go about it. Now, he felt it was time to discuss his payment. He walked towards her and placed a hand between her thighs. "This might be all I want in return."

"No money?" She looked up at him, bit her lip and stepped into his grasp.

"No money."

"Just pussy?" she asked, while acting as if she was about to climb him.

O'Shay raised her dress, felt her vulva and shrugged. "And maybe a little ass."

"You gotta handle the pussy with care, cos it's very fragile. What I mean to say is, this is my first time."

He swallowed the lump of lust in his throat. "Seriously? Ain't nobody had none of this pussy yet?"

"Not yet."

"I'm going to have to make this special for you then." O'Shay pulled her dress over her head, being careful not to mess her crowned ponytail. As she stood before him in only panties and a bra, O'Shay couldn't think of anything else, he had to have her. "You pop pills?"

"What you got?"

"I got a couple of E-pills."

Riches immediately remembered what the doctors told her aunt while she was in the hospital. "Opium."

"Yeah, they got a little opium in them, I think." O'Shay swallowed one of the pills and gave the other to Riches, who swallowed hers also. He pushed her back onto the bed and began removing his clothes. He placed the Desert Eagle on the nightstand and unbuckled his belt. The tear that fell from her cheek went unnoticed as his eyes targeted for the plump flesh between her legs.

"Can I taste it?" he asked, snaking his way from the foot of the bed. She nodded. He licked the insides of both her thighs, inhaled her scent and moved up to her stomach. "Just chill, just chill. I'm not going to hurt you," he coaxed her, feeling her nervousness.

"Wait a minute," Riches rolled over. "Lay down." She pushed him onto his back.

O'Shay smiled.

"You've been teasing me with this dick too long." She reached for her purse and when she pulled out the silk straps she watched his smile widen. "I might be a virgin, but all that soft shit ain't doing it for me." She grabbed each of his wrists, tied them to the headboard and before placing the pillow under his lower back, she pulled down his silk boxers.

"Oh, you like that surfboard shit, huh?" He looked down at his erection, he was satisfied.

With both his arms and hands above him, Riches opened the Magnum package and slid it over his throbbing erection. She looked over at the gun on the nightstand and asked, "You like big guns, huh?" With him nice and elevated, Riches stood at the foot of the bed.

"You're sick, bitch, you know that?"

"Bitches love it."

"And a trick bitch."

"Money ain't shit to me, nigga." O'Shay adjusted himself, making his penis jump.

"I'm gonna kill you, bitch."

Seeing her putting her dress back on, O'Shay's smile vanished. "Take this shit off me!" He began pulling at the restraints. "Take this shit off me, Riches!"

"I hope you rot in hell!" Riches said, and spat in O'Shay's face. Then she left the room.

"Finally, the devil is on a leash and can only bark, but can't bite," said Jay as he walked in the door.

Cain followed. "Well, if it ain't the devil himself. You don't remember me, do you?"

"Come on, Jay, it doesn't have to be this way."

Jay and Cain exchanged glances, then Jay nodded. Simultaneously, they opened fire from the guns in their hands. As the bullets poured out thunderously, piercing and ripping through O'Shay's body in places, the force of the bullets' impact caused O'Shay to jerk convulsively. Jay and Cain kept shooting until the guns were empty of bullets. It was around this time that a pregnant silence took over, smoke filled the room and when the smoke cleared, there was nothing left on the bed but the mangled remains of O'Shay's body, amidst sheets soaked and swimming in blood. Jay and Cain moved closer to the bed. O'Shay's body was hardly recognizable.

"See how creative we are, Cain!"

"Yeah. We daubed the walls of his body with graffiti."

"You can say that again. Let's get outta here right away."

Riches walked out of the room with Byrd's gun and no regrets. The huge duffle bag on the trunk of her car was the reward she was given for having to go through the pains she faced after realizing O'Shay was the one that had stabbed Byrd, and for the performance it took to get the devil himself to slip. And remembering Kay's wisdom about not taking from the game what she didn't want people to come looking for, she wasn't about to accept it. What she wanted was Byrd back on his feet again, but he was dangling on a thin thread of life. She discarded the money.

"You're forgetting the money, Riches." Kay told her after climbing into the car with her.

Riches shook her head. "I'm not going to need it, Kay. Remember what you told me about taking from the game?"

"You can only tempt a bitch so much, Riches." Kay climbed out, grabbed the duffle and hugged it.

EPILOGUE

Shannon walked out of her apartment, crossed the parking lot and found the trunk of her car opened. The lock had been busted, but from what she could see, the only thing out of place was the spare tire and the carpeting around it and since she was in a hurry, she closed it as best as she could and headed to the salon. Since she was never aware of the hundred thousand-plus O'Shay kept in the trunk of her car, it wouldn't be something she missed.

T had been calling O'Shay for the past hour because of the money he was said to have been on his way with. With reality slowly setting in with him, T was feeling used and dumped. "O'Shay is an asshole," he said to himself.

The following day, when Riches and Yousef met, she lost herself in his embrace. Just a day ago, she yearned to kill him but thanks to Kay, that didn't happen. He repeatedly confessed his undying love to her and the tears that fell from his face spoke volumes. It wasn't until he began talking about the subject of his latest phone call that she realized, despite the love he had for her and she for him, they would forever be apart and once he found the answers to the puzzle he was thinking to put together, that would happen sooner than never. Watching him cry uncontrollably, Riches held him to her, comforting him.

"You want to talk about it?" she asked him, referring to the call he received hours before.

"I'm going to get them, Riches. I've got to," he cried.

"It's okay, Yousef. It's okay, baby."

"They didn't have to do him like that." Yousef pushed his face into her bosom.

"Just tell me what's wrong, Yousef. You keep mumbling shit, but you ain't telling me nothing."

Yousef looked at Riches with a look that resembled one she would have loved to forget. Then he told her, "They found my brother dead at the Great Western Hotel last night. Whoever killed him cut his dick off and shoved it in his mouth."

"Your brother? I didn't know you had a brother." Riches backed away from him.

"I wished I didn't and despite the shit he was doing out here, he was still family and you know how I feel about family."

Riches closed her eyes, recalling Byrd's words,"Family is everything, ain't it?" While thinking of the things she'd done for her family, she had no regrets and she understood why Yousef felt inclined to do the same for his family. Hence, only one thought took form in Riches' mind. Blood is thicker than water, after all.

The End

Stay Connected with Us!

Text **LOCKDOWN** to 22828 to stay up-to-date with new releases, sneak peaks, contests and more…
Thank you!

Coming Soon from Lock Down Publications/Ca$h Presents

BOW DOWN TO MY GANGSTA

By **Ca$h & Jamaica**

TORN BETWEEN TWO

By **Coffee**

BLOOD OF A BOSS **IV**

By **Askari**

BRIDE OF A HUSTLA **III**

By **Destiny Skai**

WHEN A GOOD GIRL GOES BAD **II**

By **Adrienne**

LOVE & CHASIN' PAPER **II**

By **Qay Crockett**

THE HEART OF A GANGSTA **II**

By **Jerry Jackson**

LOYAL TO THE GAME **IV**

By **T.J. & Jelissa**

A DOPEBOY'S PRAYER **II**

By **Eddie "Wolf" Lee**

TRUE SAVAGE **III**

By **Chris Green**

IF LOVING YOU IS WRONG… **II**

By **Jelissa**

BLOODY COMMAS **II**

By **T.J. Edwards**

A DISTINGUISHED THUG STOLE MY HEART **II**

By **Meesha**

ADDICTIED TO THE DRAMA **II**

By **Jamila Mathis**

Available Now

(CLICK TO PURCHASE)

RESTRAINING ORDER **I & II**

By **CA$H & Coffee**

LOVE KNOWS NO BOUNDARIES **I II & III**

By **Coffee**

RAISED AS A GOON I, II & III

By **Ghost**

LAY IT DOWN **I & II**

LAST OF A DYING BREED

By **Jamaica**

LOYAL TO THE GAME

LOYAL TO THE GAME II

LOYAL TO THE GAME III

By **TJ & Jelissa**

BLOODY COMMAS

By **T.J. Edwards**

IF LOVING HIM IS WRONG…

By **Jelissa**

A DISTINGUISHED THUG STOLE MY HEART

By **Meesha**

PUSH IT TO THE LIMIT

By **Bre' Hayes**

BLOOD OF A BOSS **I II & III**

By **Askari**

THE STREETS BLEED MURDER **I, II & III**

THE HEART OF A GANGSTA

By **Jerry Jackson**

CUM FOR ME

CUM FOR ME 2

CUM FOR ME 3

An **LDP Erotica Collaboration**

BRIDE OF A HUSTLA **I & II**

THE FETTI GIRLS **I & II**

By **Destiny Skai**

WHEN A GOOD GIRL GOES BAD

By **Adrienne**

A GANGSTER'S REVENGE **I II III & IV**

THE BOSS MAN'S DAUGHTERS

THE BOSS MAN'S DAUGHTERS II

A SAVAGE LOVE **I & II**

BAE BELONGS TO ME

A HUSTLER'S DECEIT I, II

By **Aryanna**

A KINGPIN'S AMBITON

A KINGPIN'S AMBITION **II**

I MURDER FOR THE DOUGH

By **Ambitious**

TRUE SAVAGE

TRUE SAVAGE II

By **Chris Green**

A DOPEBOY'S PRAYER

By **Eddie "Wolf" Lee**

WHAT ABOUT US **I & II**

NEVER LOVE AGAIN

THUG ADDICTION

By **Kim Kaye**

THE KING CARTEL **I, II & III**

By **Frank Gresham**

THESE NIGGAS AIN'T LOYAL **I, II & III**

By **Nikki Tee**

GANGSTA SHYT **I II &III**

By **CATO**

THE ULTIMATE BETRAYAL

By **Phoenix**

BOSS'N UP **I & II**

By **Royal Nicole**

I LOVE YOU TO DEATH

By Destiny J

I RIDE FOR MY HITTA

I STILL RIDE FOR MY HITTA

By **Misty Holt**

LOVE & CHASIN' PAPER

By **Qay Crockett**

TO DIE IN VAIN

By **ASAD**

BOOKS BY LDP'S CEO, CA$H

(CLICK TO PURCHASE)

TRUST IN NO MAN

TRUST IN NO MAN 2

TRUST IN NO MAN 3

BONDED BY BLOOD

SHORTY GOT A THUG

THUGS CRY

THUGS CRY 2

THUGS CRY 3

TRUST NO BITCH

TRUST NO BITCH 2

TRUST NO BITCH 3

TIL MY CASKET DROPS

RESTRAINING ORDER

RESTRAINING ORDER 2

IN LOVE WITH A CONVICT

Coming Soon

BONDED BY BLOOD 2

BOW DOWN TO MY GANGSTA